Two Sisters

TWO SISTERS

LORNA HENDERSON

Choc Lit
A JOFFE BOOKS COMPANY

Revised edition 2024
Choc Lit
A Joffe Books company
www.choc-lit.com

First published as *Where Are You?* by L.E. Hill
in Great Britain in 2021

This paperback edition was first published
in Great Britain in 2024

Cover art by Nick Castle

ISBN: 978-1781897683

PROLOGUE

I killed my husband just a few days before Christmas. It was a cold and damp afternoon, and I'd been doing my best to decorate the tree he'd brought home after another night at the pub. I was sure he'd stolen it but knew better than to question him. Tinsel and baubles and blood. I ran out the door into the darkness and didn't look back.

PART ONE: NOW

CHAPTER ONE

Tara

I stare out of the kitchen window, watching the builders at the bottom of the garden. Hopefully all this upheaval will be worthwhile. My phone pings with a notification. Snatching it off the counter, I see Mum has replied to my message.

I'm sorry to hear that, Tara. No, I haven't had any health issues. No genetic conditions as far as I'm aware. X

That's it? That is *all* she can be bothered to say? I walk into the open-plan living space and throw my phone onto the sofa, furious that she's so brief. My own mother . . . though really, the voice in my head says, what was I expecting? Things had not changed a bit in all those years. If I had told her I had months to live, would it have made a difference? Why had she even bothered getting in touch in the first place? Guilt?

Tears spring to my eyes but I bite my lip. I won't waste any more tears over her. I've had enough of all of this. I've had enough of her. That's the last time I make contact with her. *Ever.* What sort of woman is she anyway? Not one that I want anything to do with anymore. Once again, I'm tempted to go and find the box of birthday cards she sent to me over the years and chuck them in the bin.

Instead, I march into the kitchen, turn on the oven and begin grating a courgette onto a plate. This is my way of making the kids eat more vegetables. Because I care about my children — unlike my own mother, who doesn't give a shit. I try to breathe in and out slowly. I will not let her ruin yet another day in my life. This needs to stop.

Tipping the grated mound into the mixing bowl, I smile when I think of Oliver and Millie's reaction if I were to tell them what's *really* in the cake. So far, I've managed to trick them with this recipe. Mind you, the thick, white icing is probably enough of a distraction. Anyway, baking always soothes me and allows me to feel as though I'm properly fulfilling my mothering duties. My heart rate settles as the actions of mixing and stirring help to soothe my mind. The fan in the oven whirs slightly and I glance over, checking whether the light's gone off to signal that it's ready.

The builders have been hard at work all day, and as it's Friday I know they're hoping to get away a bit earlier. It would be lovely to have the garden back to ourselves for the weekend at least so I can hang out some of the washing. The weather is supposed to be good too, which means we could maybe even attempt a barbecue — the first one of the year, which is ridiculous given that we're now into June. Rob, the project manager, waves his colleagues over. They've stopped for a cigarette break, which doesn't bother me in the slightest. They're all grafters. There are plenty of tales from the mums at nursery about the number of tea and fag breaks their builders take. You can hardly blame them though. It is labour-intensive work, and as long as they keep roughly to their time schedule, that works for me. My only gripe is the cigarette butts scattered around the garden. Oliver has picked them up a few times and come in with them hanging from his lips. I always whip them from his mouth and throw them in the bin. He isn't as interested in the work as Millie. She's always asking questions about how deep they will dig and how long it will take to build their den, which my supposed studio space is now becoming known as.

3

It's just after three o'clock. Perhaps I should offer them a cup of tea. I could do with one, but there's something wrong about drinking it and watching them outside. I pop the cake in the oven and set the timer. Sighing, I look at the trail of muddy boot prints across the hall. The guys do their best to wipe them at the door but inevitably crumbs of dirt fall off and get smeared into the tiles. I suppose it's no worse than having the kids traipse in and out of the house. At the end of the day it's only dirt.

Looking out, Rob is now pressing his glasses against his nose, as the group all huddle around him. They all appear to be staring down into the hole at something. One of them drops to his knees and prods it with a spade. He shouts out and stands up jerkily, dropping the spade behind him. Then Rob grabs it and gingerly touches at the ground before recoiling backwards. What on earth are they doing? I wonder if there's a problem with the roots of the tree. It's quite conceivable that they've grown under the foundations of the garage over all these years. Those apple trees have been there for ever. Do the roots of apple trees do that? Maybe I'm confusing them with weeping willows. The bottom line is that they will most probably need to treat them or do something before they start to install the work-space-cum-den. Which will surely mean a delay.

Rob looks up and sees me watching. His face remains impassive, but his eyes bore into mine. He's an unassuming kind of guy who doesn't make a lot of eye contact unless absolutely necessary. He glances away briefly at his colleagues before looking back at me. What is going on? Surely whatever it is must be fixable? I wipe my hands on my apron and make my way across the kitchen towards the front door, opening it as Rob appears.

'Is everything okay?' I say. 'I was about to come out and ask you if you fancied a cuppa.'

His face is flushed. 'Eh, no. No thanks, love. Erm, we seem to be facing a slight problem.'

I sigh inwardly. 'Mm-hmm. What is it?'

4

'Well, see, to be honest . . . eh, actually, I don't know quite how to put this.'

I smile. 'Don't worry. I'm quite thick-skinned. Whatever it is, we'll try and work out a plan. Don't tell me — it's going to cost more than you thought!' My attempt at a joke fails.

He purses his lips. 'No. Nothing like that . . . But, well . . . I think we'd better call the police.'

'The police?' Now I'm completely confused.

He nods. 'Aye.'

'But why? What's happened? What's wrong?'

'Well,' he says, turning to point to the bottom of the garden, where his colleagues are staring back at us. 'Eh, we've found something.'

'What do you mean? What?'

'Bones,' he says, turning to look at me. 'You've got bones buried at the bottom of your garden.' He thumbs back towards the men. 'That's why we need to call the police.'

CHAPTER TWO

Josie

I wake early this morning, listening to the creaks of Gran's house and the seagulls banging about on the roof. They sound like a squad of angry toddlers. I should get up but my head is spinning. I'm still in shock from yesterday's events and seeing Jason unexpectedly after so many years. I've barely had a chance to think about Dimitri's card. I'll deal with my soon-to-be ex-husband later.

My sister doesn't have any idea about my infatuation with Jason when I was a teenager. Nobody did. I was eighteen when he came home from Australia, where he had been living, to visit family. There was a five-year age gap, which seemed a big deal at the time, though nothing at all now we're in our thirties. I was working in the Italian ice cream shop selling gelato to all the tourists. Jason had come in and asked for a pistachio cone. I remember screwing my face up in disgust and he laughed at me. His blue eyes had a cheeky glint in them, and I was completely mesmerised. I cleared my throat and found myself asking if he wanted to meet later for a drink. He immediately said yes, he would. I knew it would be a brief fling as he was only home for a few weeks before returning to Sydney. I was leaving to go off to university in St Andrews. We met in secret, as we didn't want the town gossiping about us and speculating over the age gap. And our clandestine meetings tended to make things more exciting anyway. He was my secret, and I didn't want anyone to know. When he left I was devastated, and he admitted he was gutted too but promised to keep in touch. He never did. After that, things all started to spiral downwards and if Gran hadn't been there for me, I'm not sure what I would have done.

Padding downstairs, I pause and frown when I see Gran's door at the top of the stairs is ajar. Maybe she was up in the night and didn't close it properly.

'Gran?' I say when I see her sitting at the kitchen table. 'What are you doing up so early?'

'I couldn't sleep, lovely. I've been tossing and turning for hours. I thought I may as well come down and make some tea.' She gestured at the round, blue-and-white moon-and-tide phase clock on the wall. 'Full moon. That always brings up weird energies and keeps me awake.'

I glance at the clock, a present from Tara and me a few years ago. Gran's always been a believer in not making any important decisions around a new moon or a full moon. 'Things are always a bit weird. Always try and ground yourself and let whatever you're feeling pass.' Perhaps I need to go back and check the moon status when I walked out on Dimitri. I reach over to fill the kettle. 'I'll make you a fresh one, shall I?'

She nods but doesn't pull her eyes away from the window. Squeezing her on the shoulder, I ask, 'Are you okay, Gran?'

'Yes, dear, I am. Just a bit slow to start today.'

She's always so youthful and sprightly, and I don't like to think of her as getting old, despite the fact she's ninety. It's a reminder that she won't always be around, and the thought terrifies me. A tear starts to skid down my cheek, and I harshly wipe it away. To think of all the lost time that

I could have had with her if I hadn't been under the spell of *that* man. 'Are you sure you don't want some of the strong stuff, Gran?' I lift up the cafetière.

'No, a plain old cup of builder's tea will be lovely. Thanks, dear.'

I spoon some coffee into the pot for me and pour on the boiling water, savouring the smell of the Colombian roast blend as I make Gran's tea. 'Here you go.' I put her favourite mug down in front of her, from a pottery in Perth which we visited a few years ago. Her iPad is on the table next to her. 'Were you watching something?'

'No. I'm catching up with some emails and the news. Needn't have bothered with that.' Clasping her fingers around the dark red cup, she takes a sip and watches me as I push the plunger through the coffee grains. I pour the dark liquid into my cup.

'Cheers,' I say, raising my mug.

'You always were your mother's daughter.' Her words are unexpected.

'What do you mean?' It is *extremely* unusual for her to even mention my mother.

'She was always quite particular about her coffee too.'

I didn't know that about my mother. Unsure of how to reply, I take another glug of coffee, trying to hold onto this rare snippet of information about my mum.

'She always refused the instant stuff and insisted on having proper coffee.' Gran closes her eyes and is quiet for a moment. 'She used to have a small metal coffee maker which sat on top of the stove. She brewed her coffee that way. I remember it was something to do with boiling water and steam . . . Anyway, the coffee tasted quite strong and bitter. It was okay in small doses.' She smiles, her eyes still shut. 'I remember the first time she made a cup for me. It was when they lived in that house and she insisted I give it a go. It was one of the very first things that she made me.'

A ripple of sadness passes through me. 'Which house, Gran?'

'The manse, sweetie. The house you were brought up in.'

The house which is a few minutes away from here and holds so many memories of my childhood. The old stone cottage with the huge garden and wonderful views. It always seemed so magical when I was small.

Gran opens her eyes. 'The main thing is that you and your sister are friends again. That's all any mother ever wants. For her children to be friends.'

We sit for a while chatting and Gran announces she's going back to bed for a while. 'I've got a date with the bridge girls later on,' she says. 'I'd better catch up on my beauty sleep, otherwise they'll talk.'

'Okay, Gran,' I say. This will give me a chance to try and catch up on the cleaning. 'I'll potter about for a while.'

Later that afternoon, I'm about to start the hoovering when I see three missed calls on my mobile from Tara. I wonder what's wrong and immediately call her back.

She's super calm when she tells me there's been an 'incident' in the garden.

'An incident? What do you mean? Are you all okay?'

She sighs. 'Well, it's all surreal, Josie . . . The builders found bones.'

'What do you mean bones?'

'I mean bones. They're most probably animal bones, but apparently you're legally obliged to let the police know if you find bones anywhere.'

'Is it a skeleton?' I wonder if someone who lived there before us had buried their cat or dog in the garden.

'Hmm, I'm not quite sure. The builders just said it was bones. It seems serious.'

'Do you want me to come over?'

Tara sighs. 'I'm not quite sure what to do.'

'Okay, I'll be right over.' I know her uncertainty means she must be in shock. 'Where are the kids?'

'Oliver is with Dad and Millie is at her friend Jessica's house.'

'Well, that's something at least. Probably better if they're out of the way.'

Gran is dozing in the front room, like she always does at this time of the day. There's no point in worrying her, so I kiss her head gently and tuck the blanket round her knees. A rest will do her good after her sleepless night.

'I'm so glad you two are so close,' she says, opening her eyes and making me jump.

'Gran, you gave me a fright.'

'Sorry, lovely. I heard you come in.'

'I'm popping in to see Tara. What about your friends? Are you still meeting them?'

'No, sweetie. Bella called earlier to postpone. I'm quite happy here anyway.'

'I guess every cloud has a silver lining?'

'Yes, sweetie. It does indeed.' She closes her eyes again.

'Hopefully I won't be long.' Gran is definitely not herself. I'll need to try and get her to the doctor's and get her checked out. I'll do that first thing Monday morning.

By the time I arrive at Tara's, the local police officer is also there speaking into his phone, looking quite grim-faced. He nods when he sees me. Tara is handing out mugs of tea to the builders. I walk down to meet her. 'Any more news on what it is?'

She shrugs. 'No, there's not much to say right now. I mean, I keep thinking a family pet from way back. Or maybe an ancient burial site.'

The policeman walks over to us both.

'This is my sister, Josie,' she says. 'This is Brian. Or DI Thompson, sorry. His daughter is at nursery with the twins.'

I reach out to shake his hand.

'Brian is fine. Hello, nice to meet you.'

'What's happening? What kind of animal do you think it is?'

He coughs to clear his throat. 'Erm, well, that's the thing. We're not entirely convinced it is an animal.'

'Oh,' we both say together.

'In fact, I've called CID in.'

I raise an eyebrow. 'CID?'

'Yes.'

'You think it's human remains?'

'Yes. Yes, I do.'

I look over at Rob, whose face is ashen. He rakes his hands through his hair and walks towards us.

'I'm so sorry about all this, love,' he says to Tara.

'Sorry? But it's not your fault.'

'I'm sorry for digging so deep. I got the guys to go deeper than normal. If I'd stuck to the original plan this wouldn't have happened. We were digging and my shovel got caught on something. I thought there must have been a root from one of those trees,' he says, pointing towards the bottom of the garden without turning around. 'Or even a stick. But when I looked closer, I realised there was a bone and . . . well, turns out not one but quite a few . . .' He puffs out his cheeks. 'One of the guys googled what you should do if you find bones in your garden and the advice was to phone the police. That's why we called Brian in.' He pauses. 'Did I hear that right? Does he think they're human?'

'Mmm,' says Brian.

'When do you think CID will arrive?' I ask.

He glances at his phone. 'I don't think they'll be that long. They'll come down in the first instance to assess. But I'll need you all to stick around.'

'Could it be old bones?' I ask. 'As in Iron Age or something?'

'Mmm,' he says, not sounding at all convinced. 'I wouldn't like to say for certain either way. CID will take a look.'

While we wait for the police to arrive from Edinburgh, Tara calls Mark to update him. I sit at the kitchen table, sipping a mug of tea and swinging my foot.

'Tara,' I say when she comes back into the kitchen. 'If these are human remains . . . well, what does that mean?'

She shivers. 'Exactly. Who on earth has been buried at the bottom of our garden all these years?'

11

CHAPTER THREE

*It was after 4 p.m. on a freezing cold day a few days before Christmas.
I had spent the afternoon trying to make the flat look festive and inject
a bit of warmth into the dismal lounge with its threadbare curtains
and wooden floors. I reached up to drape some tinsel over the tufty
tree which he said he had bought cheap on his way home from work.
More likely he stole it. I thought the baubles and lights I had brought
from home might help me feel more settled. But they looked crap and
reminded me of my pathetic existence. Who was I trying to kid?
Maybe things would be different. Perhaps we could still make things
work and be a family.*

*Then the doorbell rang. I wasn't expecting anyone, so I ignored it
until the letterbox started rattling.*

*'I know you're in there,' she called. 'Come on! Please tell me
you're okay.'*

*I only opened the door to shut her up. I didn't want the neighbours
wondering who was making the noise. I certainly didn't want him to
arrive home and find her on the doorstep.*

*She pushed past me and demanded that I go with her. I know
she only meant well but her presence made me edgy and tense. Casting
a withering glance around the room, she told me I could do better. She
kept telling me that I should make more of my life. But my eyes kept
flitting to the clock. I knew she was right — she always was. But I also*

12

knew with certainty that he would be home any minute and he would be furious if he found her here. He hated her.

'Please, come with me. You don't have to stay,' she said.

Wiping away the tears, I admit I was tempted. How I would have loved to have started again. A fresh page and a new start. But I couldn't. Things had changed. It wasn't as simple as that. And when I told her, her eyes widened.

'Even more reason to come,' she said. 'You're not safe here. He's going to kill you.'

She clasped at my arm, begging me to go with her while I begged her to leave. I heard his key in the door. I gasped, feeling terror ripple through me. Then I saw the fear in her eyes. This would not end well.

CHAPTER FOUR

Tara

'God almighty,' I say, wrapping my arms around myself. 'This is like some sort of nightmare.'

Josie grimaces. 'Who lived here before we did?'

'I don't know. We would need to ask Dad. Though from memory I think possibly a minister who lived alone.'

'Or did he?'

'What do you mean?'

'Well, maybe he buried his wife at the bottom of the garden?'

'Don't be ridiculous. I'm sure there's a perfectly reasonable explanation.' Something dawns on me. 'Remember the house you looked at in London?'

'Which one? We viewed loads.'

'I know,' I say, and scowl. 'The one that was down a lane and cost a fortune, remember? It was tiny and the small print said there were bodies buried in the garden.'

She smacks her hand off her forehead. 'God, yes, of course. How could I have forgotten?'

I remember Josie calling to tell me about a house near Bushy Park which looked promising. She thought they could get it for a reasonable price because it needed work. I baulked because for the same price she could have bought a detached house with acres of ground here. Initially she and Dimitri were keen, and she sent me the schedule. I wasn't impressed at all. It looked so poky and shabby. But then Josie always had a better vision for these things than I did. I thought it was an awful lot of money to pay for a house which seemed to be in complete disrepair. I was reading the particulars and looking at the room dimensions wondering how on earth she would fit a double bed in, never mind a wardrobe, when I saw the previous owners' last wishes in small print. They wished to be buried in the garden. That was where they both still rested. I called her straight away. 'Don't you think that seems kind of weird?'

'No, not really,' she said, trying very hard to sound breezy.

'Honestly? You want to spend almost three quarters of a million pounds on a wreck of a house with a couple of people buried out back? You can't be serious?'

That's when she got a bit snotty. 'It doesn't bother us, Tara, though it's clearly an issue for you. Beggars can't be choosers in this area. And anyway, the house is in a great school catchment area. You should see the Ofsted report for the local primary. It certainly doesn't appear to be putting people off. The estate agent said there's loads of interest.'

'No shit, Sherlock. They're obviously going to say that, aren't they? They want to whip up some competition so they can push up the price and get more commission. The more competition and rivalry they can drum up the better.'

'Well, *we* don't have a problem with the house, Tara. And we're the ones buying.' Her tone was chilly and she abruptly ended the conversation.

I remembered speaking to Gran afterwards and asking her if she thought everything was okay with Josie. I couldn't believe she would be happy about buying a house with people buried in the garden, for goodness' sake.

'You never know what's going on with people,' she said diplomatically.

'But Gran, would having people buried in the garden not put you off buying a property?'

She shrugged. 'If it's in a desirable area where they want to live, then that's up to them and none of our business, Tara.'

She changed the subject, Gran's way of closing an awkward conversation down.

They didn't end up getting the house in the end because it went to a higher bidder and instead ended up buying the one they're in now, or at least he is.

I pour myself a glass of water, glancing out at the garden and wondering if this will all be sorted out quickly. 'Do you wish you'd got that house?' I ask.

'No,' she says, quietly. 'You were right, Tara. I couldn't see it at the time as I was so hell-bent on us getting settled to start a family.'

I try to lighten the mood. 'Well, at least you don't need to try and sell a house like that. The one you're in will be much easier to shift, I'm sure. Especially with all the work you've done.'

'Who said anything about selling?' she says, looking at me in surprise.

'What do you mean? You can't be thinking about going back there, surely?'

She doesn't answer and luckily for her, I spot another police car arrive with a van following close behind. It's lucky we don't have many neighbours close by. They would be having a field day. I hope this will all be resolved before too long and before anyone notices. Otherwise, the news will be all over Facebook and Snapchat.

I watch Brian throw away his cigarette end and walk across the lawn to greet his colleagues.

'Come on, we'd better go and find out what happens now. This is all starting to look a bit ominous.'

CHAPTER FIVE

Josie

Before too long, fluorescent-yellow police tape is fluttering in the early evening breeze. Tara could be right, maybe this does have something to do with people who lived here long before us. I've a vague sense it was church property for decades, but I couldn't think of any ministers who had requested they be buried in the garden of the manse. But why would I know that? Fortunately, the experience with the house in Teddington means all of this isn't such a shock. I wonder if I should call Dad or wait until we know more. This isn't something the kids should see. 'Tara, what about Oliver and Millie?'

'Yes, you're right,' she says, looking at her watch. 'Time is getting on and I'm not sure how long this will take. I'll call Dad and Jessica's mum to give them the lowdown.'

Another car appears in the drive, which is now starting to get a bit crowded. 'Oh God,' says Mark as he jumps out and runs towards us. Jason climbs out the driver's side.

That's when I look at him properly and realise how little he's changed. Then I rebuke myself for effectively eyeing him up in the midst of a potential crime scene. 'The builders have found bones. The police think they resemble a human skeleton. The forensics are here to dig more,' I say quickly, pointing at the small tent which has now been erected over the site of our former garage.

'Good God,' says Mark.

'Quite.'

'Why did you come home?' asks Tara, running across to greet him.

He puts his arm around her. 'I saw your missed calls and the jungle drums are already beating in the town, as you can imagine . . .'

Mark pulls his phone from his pocket and shows me the pictures which are now on the town's Facebook page.

What's happening at the old manse? Heard the police are digging up there?

Anyone know what's going on?

Never a dull moment in this town. That house is haunted.

'It would help if the police got everyone to move on for the moment,' Jason suggests, pointing over at the people gathered around the gate of the driveway.

'I'll go and have a word with Brian.' Mark heads towards the police tape.

'I'd better call about the kids.' Tara walks back towards the house out of earshot.

I'm left standing with Jason.

'How are you, Josie?'

'Slightly freaked out by all of this,' I say, spreading my hands out in front of me. 'Not quite sure what it's all about.'

'What do you think will happen now?'

'Who knows?' I shrug. 'They'll take the bones away for a post-mortem, I guess. Try to determine a cause of death or send them away for forensic analysis. Although I'm no expert. I'm only going by what I've seen on television. Can you tell?' I speak quickly, aware lots of words are tumbling

18

out my mouth. 'How are you?' I ask, desperate to try and distract myself from the drama that seems to be rapidly unfurling. His attention is firmly fixed on the scene, and he's biting his bottom lip in the way he always used to.

'Good, thanks,' he says, eventually looking at me. 'It's nice to be back at work with Mark. He's got loads of ideas for the restaurant.'

'Sounds exciting . . . though what about Sydney? I thought it was a permanent move?'

'Yes. I did too for a while and then came back a couple of years ago. I was just back tying up a few loose ends in Sydney . . . then down in Melbourne.' He pauses. 'I had some things to do.'

I look at him questioningly.

'And you? Mark said you're staying with your gran for a while?'

'Yes. Likewise. I needed to get out of London for a bit. Things were getting a bit much. I thought I would come here for a few quiet weeks . . . though it hasn't quite worked out how I planned. I think London would be quieter.' Then I remember what happened the day I fled. 'Though possibly not . . .'

He smiles. 'Yes, I'm sure this isn't quite the idyllic spot you were looking for.'

'And to think it used to be so comforting too — especially the view.'

Mark walks back towards us unsmiling. 'Jeez. This is awful. If we hadn't pulled the garage down, the poor soul would've been down there and lost for ever. The police are saying it's completely random they've been found.'

'What if they wanted the garden to be their final resting place though?'

'What do you mean?' Jason says, surprised.

'Well, remember that house we wanted to buy in London?'

Mark nods. 'Ah, yes. Yes, I do. Very weird.'

He gives Jason a condensed version while he listens in bemusement. 'Really? I've never heard of that before.'

I nod.

'Is it an English law thing?'

'No,' says Mark. 'There are no restrictions on burials on private land in Scotland either.'

'How do you know?' I ask.

'Because I remember Tara telling me about your predicament and it made me wonder if you could do it here too. Quite often there are differences because of the separate laws.'

'What, did you fancy getting buried at home then, Mark?' Jason laughs.

'No, not necessarily. I was just curious and hadn't ever considered it until Josie told us about that house she was after.'

'But wouldn't it have been declared in the title deeds of the house?' says Jason.

'Yes, you're right. It would be in the small print, surely,' I say. 'Or somewhere in the particulars. Did the lawyer mention anything to you when you bought the manse?'

'No.' Mark shakes his head. 'But it depends when the burial was.'

'Well, Dad took over the manse well before we were born, so we're going back more than thirty years. Surely he would've known if it was in the deeds?'

'And who was here before your dad?'

'We think an old minister who never married. At least, I'm sure that's what Dad said. But I would need to ask him.'

I notice the few people gathered at the gates have now swollen to a small crowd of folk obviously desperate to find out what is going on. Fortunately, the builders have left and Brian's gone over to talk to the gawkers, quickly moving them on. Tara comes back out of the house.

'Dad is going to hold onto Oliver just now, but I'd better go and collect Millie. She's still at Jessica's. I told Dad I'd drop her at his too. Better that they're out the way and not seeing any of this.'

'Did you find out anything about the old minister who was here before we lived here, Tara?'

'No, why would I have thought to ask?'

'Dad will know more. We can ask him when we see him,' I say. 'You can all head off. I'll stay here until we're a bit clearer about what's happening.'

Mark turns to Jason. 'Jaz, are you okay to head back and hold the fort at the restaurant, mate? I'll be right behind you in a few minutes.'

Jason is watching the police. He seems anxious and jumpy and agrees straight away. 'Yes, of course. I'll go back and check on things. Don't worry. Take your time.'

I give one last glance to the surreal scene in front of us all and walk back up to the house with Tara and Mark. 'I'll call you the minute I hear anything else.'

She nods. 'Of course.'

I turn to say goodbye to Jason, but he has already gone.

CHAPTER SIX

'What the fuck is she doing here?' His voice was calm and steady, even though he'd been drinking. But his eyes darted manically between us.

Instinctively I moved towards him, putting myself between him and her. I made a conciliatory gesture with my hands and did my best not to shake. But my whole body trembled.

'Come on,' she said. 'You don't have to stay here. You can come with me.' She was trying to sound assertive, but her voice wavered.

'She's not going anywhere,' he said. He stood for a moment sneering at us. 'You're an ugly pair,' he spat. Then he shoved me. I winced as I fell against the Christmas tree. The fairy lights flickered off.

She crouched beside me, trying to haul me up. The shock and terror in her eyes scared me. But I lay there rigid, bracing myself for what would come next if she didn't leave. 'Just go,' I whispered. 'I'll be okay. Go.'

She shook her head. 'No. I can't leave you here with him. I can't.'

'You heard what she said. She doesn't want you here. So fuck off. I'm getting a beer. And by the time I'm back I want you gone, bitch,' he spat at her, a glob of saliva landing on her shoulder.

'Please go. You're making it worse,' I pleaded, the tears streaming down my cheeks.

'You don't have to put up with this. You deserve more,' she said. 'Please come with me. We can start afresh somewhere else. We can be together.'

For a few moments, I caught a glimpse of a new future. Of being free and happy and with someone who loved me. I thought of laughter and sunshine and possibility. It all felt within my grasp. I managed to stumble to my feet and steady myself.

'Come on,' she urged. 'You don't need anything. Come as you are.'

I looked down at my feet — I didn't even have shoes on — and took a tentative step forward. Maybe I could do this. Leaning into her, she desperately pulled me towards the door.

'Quickly,' I said. 'Hurry.' I stopped. 'Wait, I need my bag.'

'No,' she said. 'You don't. We need to go now.'

'But . . .' I thought of what was in my bag. My only picture of Mum.

'No,' she was shaking now. 'Let's go now.'

We were almost at the door.

'Not so fast.'

I froze, feeling his hand claw into my shoulder.

'Where do you think you're going?' His face pressed up against mine and I could smell his foul breath.

'She's coming with me!' she yelled. 'Come on.'

I was like a ragdoll being pulled by the arms with her on one side and him on the other. He yelled and yanked at my arm and I screamed out as pain ripped through me.

She stood with her back right up against the door as he moved slowly towards her. He took a swig from his beer bottle and threw it to the side. 'You think you can waltz in here and start calling the shots? Stupid cow. Fuck off.'

His voice was agitated, and I knew he would hurt her. 'We're fine, the two of us. We don't want you here.'

Someone whimpered in fear. I don't know if it was her or me. But at that moment a red mist descended. I picked up the bottle and with every ounce of strength I had left in my broken body, I slammed it down across his head.

CHAPTER SEVEN

Tara

I jump in the car and make my way past the nosy folk with nothing better to do than stand at my gate staring. It's getting late, and even though there's still activity in the garden, I have to go and get the twins from Dad. This is probably the most exciting thing to happen in the town for years. Quite often there are emergency call-outs when the lifeboat is launched, which, depending on the circumstances, sometimes also warrants a search and rescue helicopter. However, touch wood, things tended to have a happy outcome. Normally it would be a kayaker who had become tired or a fishing boat with engine trouble. This was *obviously* far more exciting.

Crime is not a big problem at all in this part of the world. Until now. I stare at the faces as I pass, although I don't recognise anyone at all. Our nearest neighbours are about a hundred metres away and they aren't part of the pack. Glancing in my rear-view mirror, I'm relieved to see Brian shoo them away.

When I arrive at Dad's house in the town centre, he opens the door and waits. Which is something he never does as he lives at the top of the building, two flights of stairs up. He's clearly been watching from the window.

'Hi, Dad,' I say, immediately shocked by his grey complexion. 'You didn't need to come down, I would have come up . . . Are you okay? You're not looking too great. Are the kids playing up?'

He shakes his head. 'No, not at all. They're fine. I'm awfully tired, dear, and a bit out of sorts. How are things at the house? What did the police say?'

Clutching at my car keys, I usher him back up the stairs, watching in concern as he grips the banister which we'd got a joiner to put in last year. I was worried about him slipping or toppling down the stairs.

'Sit for a minute in the kitchen, Dad, and I'll check on the kids.' Sticking my head into the front room, Millie turns to smile briefly but then focuses again on the game she and Oliver are playing. 'Hello, poppets. Is everyone okay?'

'Yes,' says Oliver, his tongue hanging out as he concentrates on where to put his yellow disc. From what I can see, Millie's about to beat him.

'Good. Um, I'm going to go and have a wee chat with Grandpa.'

'Okay,' says Oliver.

'Did you have a nice day?'

'Yes,' he says. 'We went fishing.'

'Ah, sounds nice.' That explains why Dad is looking so worn out. Knowing them, they'll have been out all day long, and even though the weather was mild today, when the wind whips up it can take quite a bit out of you.

'When are we going home?' asks Millie.

'I'm not sure yet, sweetie. Soon though. How was Jessica's?'

'Mmm, okay . . . fishing would've been better.'

I can't argue. A day outside at the beach sounded much nicer than being with Jessica, who can be a bit bossy. I sometimes wonder if she takes after her dad, Brian, the policeman. I go back to the kitchen, where Dad sits at the table, his fingers laced together and his head bowed. 'Okay, Dad, first things first. Have you eaten?'

'Yes, I had something earlier.'

25

'Well, it's after six o'clock now. Have you drunk enough water?'

'Probably not.'

'Okay, let me sort that.' I fill a glass at the sink and place it in front of him.

He takes a sip. The silence grows heavy but still he doesn't speak.

'The police think the bones are human remains.'

'Oh,' he says, the words puffing out from his mouth.

'Yes,' I continue. Dad sits in silence listening. His pallor doesn't change and he keeps his eyes on mine. 'They had to call in CID and forensics. Anyway, Josie and I wondered if the people before us might have known anything. Maybe they decided they wanted to be buried there?'

'Why?' he says.

'Because apparently that can happen. Remember the house Josie looked at in London?'

He purses his lips.

'Do you remember who lived in the manse before us?'

'Well, the minister before me was Ronnie McDonald. He lived alone. But I'm not sure who was before him.'

His colour is worrying me. 'Dad, I think it might be a good idea to call the doctor and have you checked out. I'm worried. You look grey.'

He squirms a bit in the chair and tries to stand up, brushing the back of his hand against his forehead. 'I wonder if it's something I've eaten. My stomach's a bit sore.'

'But you said you hadn't eaten for ages.'

'I had some chocolate with Oliver earlier. It could be a touch of indigestion. I can't take too much these days, and it was the dark stuff too.'

Shit, I think, standing up as quickly as I can without alarming him. 'Dad, sit down for a minute,' I say, helping him sit back down. 'Is your chest sore?' I ask as lightly as I can.

'A bit tight. I feel a bit tense,' he replies.

I rub his shoulders for a moment and think. 'Okay, well, I think it's worth me making a call to get you checked out to be sure.'

He doesn't reply, which is unusual as he hates when anyone makes a fuss. Something definitely isn't right. I run over to grab the landline and dial 999.

CHAPTER EIGHT

Josie

Tara has texted me telling me not to panic but that she's in an ambulance with Dad on the way to hospital in Edinburgh. The paramedics are treating him for a suspected heart attack. I call her immediately.

'Oh God, Tara,' I say. 'Is he okay?'

The line is patchy, and she sounds as though she's in a plane speeding down a runway. 'Thank God you called them when you did. Is he okay?'

'Hmm, well, I hope so. At least he's in the right hands for now.'

She sounds non-committal, which makes me wonder if there's more to this than she's letting on. 'What about the kids?'

'Mark is at Dad's house with them now. I couldn't let him go on his own.'

'Of course,' I say.

'Are you still at our house?'

'Yes. It's all quietened down, thank goodness, apart from a couple of officers around, but at least the circus from earlier is gone . . . Can I do anything now? What should I do? Poor, poor Dad.'

Tara's voice croaks slightly. She's doing her best to put on a strong front. 'I'm leaving it up to Mark to decide what to do with the kids. I reckon he'll bring them back to the house when the coast is a bit clearer. Will you fill him in?'

Sitting down on the back step, I suddenly feel exhausted. 'Yes, of course. I'm so sorry that you're having to deal with all of this, Tara. How lucky you went when you did, otherwise . . .'

'No point in dwelling on that now. The main thing is that he's okay, and hopefully when we go to the hospital, we'll get a better idea of what's happening.'

'Okay. Well, let me know as soon as you hear anything. In fact, do you want me to come up now?'

'No . . . but thanks. Anyway, you'll need to go and check on Gran. She must be wondering what on earth is going on.'

'You're right. No doubt one of the bridge ladies will have been in touch to tell her the gossip.'

'Josie, she probably already knows. She's always lurking about the Facebook page. Half the time she's more aware than me about what's going on.'

I stifle a laugh. 'You're right. I'll go down and see her as soon as I can.'

Ending the call, I stand up and stretch. The sky is turning a deep pink and I look at my watch. It's after nine. Walking over to Brian, I tell him I need to leave to check on Gran.

'Oh dear,' he says. 'That's rotten about your dad. Never rains but it pours.'

'Yes, you're right. I'll go and check on her, if that's okay?'

'I'll probably be here for a while. But come and go as you want to for now. That area—' he gestures to the garden — 'will remain out of bounds for a while.'

'Okay, thanks. I'll let my brother-in-law know so he can bring the kids back.'

'No worries,' he says.

When I pull up outside Gran's house, she's standing at the window staring out. Her hands are clutched to her chest, and she holds one up to wave when she sees me.

'Come on in, dear.' She beckons me in and closes the door behind, sliding the safety chain across, something I've never seen her do before.

'I'll make a nice pot of tea, shall I?' she says. I follow her into the kitchen. I dump my bag on the floor and slip my coat off and hang it over a chair by the table.

'Here, let me sort that, Gran,' I say when I realise she's standing staring into the open fridge.

'Oh . . . okay, dear. Thank you.'

'Would you like Earl Grey?'

'Yes please, that would be perfect.' She sinks into a chair, her normally rosy cheeks drained of colour.

'Are you okay, Gran?' For the second time in a few days, I think that she looks her age.

'A bit tired, love. I wasn't sure what was happening up at Tara's and I was getting a bit anxious . . . I looked at Facebook . . .' Her lips twitch together.

'Here you go. Have a wee drink of that and I'll tell you what happened. But please don't worry. I'm sure everything will be fine.' I wonder about pouring her something stronger. 'I'm going to pour us a wee gin and tonic. I could certainly do with it.' I need to tell her about Dad, but a huge part of me is worried that she will have a heart attack too. I jolt in fright when her teacup clatters back to the saucer.

'Oopsy, silly me,' she says, wiping up the spilled tea with the edge of her sleeve. 'Where's Tara?'

I reach for two glasses, quickly slice a lemon and pour a generous measure of gin into hers. She always keeps tonic in the fridge in case, so I open a bottle and fill the glasses to the top.

'She's with Dad . . . the thing is, he's not feeling too great.'

'Oh,' she says, quietly.

'Gran . . .' I begin to say.

'It's okay,' she says, taking a sharp breath. 'I already know.'

'Oh,' I say surprised. 'But how? It was all very sudden. Did Tara call you from the ambulance?'

'The ambulance?' she says, looking startled. 'Why the ambulance? Who's in the ambulance?'

Reaching out, I touch her arm gently. 'Gran, it's Dad. He's been taken into hospital with a heart attack.'

She gasps. 'But is he okay?'

'We think he should be, but Tara will call with news as soon as she can. They're taking him to the Royal. They should have arrived by now, so hopefully it won't be long until she's in touch.' Pulling my phone from my pocket, I sit it on the table, checking that the ringer is definitely switched on. I rub my eyes and yawn.

'Oh dear.' Her voice is small and distant. 'What a day.'

'It most certainly has been, Gran. I won't forget this one in a while . . . I could certainly do with a drink.' I take a long gulp and notice she copies.

We sit in a comfortable silence for a few minutes before Gran speaks. 'What happened up at the house then?'

I inwardly curse, completely forgetting what Tara had said. Gran likes a wee nosey around Facebook so she knows who's saying what and what's going on. Probably gives her something to talk to her bridge ladies about.

'The builders had knocked down the garage and were digging the new foundations of the office. They went a bit deeper than they normally would, and that's when they found them.'

Gran takes another chug of her gin. 'Were there many?'

'Quite a few.' I don't really want to go into too much detail and give her a sleepless night. 'The police have taken everything away to analyse. They'll hopefully be in touch again before too soon.'

CHAPTER NINE

My hands were sweating as I stared at him lying momentarily stunned on the floor. He no longer seemed so looming and scary. He looked pathetic.

'Come on. Now's your chance. Let's go,' she urged. 'Come on.' She'd managed to unlock the door and stood with one foot inside and the other across the threshold.

He twisted slightly and groaned.

'Okay, but let me grab my bag.'

Her face was white. I guessed I had about twenty seconds to get out of there before he moved. Running into the kitchen, I couldn't see it in its usual place, slung over one of the chairs at the rickety table. Shit. Where was it?

'Hurry up!' she yelled.

Then I remembered. I'd brought it through with the decorations. I raced back through into the living room to get it. Turning, I rushed to the door, taking a second too long to realise he wasn't there. I spun round and saw her standing there at the door, her eyes widening in horror as he pounced. Grabbing me by the neck, he started squeezing harder and harder. I gasped for breath, desperately trying to wrestle free. I kicked out with my feet but it was a waste of time. This was it. He was going to kill me. I started to black out, thinking how close I'd been to getting away. Suddenly he let go and I gulped in air, rubbing my raw neck.

Opening my eyes, I saw him on top of her. That's when the red mist descended again. I threw myself on top of him, screaming at him and battering at his back with my fists. She managed to wriggle free and move to the side and then things went blurry. All I could see was blood.

Red baubles and gold tinsel and blood. Lots of thick red blood. Everywhere. Screaming. Then silence, apart from the tick of the white plastic clock on the mantelpiece. She stared at me, her eyes glazed.

'What happened?' I whispered, my throat hoarse and sore.

'He's dead.'

'What?' I couldn't understand how he could be dead. Glancing at him again, I waited for him to rise up.

'He. Is. Dead.'

'But . . . how? What happened?'

She looked at me for a minute before she spoke. 'You . . . you killed him.'

CHAPTER TEN

Tara

It is almost midnight by the time I get home from the hospital. Dad was settled when I left and his colour had returned. The doctor said it was a good job the paramedics had arrived when they had. 'You did the right thing by calling,' she said. 'Otherwise, he might not have been quite so lucky.' Her face remained serious. 'But he'll need to stay here for a couple of days so we can keep an eye on him.'

He looks so weak and vulnerable, lying against the stiff starched sheets with the pillows propped up behind his head. Up until now he's always kept fairly healthy and now there's been this seismic shift in our roles. He's always been my parent, there to help me and to look after the children, but now things are definitely changing, and it's my turn to care for him. I know Josie's here to help and it would have been nice if she'd been there too for some moral support at the hospital. But it was important she be with Gran, especially after all that had happened.

My sister is used to her independence, having lived away for so long, and she doesn't need to think or worry about Dad or Gran in the way that I do. They don't feature on her radar in the way that they do on mine when we all live in such close proximity. Josie also knows I'm around to do all the worrying and checking. That's something she's always taken for granted. I can't help feeling a surge of resentment towards her and guilt that I'm thinking badly about my own sister. Especially with everything she's currently going through. Poor Josie has fled one domestic drama and fallen straight into another. I wonder if life with Dimitri now seems more appealing after all, although I hope not.

When I pull into the driveway, the house is in darkness apart from the glow of the lamp in the living room. Walking in the front door, I quietly place my bag on the floor, kick off my shoes and pad through. Mark is fast asleep on the sofa, holding the book he's been reading gently in his hand. He jolts when I lean over to kiss his head. 'Oh.' He rubs his eyes. 'I didn't hear you come in. Sorry, love. I meant to sit up.'

'You must be shattered. You should have gone to bed.' I sit down next to him.

'Don't be silly,' he pulls me into a hug.

I finally burst into tears, after spending most of the day biting my emotions back.

'Ssh, you're okay.' His voice is soothing as he strokes my hair. 'What a day, eh?'

Reaching into my pocket, I pull a tissue out and noisily blow my nose. 'You couldn't write it. Dad in hospital is bad enough without all this mess in the garden and police business . . . To think a week ago life was relatively quiet and dull.'

Mark laughs. 'There's a lot to be said for a quiet life. It's difficult to know what to make of everything. Hopefully there'll be a straightforward explanation to the stuff in the garden.'

'Yes, hopefully. Though a body's not "stuff", is it, Mark?'

'Come on, Tara. Let's get you to bed.' He stands up and holds out a hand, which I gratefully grab.

I turn to follow him and we climb the stairs, pausing at the top to check on Millie and Oliver, who are both sound asleep. 'Did they ask much?' I rub my eyes and yawn.

'No, not really,' says Mark. 'I managed to distract them.'

'Oh well, I suppose tomorrow is another day. We can deal with things then.' I'm actually dreading a new day. I've managed to avoid all the messages on my phone from well-meaning friends, not to mention those from people who are clearly just being nosy. I'd sent a quick text to Jessica's mum, given she had been looking after Millie today when things all kicked off, with a brief explanation of what was going on. I knew she could be relied on to disperse the news accordingly, and Brian would no doubt have provided her with more details.

I give my face a quick rub with a cloth, brush my teeth and haul my pyjamas on. Climbing into bed, I lie for a while thinking about the day and how this morning had started. Never in my wildest dreams would I ever have imagined things turning out like this. How I would love to travel back in time and start the day again.

Mark quickly falls asleep and I envy his ability to switch things off, close his eyes and find peace somewhere. He's always been a sound sleeper, even when the kids were babies, and could sleep through anything. My mind is far too busy to switch off. Fidgeting with the covers, I toss and turn and force myself to count to a hundred. But I reach fifty-six and feel agitated. I kick off the duvet. Mark is now snoring gently and blissfully unaware of the turmoil in my head. I list all the things I need to do in the morning and wonder what time I should head back to see Dad at the hospital. I also need to pick some things up at his flat. Maybe some fresh pyjamas and underwear. What else? I should ask Mark what sort of things a man would need for hospital. Would he want his razor? My mind is whirring.

Then I remember how determined he was that I shouldn't bring Gran to visit. I was *not* looking forward to telling her that she was barred from the hospital.

'Please don't, dear. You mustn't bring her all this way. That won't help any of us. Especially her, if she sees me like this.'

'But she'll want to,' I said. 'You know how stubborn she is. She'll insist.'

'That doesn't matter. She's not that great in hospitals, trust me. It will only trigger memories of my dad being ill and dying.' He paused to take a sip of water through the straw sticking out of the cup I held for him. 'And of the times she's been in too.'

'Okay. If you're sure?' I said, suddenly remembering my own predicament.

'Yes,' he said. 'Thank you, dear.'

'I'd better be going, Dad. You need your rest. In fact, I probably shouldn't even be here.' I knew the nurses were turning a blind eye to my presence and I didn't want to take advantage any longer. I stood up to leave.

'Wait,' he said, his voice low, and he beckoned me closer. 'Can you do something else for me, please?'

'Of course,' I said, thinking he was going to ask me to bring in some contraband food or something.

This time his voice was barely a whisper. 'Please make sure she doesn't go anywhere near my flat.'

'Who?' I said.

'Your gran.' He clutched at my hand. 'Promise me.'

'I promise you.' This was weird. Why on earth did he not want her in the flat? Did he think she was going to rifle through his drawers?

Dad was still gripping my hand and I gently uncurled each finger. 'I need to go now, Dad. I'll be back in tomorrow.'

He managed a small smile and raised his hand in a small wave.

I was so exhausted I couldn't give it much more thought as I drove home. But now as I lie here, restless, my mind a blur of emotions and thoughts, I can't help but wonder why he was so adamant. Is there something he's hiding?

CHAPTER ELEVEN

Josie

The next day when I'm sure Gran is asleep in her chair, I walk along to the Co-op in the high street to pick up some milk and bread. Unsure whether to buy a loaf of brown or a seeded batch, I stand staring at them both. Lately, it seems making the simplest decisions is a bit too much. I sense a presence behind me and I jump. I spin round to find Jason standing there.

'Hi, Josie,' he says, almost shyly. 'Sorry, I didn't mean to give you a fright.'

'That's okay,' I say, realising how on edge I am. Aside from a few silver hairs in his dark cropped hair, he's hardly aged. His smile is warm and welcoming and . . . my face flushes with embarrassment.

'Are you okay?'

'Yes.' I give myself a shake. 'A bit hot and bothered.'

'I heard about your dad.'

I laugh nervously. *Seriously, Josie?* I'm like a teenager again, which is *not* good. And anyway, he's asking after my sickly father, he's not asking me out. 'Oh. Can you believe it? Yesterday kept getting better and better.'

He frowns. 'But how is he?'

'Still in hospital. They're keeping him in for a couple of days to keep an eye on him. I'm going to go up and visit him later.' I shrug. 'I'm getting a few things for Gran.'

'How's she bearing up?'

'I think she's had a bit of a shock. She's not saying much, which is not like her. Normally she doesn't stop talking.'

'Well, if I can do anything to help will you let me know?'

'Thank you, I will.' Although what he can possibly do to help, I'm not entirely sure. 'Well, nice to chat.' My voice is now clipped. 'I'd better go check on Gran.'

'Sure, of course,' he says, reaching and patting me on the shoulder.

His voice is kind and I want to tell him everything. But I'm too late. Years too late. 'Bye.' I grab a loaf of bread, not caring what type, and head straight to the till. The touch of his hand on my shoulder still tingles, which is unsettling. Especially as I noticed the wedding band on his finger. Not that his marital status should matter a bit . . . but, well, of course that's all I can think about now. Where is his wife? Who is his wife?

As I walk down the high street back towards Gran's house I shiver and pull my jacket around me. My stomach starts churning and I walk faster. Turning around, I quickly scan the pavements. They're busy and bustling with people out doing Saturday morning errands. *Calm down, Josie, breathe slowly and concentrate on getting back to Gran's.* I think I'm being watched, and I jump when the church bells chime.

Bloody Dimitri, he knew exactly what he was doing by sending that card. A technique designed to unsettle me so I would be walking on eggshells not knowing if or when he was going to appear.

I slow down and try to settle my heart rate. For a moment, I think about Jason and wonder about what could have been. But we were a summer fling, that's all. We both agreed that when we started seeing each other. Yet our brief romance felt like so much more to me. Afterwards, I don't know how I could have coped without Gran. She was my rock throughout and helped me to hold everything together even though my world was falling apart.

Slipping the key into the lock, I go through to the lounge, where Gran is still dozing. I've always loved this room, with its off-white walls and cosy sofas with bright-blue scatter cushions. I gently shake her arm and she opens her eyes, blinking. 'Hi, Gran.'

'Oh, hello, dear. Is everything okay?'

'Yes. I was at the shops.'

'Oh,' she says, straightening herself in the chair. 'Thank you. Though why?'

'Well,' I say, slightly puzzled by her question, 'we'd run out of bread and milk.'

'But your dad normally gets things for me.'

I sit down next to her, reaching out to pat her shoulder. 'Yes, he does. But remember he's not feeling well?'

She rubs her eyes. 'Yes, of course, right. Silly me. I remember now. He's in the hospital.'

I sigh a breath of relief, though I'm still worried she's becoming muddled with what's going on.

'Can I go and see him?'

'Well . . . I think we need to wait and hear if he's up to visitors.' Tara called me earlier to tell me he had insisted she didn't visit him. But Gran would be devastated if we told her.

'But I'm his mother,' she says, becoming quite indignant. 'I should be there with him.'

This is uncharted territory with Gran and I'm not quite sure what to do or say. I wish Tara was here to handle this, which is extremely selfish of me. I'm now guiltily realising how much responsibility Tara's had to shoulder in my absence. My sister has far too many things to try and juggle right now.

'You're right, Gran. But let's wait and find out what the doctors say. They might suggest a couple of quiet days of rest will do him the world of good.'

'But . . . I should be there. Please take me, Josie.' She stands up and walks towards the doorway of the room. 'I'm going to go and change and I'll be ready.'

I pull my phone from my bag and check the time. Shit, how do I deal with this? 'Okay, Gran,' I say, trying to keep my voice calm and steady. 'But it's not visiting hours yet. And I really think we need to take advice from the hospital . . . There's no point in driving all the way up there only to be turned away at the door.'

She folds her arms, a look of something crossing her face. 'I need to talk to him.'

God, I need to distract her. I've never seen her so keyed up before and so serious. 'Gran . . .' My voice trails away as I desperately think of something to say. 'Why didn't you tell me Jason was back?'

'Jason?'

'Yes, Jason. Remember?'

'Jason?' she says again, confused.

'From way back. When I was a teenager. It was before I went to university.'

She purses her lips. 'Jason. Of course.'

'He's back in town, working with Mark at the restaurant.'

Her face is blank. 'Oh. I wasn't aware, dear.'

'But didn't Tara say anything to you about Mark's new business partner?'

She shakes her head abruptly. 'I didn't realise it was *that* Jason. It is quite a common name.'

Seized by another wave of confusion, I study her face and notice guilt flow across it. I'm certain she's keeping something from me.

CHAPTER TWELVE

I looked at my bloody hands, which I was rubbing together. 'But how . . . I didn't. No.' I stuffed a bloody fist into my mouth trying to stifle a scream. I couldn't believe this was happening. How did I kill him?

'It's okay,' she said softly. 'You're okay. He had a knife. He had a knife. He was going to kill me . . .'

'Oh God. But what about . . .'

'Ssh,' she said, putting a finger to her lips. 'It was self-defence.'

I shuddered in fear. 'But they won't see it like that. They'll say I killed him on purpose. Murder. I'll go to jail. I can't go to jail. Not now. I can't. I can't.' I was weeping while grief ebbed out of me and the metallic scent of blood invaded my nose. The blood felt dirty and oily on my skin. I wasn't a murderer. I couldn't even kill a spider. There was no way I could've killed him. Was there?

'Listen to me,' she said, her voice now firm. 'You need to go.'

'I can't . . . we need to call the police . . . surely they'll be here any minute anyway.'

She shook her head. 'Nothing new, there are always domestics around here. The neighbours won't care.'

'But we can't just go.'

'You need to go now.'

I shook my head violently. 'No, no, I can't . . .'

'Listen to me. You can and you will. You've got to think about the future,' she said. 'There's too much at stake.'

She stood up and wiped her hands against her trousers, leaving a trail of blood. It seemed to be everywhere.

'But I can't run away.'

'You can. And you will. You need to. I'll sort all of this out. Go and wash your hands. Pack lightly and only take what you need.'

CHAPTER THIRTEEN

Tara

When I reach the bottom of the stairs this morning, I gather up the mail from the mat, automatically rifling through it on my way through to the kitchen.

Mark and the kids are sitting at the table, eating porridge. I spot the dirty pot in the sink and hope he'll wash up.

'Good morning, Mummy!' shouts Millie.

Oliver slips off his chair and runs to give me a hug.

'How are you this morning?'

'Okay,' he says, sticking out his bottom lip.

Looking over at Mark, I raise an eyebrow.

'I was just telling the kids Grandpa is fine and he'll be in hospital for a few days so the doctors can keep an eye on him.'

Kissing Oliver's head, I take his hand and walk him back over to the table. 'That's right. He's fine and he'll be home soon.' I've not had a chance to process the fact the kids will have had a fright when they saw their beloved grandpa wasn't his usual self. Not to mention me telling them an ambulance was coming to collect him. Thank God Mark had arrived when he did and was able to distract them before

44

the paramedics came running up the stairs. It would've been awful if they'd seen him being taken out on a stretcher.

'Can I make him a card?' says Millie, showing her practical side.

'That's an excellent idea,' I say. 'How about you eat up your porridge and I'll fetch the craft box out?'

Oliver nods and I stand up to walk back to the sink, where I've left the mail. Sifting through the bills, I spot a card addressed to Josie, which seems strange, and a white envelope addressed to me. Ripping it open, I quickly scan the contents.

An appointment at the breast clinic at the Western General for Wednesday. Carefully folding the slip, I pop it into my handbag, which is still sitting in the hallway from last night. My hands are shaking, though I'm not sure whether in terror or relief. There's nothing I can do until next week, so I need to put this well out of my head and focus on Dad.

Later, I drive to Dad's flat to pick up some bits and pieces for him. I let myself in with the spare key. Bending down, I pick up his mail, leaving neat bundles for the two ground-floor flats and climb the stairs to Dad's flat. I never normally come here alone. I've never needed to.

Opening the door, I step inside and pause, listening to the rumble of the boiler starting up. I walk through to the kitchen and fill the kettle. I've not had my usual cup of tea this morning and could do with sitting quietly for five minutes. Reaching into the cupboard above the kettle, I take out a mug, which is covered in sunflowers, designed by Millie. I open the next cupboard and see boxes of Special K and Coco Pops. We were never allowed those when we were younger. Dad's been a changed man since the twins' arrival, and I smile. Dunking a teabag in the mug, I throw it in the overflowing bin, which I make a mental note to empty.

The kitchen is tidy enough but, while my tea cools, I quickly wipe everything down with a wad of kitchen roll and squirt some bleach down the sink. I open the fridge and give the contents a quick inspection. There's some yellowing broccoli and a carton of out-of-date milk. Sadness ripples through me as I think of my poor dad living here alone all these years.

I tip the broccoli into the bin, then pour the sour milk down the sink and rinse the carton. I sit down and sip my tea. Everything about the flat is sparse and there's no clutter at all. The only dashes of colour are Millie and Oliver's paintings, which are neatly pinned to the fridge with a magnet.

My poor dad. All these years he's been alone, waiting for my mother to return, and she never has. How could she? And how could he have waited? Was he *so* devoted to her? Would I have been able to do the same if I had been in his shoes? Would I wait for Mark to return?

I think of Dad, always insistent he's happy with his own space, and wonder how he fills his evenings. I know he's busy with volunteering at the church and the odd game of bowls. But what does he do in this flat? What does he eat? What does he watch on TV? I'm ashamed to be so unaware of the intricate details about my father's life. I drain the rest of the tea, wash the mug and set it on the rack to dry. He's always refused to buy a dishwasher, saying that he prefers to wash the dishes himself to keep himself busy. I pull some antibacterial wipes from the cupboard under the sink and give them a quick rub across the floor, noticing they aren't too dirty when I finish. That means he does keep quite a clean and tidy house. Satisfied the kitchen is clean enough, I quickly wipe the surfaces in the hall and in the living room and give all the carpets a good once-over with the hoover. The upright piano sits against the wall in the living room. That had been our piano — or rather, Mum's piano. I run my hand along the top, unsettling a layer of dust which I've missed. I always wondered why he kept the piano. Nobody's played it since Mum left. She was the pianist of the family, with her long, slender fingers. He doesn't even let Oliver and Millie mess about on it. That's the only time he gets cross with them. If they dare to open the lid, he immediately tells them off. Fortunately, they don't go near it now as they know he gets cross. Yet Dad is rarely sentimental about things. I sit down on the stool and open the lid, brushing my fingers against the keys. Playing the piano was never one of my talents, although I did try so hard as a child when I was sent to lessons. Leaning forward, I rest my forehead on the piano and close my eyes. A memory of a gentle tune comes back, mellow and warm and uplifting. I imagine Mum's graceful fingers stretching across the keys, her head dipped slightly and her eyes narrowed as she immersed herself in the music. I can hear the notes so clearly. She used to play the piece all the time for Josie and me. The theme from *Forrest Gump*. Music I had completely forgotten until now as I sit here by the piano. I open my eyes and sit back for a moment, rolling my shoulders and shaking myself. Reminiscing is pointless and I've more pressing matters to attend to.

I push the door open to the spare room where the twins always sleep, and give it a quick dust and hoover the carpets too. The room isn't at all dirty, but there's something reassuring about being able to freshen everything up a bit. I'm assuming when Dad does come home, he'll need to take things easy for quite some time. Anyway, I'm actually finding the whole process quite cathartic. Cleaning tends to do that to me and helps me sort out my jumbled thoughts.

My hands are clammy as I stand at the threshold of Dad's bedroom, wondering if he will be annoyed if I go in. I push the door handle to his bedroom. Light floods into the room from the window at the back. I'm uncomfortable about being in here, a room I've never had any need to go into before. I strip the bed, dumping the sheets in the hallway, thinking it will be easier to take them back to my house to wash and dry out in the garden. That is, I assume, if the police are all finished. I hoover under the bed, amazed how easily it slides in, unlike in my house where we keep an assortment of stuff stashed there. I put a fresh set of linen on, wipe the bedside table and the chest of drawers and open the window to let a blast of fresh air in. Onto the bathroom next, to give it a quick once-over.

When I finish wiping down the shower, I gather up the laundry and give the rest of the flat a cursory glance, remembering to take the rubbish bag out of the bin. I'm about to leave when I realise I've left the bedroom window open and forgotten Dad's things. He needs pyjamas and his razor and some clean clothes. Honestly, what's wrong with me? My head is all over the place.

He keeps a holdall in the hall cupboard, so I fetch it and stand looking at his drawers, which is weird. The first drawer I open has his underwear and night stuff all folded neatly. I select a few fresh pairs and put them in the bag. I spotted his washbag in the bathroom earlier and add in some of his toiletries from the bathroom cupboard. His glasses are on the bedside table, so I pick them up and wonder if he would like a book. Looking around, there's no sign of any, unlike in my bedroom where they're stacked in a pile on the floor next to the bed.

Reaching to pull open the top drawer beside his bed, I notice a Val McDermid book. That will do. I'm about to push the drawer shut when I spot a small box. I shouldn't be rifling about or being nosy and I should shut the drawer. But I can't help myself. Curiosity gets the better of me and I reach for it. Holding the box in the palm of my hand, I study it for a moment. The box is wooden with a delicate carving on the front which is like some kind of symbol. Frowning, I trace my finger over the symbol. It's not something I've ever seen before. Mind you, I'm not in the habit of going through my dad's things. I should put the box back and leave well alone. But I gently prise it open, promising myself I'll just take a wee peek inside. Its contents might even give me more of an insight into Dad's life and help me understand him a bit more.

The lid opens and I stare inside, momentarily stunned. That's when my world starts spinning on its axis. I can't believe what I'm looking at.

CHAPTER FOURTEEN

Josie

With all that's going on, I've just about managed to put Dimitri out of my thoughts. However, now I find myself upstairs sitting on my bed, staring out the window and thinking. Reflecting and processing my thoughts is something I rarely do. It's far easier to keep busy and distract myself with everything else and everyone else's problems. Gran is downstairs watching a new crime series on Netflix and invited me to join her. But my restless mind meant I couldn't focus on the plot, whereas she was completely hooked. I made my excuses and said I would go for a lie-down.

By all accounts, after what happened between us, I *should* be heartbroken, yet I don't have a particular ache eating away at my insides. Nor do I have a sense of longing for my husband or feel any loss. Maybe that's still to come? I actually enjoy having the bed to myself without him snoring next to me. Admittedly, I'm emotionally washed out, but I just don't think I'm as devastated as I should be. Does that mean I didn't ever properly love him? Isn't heartbreak supposed to be about love and losing that love? I think about Mum and how devastated I was as a child when she left. I was

49

broken, confused and bereft. And so much more. Of course, as I grew up those feelings diminished and faded with time. But the heartbreak and the sense of loss never disappeared altogether. Nor did the longing I have when I go to places here, in North Berwick, which remind me of her: the walk up the Law, the apple trees in our old garden — or should I say Tara's garden now — the scout hall where she used to take me for gymnastics and would always be waiting by the creaky swing door to collect me. Sometimes when I pass these places, though I do try to avoid them as much as I can, I have a physical yearning for her that threatens to overwhelm me. Sometimes I will randomly recognise a smell — her perfume or the laundry powder she used — and it will stop me in my tracks, taking my breath away. I close my eyes, and a raw sense of longing for the love of my mum hits me. I feel the sadness surrounding her loss once again. That's never left me and never will. It will for ever be part of my soul.

My thoughts about Dimitri feel completely different to how it was after Jason left and we went our separate ways. I remember the clawing agony and how much I missed him. The feelings are all still as raw and intense as they were fourteen years ago. I was heartbroken because I had been rejected by the man I loved. Unrequited love is, according to the experts, the most heart-breaking. I remember so many times when I thought I had learned to cope, then the heartache about what had happened between us would crash down on me. It felt like I was drowning. Although it was surreal to see him again — and, I admit, kind of nice — it overshadowed the sadness and grief that took over back then.

I certainly don't long for Dimitri in the same way and I don't have any sense of loss over my inability to conceive a child with him. I'm relieved and so very glad.

CHAPTER FIFTEEN

My pulse quickened as I started to do as she said. Rushing into the bedroom, I pulled a holdall out from under the bed and threw in some underwear. Then I caught sight of myself in the mirror. I was covered in blood.

'Change your clothes and take them with you,' she said.

Peeling off my sweatshirt and jeans, I shoved them into a side pocket of the bag and quickly hauled on a fresh pair of trousers and a top.

'Don't take anything else,' she said. 'Buy what you need when you get to wherever you go.'

'But what about my toothbrush . . .'

'No. You buy what you need later. Just go as far away from here as you can and don't look back. You need to think of the future.'

'But I don't have any money . . .' I knew he did, and I reached under his side of the mattress and pulled out a brown envelope stuffed with cash.

'Take all of it,' she said. 'Come on, you need to go.'

Wincing, I bent down to slip on some shoes. 'But what will you do?'

'I'll call the police. I'll explain what happened and tell them I acted in self-defence.'

I threw myself into her, clinging tightly and sobbing until she gently unfurled my hands. 'Time to go. Grab the first taxi or bus you see and keep moving.'

Dazed, I stepped away from her.

'Here, take my jacket,' she said. It was warm and smelled of her, which made my cry even harder.

'Things will all be okay, I promise,' she said.

'Are you sure he's dead?'

She nodded. 'Let me know when you're safe.'

Those were the last words I heard her say.

CHAPTER SIXTEEN

Tara

Too shocked to move, I stare at the items nestled together in the corner of the box. My world seems to stand still for several long minutes, anxiety twisting at my stomach. Why does Dad have these? And why hasn't he ever said anything to me or Josie? I had no idea Mum had left them behind. That must have been devastating for Dad and made things real and final. Yet why did he never tell us he has her jewellery? Did she leave them behind for Josie and me? Or to make sure Dad knew her departure was final, and their marriage was over?

I tip out her engagement ring, with its large emerald, and the slim gold wedding band into my palm. They seem so delicate and small in my big hand. Rubbing them between my fingers, I think of Mum and her beautiful, slender fingers. Her nails were always polished in a pale shade of pink, and I remember how I would watch her paint them and push back the cuticles with an orange stick. She used to try and give me manicures too, but I could never sit still for long enough. Instead, I would ask her to paint my nails and walk about with my hands on my hips in a bid to show them off.

Looking at the rings, I remember how much I admired them when I was younger and how I wished I had smooth hands like her. I couldn't wait to be able to wear sparkly jewellery too. Back then, when I did try and slide them on my fingers they wouldn't go past my knuckles. Sadly, I had inherited Dad's fingers. I take the engagement ring, holding it between my thumb and forefinger. Once again, it refuses to budge past my knuckle. Smiling sadly, I'm reminded of the little girl I once was all those years ago. The fact they won't slide onto my finger confirms they are definitely hers. Feeling a wave of sadness wash over me, I'm suddenly exhausted and light-headed. Lying back on the bed, I close my eyes. Poor, poor Dad.

I'm now beginning to realise just how much I've taken him for granted over the years. He had to get on with life after she'd gone and keep things going for Josie and me. He kept the house tidy, cooked for us, helped with homework and did all the practical things Mum used to do. However, he was useless when it came to emotional things, leaving Gran to do the best she could. She made up for the cuddles and emotional support he seemed unable to provide. We're so lucky to have family in our lives who care.

My phone beeps.

Hope you're okay. Do you want me to come to the hospital this afternoon? J x

I quickly type a message back.

Yes, okay. At Dad's flat getting some stuff. Be great if you can come if not too tricky leaving Gran x

My phone buzzes again.

I'll let you know! x

Sitting a few minutes longer, I stare at the rings and put them back in the box. What's the point in being angry with Mum? If she didn't want to be with us, she did the right thing by leaving rather than staying through a sense of duty. The truth hurts, of course it does, but now in the light of day as I sit there holding something that belonged to her, I feel a bit more at peace. At least she was being true to herself and

54

leading the life she wanted to. Isn't that the most important thing we can do in life?

Carefully placing the rings back in the box, I tuck it back in the drawer hoping Dad won't notice it's been moved.

CHAPTER SEVENTEEN

Josie

Over the next few days, Tara and I do our best to distract Gran and keep her from visiting Dad in the hospital. We take it in turns to go and visit him, so one of us is always around and on hand to keep an eye on her. She isn't at all happy, but we manage to concoct a few white lies to keep her contained.

'There seems to be a virus in his ward, Gran, and they've asked we don't take any children or elderly relatives in. Tara can't even take the kids in.' Eventually, she seems to accept she isn't going to be taken in to see him and stops asking. But she's extremely agitated and jumpy and, once again, I wonder if I should ask the doctor to come out and see her. She insists she's fine, and she made me cancel the appointment I made at the start of the week.

Tara is always subdued when I see her, understandably, but I can't help worrying something else is wrong and she isn't telling me. I suggest we meet for a coffee in the high street when the twins are at nursery. At first, she's reluctant because of people gossiping and asking questions should she bump into anyone she knows. But with a little persuasion, she agrees.

I'm waiting, sitting at a small table at the back, when she arrives. Waving her over, I stand up and give her a big hug. Her face is pale, her hair pulled back in a ponytail and her sweatshirt swamps her small frame.

'How are you?' I say, sitting down.

'I'm bloody exhausted,' she says. 'With everything.' She chews the nail of her index finger, which surprises me. I haven't seen her do that for years, not since she was a teenager and sitting her exams at school.

The waitress comes over. 'What would you like?'

'Tara?'

'I'd like a flat white, please.'

'And I'll have a large skinny latte, please,' I say.

'Anything else?' asks the waitress.

We both shake our heads. A marriage breakdown, an ill father in hospital and a body in the garden are the perfect tools for diminishing our appetites.

A group of shrieking women have replaced the quiet woman who had been sitting alone at the table next to us. There's no danger that our conversation will be overheard.

'Are you sure nothing else is the matter?' I press when the waitress walks away.

She avoids meeting my eye. 'No.'

'I'm here for you, Tara, if anything else is on your mind.' I decide a supplementary statement may be better than another question.

I watch with interest as she reaches into her bag and pulls out an envelope. 'This is for you. It came the other day.'

'Oh no,' I say, immediately recognising the handwriting. A muscle twitches in my cheek.

'What?' says Tara, looking at me with concern.

'It's from *him*. Dimitri. Another letter or card.'

'Another one?' She watches me tear open the envelope and study the card with a sunflower design.

I nod. 'Yes. He sent one a few days ago.'

'Saying what?' Her smooth brow is wrinkled by her frown.

'He's basically saying I should forgive him and come to my senses and come home. Or he will come and fetch me.'

She raises an eyebrow. 'That sounds like a threat to me, Josie.'

'Yes, you're absolutely right. And . . . this is not the first time it's happened.'

'He's threatened you before?' Her jaw drops.

'In a passive-aggressive way. He's never been violent. But I now realise that doesn't matter. He's trying to do the same again.'

'Bloody hell.'

I wave a dismissive hand. 'Quite. But all his pathetic actions are currently paling into insignificance, don't you think? I mean, Dimitri is the least of my worries right now.'

'But Josie, what if he turns up here?' She sounds slightly panicky, which, again, was not like Tara at all. She's normally the calm and collected one.

'I've been worrying about that and wondering if he's watching me. But he's a coward. I don't think he'll pitch up here. At least, I hope not.'

The waitress places our coffees in front of us and we both sit silently for a moment, taking a drink from the mugs.

'Is it definitely over with him?' she asks, her voice quiet.

'Yes. I'm not going back.'

'What will you do?'

'I'm not sure yet, Tara. But I'll be here for as long as you need me to be . . .'

The women cackling at the next table are quieter and I'm aware of questioning looks being thrown our way. We've obviously been recognised and I'm very glad when they eventually pay up and leave. Tara and I keep our eyes trained on our own table and on each other.

'Do you remember any of the gossip when Mum vanished?' I say, eventually breaking the silence.

'No,' she starts and is pensive for a minute. 'I don't. I mean, I was only ten. We were so young. Dad must've kept us shielded from things. In which case, he did a good job.'

I nod. 'How did he cope?'

'He had to try his best and manage with things, I suppose. That's what happens with kids. They give you focus . . . Aw, shit. I don't mean it like that at all. Sorry. That was a bit crass of me, Josie. Sorry, I didn't mean it like that.'

'Don't worry. No offence taken.' I don't want her filtering everything she says to me in case she hurts my feelings.

'Do you still think about her a lot?' asks Tara.

Shrugging, I stall for a moment unsure of quite how to answer. 'Yes and no . . . if I'm being honest about it. I mean, yes, I do think about her, but not all of the time and only when I wish I could ask her advice. Like now with Dimitri, for example. I'd love to know what she thought and what she would say to me. I'd like to ask her opinion of him.' I bite my lip. 'How about you?'

'A bit like you,' she says in a low voice. 'I used to think about her all the time and then it waned. When I was pregnant and had the twins, I really missed her . . . in fact, I got a bit obsessed about her.'

I was aware of this as that was when Tara set up her Facebook page and started posting regular updates on it with news of her pregnancy, then the birth of the twins. I knew she was desperate for Mum to get in touch. There was no excuse for Mum not to. If she had wanted to find us, she could have. Especially when Tara was struggling and really needed her.

'Why do you think she stopped sending the birthday cards?' asks Tara, taking another mouthful of coffee.

'I don't know. I mean, I guess lots of people stop sending cards to people when they reach twenty-one. Maybe she thought that was a good age to draw a line under it. Maybe that made more sense than her keeping on sending them until we reached our thirties and it randomly stopped . . . when something happened to her?'

'True,' agrees Tara. 'The fact you got your last one at twenty-one and mine kept coming until I got to twenty-one meant there was a clear reason for it and a purpose to it.'

'Did you keep them?'

'Yes. They're all in a box under my bed . . .'

I spread my hands on the table. 'Tara, I sometimes wonder if she's even still alive.'

She reaches across and clasps my hand. 'You must keep believing that she is.'

'Then why doesn't she come back?'

'I would love to tell you the answer,' she concedes softly. 'And sometimes, until lately, I hated her. I actually hated her. But what's the point? She obviously had to do what she had to do. If she's happy, surely that's the main thing.'

'Oh.' I'm surprised. This is a change in attitude from Tara and I wonder what's happened for her to suddenly become more forgiving.

'Yes. I'm not saying I condone what she did or understand it,' she says, shuddering. 'I mean, I can't begin to imagine walking out on my kids. But it's easy to judge people, isn't it? We don't have any idea of what her state of mind was or her reasoning.'

'You're being very measured.'

'Well,' she says, 'life is short. Everyone should be happy.'

I cock my head to the side. 'Do you think she's still alive?'

'Yes. Without a doubt, I definitely think she's still alive.'

'How can you be so sure though?'

Tara opens her mouth as if she's about to say something.

'What?' I wait for her to continue.

She flicks her hand dismissively. 'It doesn't matter . . . I was just going to say that sometimes things are better left in the past.'

As I look at my little sister, there are so many questions that I don't have the answers to, and I wonder if I ever will. But as I look at her closely, I can tell she's hiding something.

60

CHAPTER EIGHTEEN

Feeling unsteady on my feet, I kept my head down and walked. Hopefully nobody would notice me in the darkness. I pulled up my hood and kept moving. I had to get as far away from him as possible. Him. The man I loved. The father of my unborn baby. I'd been planning to tell him on Christmas Day. It would've been my gift to him. The pavement heaved with people rushing past. I tried to walk purposefully, my head down, and I didn't look back. Crossing the street, I darted between cars and ran over to the bus stop. For once, two arrived at the same time but I decided to keep walking. A tear slipped down my cheek.

I felt guilty and ashamed. Like a coward. Everything was all my fault. I should never have married him. I should have left him months ago. I was stupid. And weak. How did I know he was definitely dead? Maybe I should have checked. A couple of times I stopped and turned around to go back. What if there was a chance he was still alive? I walked in circles, my head throbbing as I realised if he wasn't dead then I soon would be.

I couldn't let her take the blame. Could I really leave her to deal with everything? True to form, I'd been my obedient self and done as I was told. Like a good little girl. What sort of person did that make me?

I remembered her face, pleading and kind. She would do anything for me and I knew I had to leave, there was no other option. I couldn't risk going to jail and having my baby taken away from me. If I could do something right, I would be the best mum possible to this baby. I had to see this as an opportunity to make a fresh start. She'd given me a chance and I had to seize it. But something niggled at the pit of my stomach and I kept asking myself, would I do the same for her?

A bus whooshed past and I jumped as spray from the road hit my legs. Shivering, I clutched my bag closer to my body and kept going. One step at a time. I expected to hear the sounds of footsteps running after me, a hand on my shoulder. When I heard sirens and saw the flashing lights of a police car speed past, I shrank into the shadows. I kept muttering her words to myself. Just go as far away from here as you can. But where? I stepped around groups of people on their way to the pub, tried to block out the sounds of screaming Christmas tunes drifting from open doors of bars. Decorating the Christmas tree this afternoon felt a long time ago. Now I was roaming the street with blood on my hands.

CHAPTER NINETEEN

Tara

I'm on the verge of telling Josie all about my discovery of Mum's jewellery at Dad's house and of the messages from her over the past few years. As we sit together having coffee and talking about the past, I'm so close to offloading everything and telling her. That's what family is for. It's on the very tip of my tongue. I could show her the messages and tell her how happy they made me initially and how angry they made me after a while. I want to tell her how much I longed for Mum to get in touch, and when she finally did, I was ecstatic. But how can I explain why I've kept it a secret from her? She'll be devastated, as I would be with her if the roles were reversed. Will she understand I wanted to keep a little bit of Mum to myself? I mean, Josie had her for longer than I did. I was only ten when she left, and Josie had two whole extra years. But I'm not sure whether she'll understand any of that now. Will she appreciate my need to keep a part of Mum to myself? I'm not quite sure. And where do I begin with the box of jewellery? Instead I keep quiet and say nothing.

There are so many things I want to tell my sister. How I wish I could talk to her about the lump in my breast and the appointment at the hospital in a couple of days' time. I also want to ask her about Jason and why things are a bit awkward between them. I can't believe I had no idea something had happened between them in the past. The only reason I know now is because of something he said to Mark. Why didn't I notice? To think she managed to keep things a secret makes me wonder what other things she's kept from me. Jason only indicated to Mark quite recently he and Josie had a wee fling back in the day. He made things clear he didn't want to cause Josie any embarrassment, which is why I promised not to bring it up. I thought she might have said something to me after her obvious shock from seeing him the other night. But something holds me back from saying all of this to Josie. Because, try as I might, I know she's keeping something from me. Yes, she opened up about Dimitri and his appalling behaviour over the years. But I'm sure there is more to tell. That's another reason I don't want to tell her about my discovery in Dad's flat the other night. I haven't told Mark, and that's what I hate most of all in this mess. I'm starting to keep secrets from him, which we always said we would never do. We always said we would be honest with each other, no matter what. *No matter what.* But I don't want to tell him about the lump because he'll worry. Telling him about the other stuff feels a bit strange and raw just now and I'm not ready to share with him. Once I do, things will all start to spiral downwards and I'm not quite sure what will happen afterwards.

I haven't raised the issue with Dad either yet, despite having seen him in the hospital several times since making the discovery. I wonder if that's why he's so adamant he doesn't want Gran in the house. What is he afraid of her finding? And why is he not afraid of me finding something? Is he more confident I won't go rifling through his private stuff?

Josie and I say our goodbyes and I drive home to find a car parked in the driveway. *What now?* I think irritably. So much for the rural lifestyle. This place is getting more like Princes Street every day with the number of so-called passers-by and vehicles. Wondering if it's the police, I walk over to the car just as the driver gets out.

'Hi,' says the woman, smiling at me and holding out her hand. I can't take my eyes off her extremely long eyelashes. With her glossy bobbed hair, she looks as though she should star in a BBC drama. 'Are you Tara?' she asks confidently.

'Uh-uh,' I manage.

'My name is Amy Rodriguez and I'm a reporter with STV News.'

I drop her hand. 'I'm not interested. Please leave.'

'It must be a difficult time for you just now, Tara. But we would like to give you a chance to tell your story . . .'

I glare at her.

'There's so much speculation, as I'm sure you're aware.'

Actually, I'm not, because there's not been much time to think about that or look at the online gossip which I'm sure is picking up momentum by the day.

'Please think about it and give me a call any time.'

I'm unsure of what to say and really, if I'm quite honest, I'm taken aback by her ballsy approach yet quite mesmerised by her eyelashes. Perhaps it's a trick. If I'm lulled by the lashes maybe I'm more likely to agree to something, anything, that she's suggesting.

'Erm, why don't you leave me your card and I'll consider it.'

'Super,' she says, her eyes shining with excitement, obviously telling herself she's made the deal, job done. 'You can use this as a platform, Tara. Try and reach out . . . perhaps to your mum?'

Once, her words might have been a deal-breaker, but the way I'm feeling towards Mum right now makes it a conversation stopper. 'I'd like you to leave now.' I can't look at her.

'No problem, Tara.'

Her constant use of my name is starting to irritate me. 'Call me, Tara.'

Unlikely, I want to say. I can't discuss it with my family, the people who matter and are part of this. I watch her drive away before I let myself into the house. Once upon a time I might have jumped at the chance to make a televised appeal for Mum to come home. But because she left of her own accord and the police didn't regard her as an official missing person, there was nothing we could do other than wait. If she hadn't sent the messages, I would definitely think she was dead. I'm not sure how Dad and Gran and Josie still kept hoping.

Unless they know something I don't. Which is a strong possibility, because I know something they don't. It seems we're all keeping secrets.

CHAPTER TWENTY

Josie

Scooping some mashed potatoes out of the pot, I put them onto a plate with some chicken casserole and green beans. 'Here you go, Gran,' I say. She's been picking at food for the past few days, and she's a petite lady anyway. She can't afford to lose any more weight.

'It's super you're here to look after me, Josie,' she says. 'Thank you, dear.'

'Well, you can tell me what you think. It's about time I learned to cook properly.'

'Didn't you cook for Dimitri?'

'I did, Gran. But he never liked what I made him . . . and so I lost all my confidence. It put me off cooking.'

Gran carefully cuts a piece of chicken and puts it in her mouth, chewing thoughtfully. 'I hope you divorce him asap.'

She actually says it like 'asap' rather than 'ASAP', which makes me chuckle. She used to always try out new phrases on us when we were younger, which always had Tara and I clutching our sides with laughter.

'Don't worry. I won't be going back to him, if that's what you mean.'

'But what about your job?'

I spear a green bean, sucking it into my mouth, and swallow. 'I can ask for some more leave. But I think perhaps the time is right for me to broaden my horizons and look elsewhere. There are so many other universities, surely. I must be able to find something else.'

Gran looks at me thoughtfully. 'I'm sure you will, dear. You must do what is right for you. I think you're in a fortunate position because you don't need to think about anyone else. But you must always make sure you hang onto a job and your own money.'

I wince, knowing she's right, but once again I'm reminded of how alone I am.

'Do you think Mum will ever come back?' I ask suddenly.

Gran puts her knife and fork down. 'I'm not sure,' she says, her voice solemn.

'Tara and I keep hoping and wondering. But then part of me wonders if she's actually dead.'

Gran sighs. 'You need to keep believing in her and thinking she will come back until we know otherwise.'

'Does Dad ever talk about her?'

She shakes her head sadly. 'No. Not anymore. He did to begin with . . .'

I fork some casserole into my mouth and watch her do the same.

'Do you think he wanted to meet someone else?' The thought actually never entered my head until this moment. Dad has always been on his own and alone. I can't imagine him with anyone else. It seems so odd and wrong.

She pauses. 'I think he had some friendships over the years. But never anyone who could replace your mum. She was such a special woman.'

'Friendships? Did he? But when? I didn't know . . .' I say, feeling confused as to why I was never told or didn't notice any other significant women. Racking my brain, I try to think of the eligible women in the town or Dad's congregation who could be contenders.

'Nobody in particular, dear, and your dad was always discreet. He wouldn't introduce you to anyone until he was sure they were right. I always hoped he would stay faithful to your mum.'

'Remember and make sure you drink some water too.' I push the glass towards her.

'Thank you.' She takes a sip. 'Do you think I'll be able to go and visit your dad tomorrow, perhaps?'

'Hopefully,' I say. Dad is due to come home tomorrow and is making impressive progress, the doctors say. He must attend the GP regularly and is signed up for some health and well-being classes at the medical practice. He's also going to need to cut out sugary snacks and the junk food he enjoys. He wasn't too happy about it when the nurses told him he needed to start looking after himself properly.

'You could start walking more, Dad,' I suggested. 'Or join the gym and go swimming a few times a week?'

He nodded and smiled. Although he still looked tired, at least he had regained some colour in his cheeks. Yet I detected a flatness to his mood which worried me. The nurses reassured us this was quite normal with those who had suffered a heart attack. They also suggested we keep a close eye on him in case he became depressed. Dad has never exactly been the life and soul of the party — he is in fact quite dour, so it might be tricky to measure that. But Tara and I promised we would do all the things we should. Mark took the chef, at the restaurant, up on his suggestion to batch cook a load of healthy meals which we could put in Dad's freezer.

'It will be a relief to finally check in on him,' says Gran. 'I miss him. Feels strange not having him around.'

The next day when I go to collect him, to give Tara a break and let her spend some time with the kids, I update him on it all and tell him about the clean flat and fully stocked kitchen. 'There's no excuse not to be healthy,' I tell him. 'You're a lucky man.'

He doesn't reply. Instead, he clasps his hands. Perhaps he is saying a silent prayer. He seems relieved Gran is okay and I'm looking after her. 'She's not getting any younger. And I worry sometimes she's getting a bit . . . forgetful,' he says in a hushed voice.

'Well, she is ninety. I think she's allowed to forget things once in a while.'

'Yes, you're right. But sometimes some of the things she says don't make sense.'

I have noticed sometimes Gran does get a bit muddled, but then don't we all?

'What about all that business at the manse?' he asks. 'Is Tara okay?'

'I think so,' I lie. 'We're waiting for the police to get back to us, but who knows when or even if they will. It would seem they're rather under-resourced and over-stretched at the moment.' I think of my call to Brian the other day, to check on developments. He told me in a convoluted way that he didn't know much. Things were taking longer than usual due to administrative issues, which, reading between the lines, meant nobody had done anything yet due to the backlog. This was a historic case and therefore not urgent, he said. 'I'll call you as soon as I hear anything though. Don't worry.'

I'm waiting for Dad to use the toilets before we leave the ward, when my phone buzzes. It's a message from Tara. *Call me when you can talk.* X

I phone her straight away while I can. 'Is all okay?'

'Is Dad around?'

'No, he's in the loo. What's up?'

'Brian bumped into Mark in the high street and told him forensics may take a while. Mark said he was a bit cagey. As if he knew something.'

I frown. 'Maybe he does. But what can we do? We'll have to wait until they're ready to tell us.'

'That's the thing. He then asked if we were around, and he would be in to speak to us.'

I feel myself clenching and unclenching my free hand. 'When do you think that will be?'

She pauses. 'Possibly in the next couple of days.'

70

'Wow. Okay . . . But should we say anything to Dad?' My heart sinks as I think about having to give him this latest update as we drive home.

'I wouldn't. There's no point in upsetting him until we're certain what the news is.'

'You're right,' I say, watching as Dad walks down the corridor towards me. 'He's coming back now. I'd better go, Tara.'

'Okay,' she says. 'Let's wait until we've spoken to the police.'

police.'

CHAPTER TWENTY-ONE

I'm not sure how long I walked for, but eventually I found myself at King's Cross station. It was heaving with bodies, and I stood for a moment scanning the board looking at all the destinations and possibilities and places I could go: Cambridge, Birmingham, Nottingham, Edinburgh, Newcastle, Durham, Glasgow. The passenger announcements echoed from the tannoy and I watched a pigeon hopping around the concourse. I had to decide where to go and fast. I made my way to the ticket booth still deciding where to go. 'Single to Newcastle, please.'

'Okay love. Are you coming back soon?'

'Erm, no.'

'It's just that I can do you a saver return if you go after 6.30 p.m.'

'No. A single, please. I need to go now.' I tried to keep my voice steady, so I didn't sound impatient. The man behind the glass partition banged down my change and shoved it under the counter. I moved out onto the concourse and walked purposefully towards platform four. Someone banged into me, which made me jump. I let myself be carried by the throng. I was petrified the police would come for me. I was still convinced he was watching me and would find me.

'The next train to Newcastle will be the seventeen hundred hours service departing from platform four,' said the nasal-voiced announcer. My stomach growled and I needed the toilet, but I kept going towards the top of the train. I slumped into a seat in the corner of the carriage.

72

I didn't want to make eye contact with anyone, so I kept my gaze down, looking at the speckled flooring. I checked my watch. It was 4.55 p.m. I tried to focus on my breathing, slowly in for four counts and exhaling for four counts, in a bid to make the seconds pass quicker. Then I heard a tinny whistle and a puff. When the train finally pulled away from the station I closed my eyes and allowed myself a small sigh of relief.

CHAPTER TWENTY-TWO

Tara

I squat down to pick up some of the Lego which is scattered across the kitchen floor. Anxiety swirls around my stomach as I think about the impending hospital appointment which I've been trying so hard to forget.

I should've gone with Josie to collect Dad today. I know she is doing her best to share the load and I do appreciate her offer to collect him. But if I'd gone with her, it would have kept my mind busy. I don't like being at home alone with my thoughts. Oliver and Millie spent the morning building the Lego Friends Nature Reserve and are now curled up on the sofa watching a movie together. Normally I monitor their screen time fiercely, but really, they aren't so bad and do spend most of their time outside playing. But the voice on my shoulder is usually muttering that I'm not doing enough to raise them as well-balanced children and that I'm failing. Fortunately, I've managed to mute that criticising voice today and the light smir of rain outside makes me more relaxed about them being inside and watching TV.

I poke my head into the sitting room. *Frozen 2* is on and I smile as I watch Olaf dancing around the screen. Oliver is sucking his thumb and Millie is enthralled, a blanket draped across her, while she leans forward with her elbows on her knees and her head in her hands. I'm so tempted to sit down beside them on the sofa and close my eyes for a minute or two. Oliver flicks his glance over to me as I stand in the doorway. I almost start to walk towards them as my favourite thing is having Oliver on one side and Millie snuggled into the other, but my feet are stuck to the spot.

'Come and watch with us, Mummy,' he says, pulling his thumb out of his mouth briefly, before putting it back in.

'Aw, thanks darling. Maybe in a wee while. I have a few things to do.'

Millie doesn't move her gaze away at all. I turn and walk back into the kitchen, smiling at the sounds of their giggles.

Looking outside and towards the bottom of the garden, I'm relieved that the police tent is now gone. I've been so caught up with Dad that I haven't even noticed. I keep thinking about the police and wish they would hurry up with their investigations so our lives can go back to normal. I know, it is a selfish thought. All I can think about is getting on with the renovations. It's awful to think that our garden has effectively been someone's grave for so many years. I wince as I think of the poor family somewhere who are going to be on the receiving end of some bad news. Hopefully it will give them closure if they have spent all these years waiting and wondering.

My phone buzzes.

All fine and Dad home safe and sound. Leaving him to rest and will check on him later. J x

That's a relief, I think, reaching into the big cupboard by the doorway to get the bucket and mop. Squirting some detergent in, I wait for it to fill with warm water and start to go over the floors. Twenty minutes later I'm finished and stand back for a moment admiring the clean floors which I know will be grubby again within an hour or so. I open the back door and am about to pour the water down the drain when I hear the faint sound of a siren in the background. Usually, the only time I notice a siren is when the Coastguard's Land Rover is on duty. I glance down towards the sea, which looks calm today. Despite the light rain, it's very still.

I panic and think of Dad on his own at home. What if something is wrong with him? I chew my lip and try to rationalise that he's fine. He's probably sleeping. It's a sign I'm stressed and tired. Even the smallest little worry is becoming a huge deal.

The landline starts ringing, which is unusual, as most people call us on the mobile. I run to the hallway, almost slipping on the wet floor, and pick it up.

'Hello?'

'Tara?'

It's Dad and his breathing is ragged. 'Is everything okay?' I try to keep my voice calm.

'Yes. It is,' he says. 'Don't worry.'

'You sound a bit funny. Are you feeling okay?'

'I'm okay, dear. I need to speak to you.'

'Oh.' That is strange. 'Can I get you anything?'

'No,' he says, his voice slow. 'Just you and your sister.'

'Okay. Well, the kids are with me at the moment.'

'Don't bring them, please. This is only for you and your sister.'

'Okay.' I don't like the sound of any of this. What on earth is the matter with him?

'When, Dad?'

Silence. 'Dad?'

'As soon as you can, dear,' he says. 'There's something I need to tell you.'

My heart is racing. 'Okay, I'll be with you as soon as I can.' I put the phone down and quickly call Mark's mobile. He doesn't pick up, so I ring the restaurant.

'Hello,' says Jaz.

'Hi, Jaz. It's Tara. Is Mark around?'

'Hi, Tara. No, he's out at the market. Can I help with anything?'

'Shit. No. Actually, yes. I need to go and see my dad urgently and I can't leave the kids here on their own and I can't take them.'

'Woah,' he says. 'It's okay. One thing at a time.'

'Sorry . . . it's just that . . .' I choke back a sob.

'You're not okay, are you?' He doesn't wait for me to reply. 'Sit tight and don't worry. I'll come up and sit with them,' he says. 'I'll be there as soon as I can.'

I don't have time to argue or disagree. 'Thanks, Jaz.'

'It's all right. I'm on my way.'

I quickly punch a message in my phone to Josie.

Dad wants to see us now. Something he needs to talk to us about? Meet you there ASAP. X

She's quick with her reply.

See you there. X

Oh — what about the kids? Leave them with Gran?

No, Jaz is coming here.

She doesn't respond. I tell the twins that I'm nipping out but Jaz is coming and they have to be on their best behaviour. Then I pull on my jacket and shoes and wait by the door. I try not to panic but my mind is in chaos. What does Dad need to talk to us about? And why the urgency?

CHAPTER TWENTY-THREE

Josie

After dropping Dad at home and making sure he's okay, he insists I leave him alone. He's tired and promises me he'll take a nap.

'There's no point in you hanging around here,' he says. 'I'll be fast asleep.'

'Okay, Dad, if you're sure.' The flat is clean and tidy, and it would be strange to hang about while he sleeps. So, I return to Gran's house.

It's probably stupid, but I'm desperate for answers and can't help myself. I sit down at Gran's kitchen table and begin trawling the internet for situations where bodies were found buried in gardens. The stories don't make pleasant reading — articles about serial killers or people who had murdered their parents. One man was charged with murder after the body of his mother, who hadn't been seen for years, was found buried under the patio. Police said the man had walked into the station and admitted to the killing. Another article described how a woman had killed her parents then buried them at the bottom of their garden because she wanted their money. She told the neighbours that her parents had moved away and nobody questioned it.

As I sit, I think about our family and the gossips that talked so much about us over the years. Who really knows what goes on behind closed doors. Everyone has secrets, don't they? Tears sting my eyes and I lean forward briefly to rest my head on the table. I'm so tired. I must have dozed off for a while because the buzzing of my phone wakes me with a jolt. I glance around for a moment wondering where I am. When I realise I'm in Gran's kitchen, everything else comes flooding back.

Dad wants to talk to us now. Something he needs to talk to us about? Meet you at his ASAP. X

That's strange, I think. Why didn't he tell me earlier? What on earth is suddenly so pressing that he wants to see us both in person right now? Unless the hospital told him something? Or maybe he's feeling ill again? But shouldn't he call an ambulance? I leap to my feet, closing the lid of my laptop and slip it into my bag.

'Gran,' I call, 'I'm nipping out.'

No reply.

'Gran . . . ?'

I poke my head into the living room but she's not in her usual chair. I run upstairs to check her bedroom.

She's sitting on the window seat looking out at sea.

'Gran! There you are. Didn't you hear me call you?'

She doesn't turn round.

'Gran?' I say, walking over to her. Placing a hand on her shoulder, I give her a wee tap.

'Oh, hello, love.'

'Are you okay? I've been calling you.'

She smiles and puts her hand on top of mine. 'Sorry, lovely. I was miles away. I was having a wee daydream.'

But as I study her face, I can tell she hasn't been day-dreaming about anything nice. Her expression is distant, and I know something is troubling her.

'I need to pop out. I won't be long. Will you be okay?' I say, crouching next to her.

'I'll be fine, dear. Don't worry about me.'

'Okay. I won't be long. Call me if you need me.'

She nods.

When I get to Dad's, Tara's car is already parked outside. When she sees me, she jumps out with a strained expression on her face.

'What's this all about?'

She shrugs. 'I have no idea. He called and said he needed to tell us something.'

I slot his key into the lock.

We jog lightly up the stairs and into the front room, where he sits on his wingback chair in the bay window. The light is shining in from behind and he seems almost ethereal.

I gingerly sit down on the sofa and Tara joins me.

'What's up, Dad? Everything okay?'

He's nursing a tumbler of whisky in his hands. He takes a sip of the honey-coloured liquid. Shit. This is not a good sign. Even if he hadn't just come out of hospital, Dad rarely drinks and certainly not during the day.

'Do you think that's a good idea, Dad?' asks Tara.

I nudge her. What's the point?

'I'm sorry, girls. I'm sorry to have to do this. Especially after all you've done for me over the years.'

I hold myself rigid as Dad leans a bit closer towards us.

'There's something I need to tell you girls.' His voice is steady and calm.

'What?' says Tara, taking a shocked intake of breath.

'The body in the garden. I know about the body in the garden.'

'What do you mean?' I say, my voice a whisper.

'I know who it is and I take full responsibility.'

'For what?' I'm pressing my nails into my palm.

He looks at us both, first at me and then at Tara. His voice falters as he speaks. 'I'm so sorry, girls. I never wanted this to happen. I didn't want any of this to ever happen.' He dabs at his eyes with a cotton handkerchief embroidered with his initials, one from the set I sent for him at Christmas. Why is that all I can focus on?

'Dad?' says Tara. 'Take responsibility for what? Do you know who it is? Do you know who was buried in the garden?'

'The body . . .' He sighs. 'The body is your brother.'

'Brother?' say Tara and I together.

'What brother?'

'What are you talking about?' says Tara.

'It's your brother. And I'm so sorry that you never got to meet him.'

I'm reeling in confusion. What is he talking about? Is he having some sort of funny turn?

'Girls, I need you to listen to me.'

Tara shrinks back in the seat.

'I need you to listen to what I'm going to say. Because the police are on their way now.'

'The police?' I say, jerking my head in surprise. 'What do you mean, the police?'

'The police are on their way here. I called them a little while ago and told them I'm ready . . .'

'For what?' says Tara, confused.

'I told them that I'm ready to confess.'

CHAPTER TWENTY-FOUR

There was no plan. I've no idea why I chose Newcastle. I stood on the platform wondering what to do and found myself in a snack bar with a strong tea in a polystyrene cup and a ham and cheese sandwich. Sitting nursing the tea and nibbling on the bread, I needed to think of my next step. It was cold and dark outside and the strip lighting above now started to aggravate my headache. Should I call her? Would she be home yet? Would everything be okay? Shit. Of course it wouldn't. He was dead. What a mess. The guilt squeezed at my insides. Still, the small voice in my head grew louder. You didn't ask to be hit or beaten. You didn't ask for food you'd made to be thrown across the kitchen. You didn't ask to be ignored for days and days and be walking around as if on eggshells. *But if I had been better at cooking, he might not have been so cross. Maybe if I had been a better wife, he would have been happier. Maybe, maybe, maybe . . .*

The woman at the table next to me smoked a cigarette and I inhaled her nicotine wondering if I dared ask her for one. I gave myself a shake. I needed to stop stalling. I couldn't stay sitting in the station all night smoking and drinking tea. But where could I go? Gathering my things together, I stood up and tentatively walked back onto the concourse. Standing, feeling lost, exhausted and broken, I didn't know what to do. Should I take a taxi somewhere? Though where to? I'd never been to Newcastle before. My legs were like jelly as I urged myself to move towards the exit, forcing myself to stare straight ahead. A few groups of men stood in a group, fresh from the pub. I could feel them watching me, sense their eyes crawling over my skin. My heart stopped as a man sidled up next to me.

'Hi, love. You okay?' he slurred, his breath sour and his eyes glazed. I kept walking, trying my best to ignore him.

'Come on, love. There's no need to be like that. I want a chat. I'm just being friendly,' he slurred.

When I saw a policeman, I almost cried in relief. Then I remembered what I had done. There was nowhere to run. I trembled as the man pawed me with his hand.

'Oi!' said the policeman. 'Leave the lady alone.' He gave the drunk man short shrift and checked I was okay.

Remaining calm took all my strength. I have no idea how I managed to speak to him when the voices in my head were screaming out, You are a murderer! You killed a man this afternoon! He might arrest you! I kept trying so hard not to cry. I wanted to lie down and sleep. But I managed to mumble my thanks and say yes, everything was fine.

'You sure, love? You look a bit tired and upset,' he said. He looked like a kind man. Though what did I know? 'Are you heading home?'

'Yes . . .'

'Do you have far to go?'

'Um . . .' I cast my eyes to the floor.

'Take this, love.' He pushed a small business card into my hand. 'This isn't a nice place to hang around at night. Not for a woman on her own.' He paused. 'If you need help, go there.'

I glanced down at the small card in my hand. It was for a women's refuge.

'It's not far. Five minutes from the station. Here, let me put you in a cab.'

I allowed myself to follow him, and within a few minutes I was slumped in the back of a taxi.

CHAPTER TWENTY-FIVE

Tara

I'm silent as I listen to Dad talk and talk. The words coming out his mouth seem jumbled and wrong and I want to scream at him to shut up. I stare at this man, my father, in the chair with his beige sweater and dark trousers. Looking at his slippers, I wonder if I should have bought the other pair I had dithered over when I was in Marks and Spencer. Should I have bought him the fur-lined ones? Would that have made a difference? The man in front of me is the father who I nursed in hospital and have left my children with so many times over the years. He is a devoted grandpa and I never ever thought my kids would be anything other than safe with him. Yet, as I look at this man, my dad, sitting across from me, I can't help thinking he's a stranger. All I can think about is what he has done to us all.

My sister's gentle hand is on my shoulder, reassuring and calming. She knows I can't take in what he's saying. I have no idea how to respond. Instead, I just listen as he continues to talk.

'Your mum must have been six months along when she lost the baby,' he says. 'When I met her, she was already pregnant.'

'The baby wasn't yours?' says Josie.

'Correct,' he says. 'But I didn't mind. I would have raised the wee mite as my own.'

'Who was the father?' I ask, finally able to break my silence.

'She didn't say.' He fails to meet our eyes.

I watch him dig his fingernails into the arms of the chair. 'Why didn't she tell you?'

He takes a sharp inward breath. 'She didn't want to.'

Is he trying to protect Mum?

'She told me that she had moved here from Surrey and she had come to the church for help. We used to have a refuge, for people in need.'

'She was vulnerable. And you took advantage. Is that what you mean?' My words are cruel and stark — but I want to shake him and scream at him to tell us the whole truth. I clamp my hand over my mouth so no more words will come out.

'She had been helping me in the garden at the manse. Nobody else knew she was pregnant. She'd managed to conceal it from everyone — even me.'

'How could you not have noticed?' I think of my own swelling bump when I was pregnant with the twins. There was no way I could have kept that secret. From about four months, I was undeniably expecting.

He pauses and closes his eyes, clearly finding the process of remembering and telling the story a challenge. 'It just wasn't that obvious. She always wore loose-fitting clothes. I never noticed, and she never said.'

'What happened next?' says Josie.

'It was late and it had started to rain. I said she was welcome to stay in the spare room if she wanted to rather than walk back down the road to her accommodation.'

'Couldn't you have driven her?' I raise an eyebrow and glance at my sister, who throws me a warning look.

'Yes, but the car had been in the garage for repairs. If we had walked, we would have got soaked. Asking her to stay seemed obvious, especially when I had so many rooms.'

Josie is looking at me, but I keep my eyes trained on Dad.

'Anyway, we went off to bed . . . in separate rooms . . . and I fell asleep straight away. I didn't hear anything at all in the night. Not the slightest sound. Mind you, I always did sleep though everything. Storms, alarm clocks, children fighting over the bathroom.'

'Yes,' says Josie, nodding, 'that is very true.'

He smiles sadly. 'When I came downstairs in the morning, she was distraught . . .'

Dad shakes his head in disbelief, as if he's still in that moment, suspended in time, back in the house with Mum. 'She told me she had given birth to a baby during the night . . . and the baby was dead. He had been stillborn.'

Josie gasps. I reach for her hand and hold it.

'I couldn't believe it. I didn't know she was expecting.'

'What did you do?' I manage to say, my voice croaky.

He slaps his palms against his legs. 'I didn't *know* what to do, girls. I mean, I hadn't ever been in a situation like that before, obviously. I wanted to call for the doctor to get her checked out. And, of course, to get the baby checked out. I pleaded with her, desperately. But she was adamant nobody must hear about any of it. She didn't want to tell anyone about the baby.' He is clasping and unclasping his hands. 'She made me promise.'

'What happened next?' asks Josie.

'We said a little prayer for him.' He inhales sharply.

'Did she give him a name?' I ask.

Dad nods. 'Yes. Jonathan was his name. She called him Jonathan. Then we wrapped him up in a blanket and we buried him at the bottom of the garden by the apple trees. That was what your mum wanted. It was her favourite spot.'

As I try to make sense of what he is saying, I think about other poor women who have given birth and left their babies in doorways or in hospitals. Whenever I read a newspaper story about an abandoned child, I'm always desperately sorry for the mother. It makes me wonder what sort of state they must have been in to do that. How can I be cross with Dad when none of this is his fault? Was what they did so wrong, especially as the baby was dead? *Jonathan*. My poor mum, she clearly had good reason for keeping her pregnancy a secret. Had her family disapproved? Or had she been attacked? Was she fleeing an abusive marriage? Then I pictured her lying in her hammock by the apple trees and how she spent so much time in that part of the garden. She always said she loved it because of the view and because it was a special and peaceful place, and now we know why. It was his burial place. Jonathan. Her son and our brother.

Looking at Dad sitting in his chair, he seems to have shrunk in the time he has told us the story. How can I be anything but compassionate towards him?

CHAPTER TWENTY-SIX

Josie

I'm still reeling from Dad's confession as we wait for the police to arrive. They seem to take for ever, and rather than sit around in limbo, I make myself busy with washing and ironing. Anything to take my mind off what he has told us. Tara insists she make Dad a cup of tea and tells him to close his eyes for ten minutes or so and rest while he can. When the doorbell eventually rings, I open the door to find Brian and a female colleague.

'Hi, Josie,' he says. 'This is my colleague DI Sam Duguid.'

I extend my hand to shake hers. 'Hello. Come in.'

'Hi. Thank you,' says Sam.

They follow me up, their feet heavy on the creaking stairs. 'Would you like a tea or coffee?'

'Coffee, please,' says Brian. 'Milk and two sugars.'

'A black tea, thanks,' adds Sam.

I gesture through to the front room, where Tara is sitting with Dad. 'He's through there. Do you want us to be with him?'

'That's entirely up to yourselves,' says Brian. 'At the moment, this is about your dad helping us with some enquiries.'

'Oh,' I say, confused. 'Even if he wants to tell you something specific?'

'Well, yes, I believe he does. But we won't be taking him to the station at this stage.'

'The station? I should hope not. He's out of hospital today after having a *heart attack*.' I lower my voice. 'If the doctor knew the police were bothering him, she would not be happy. He's supposed to be resting.'

Brian strokes his chin and then coughs to clear his throat. 'We are aware,' he says, 'and we won't put him under any pressure to talk. But if a member of the public says they have information about recently exhumed remains, then it is our duty to act. And your father did call and ask us to come as a matter of priority.'

I stop myself from shaking my head in disbelief. He sounds like he's swallowed a police manual. 'Fair enough,' I say, my voice clipped. 'Let me get your drinks for you. Please, go and join my sister and Dad through there.' I watch them walk into the room and Tara stands up to greet them. Poor Dad. He hasn't done anything wrong yet obviously feels as though the weight of the world is on his shoulders.

He had tried to do the right thing and respect Mum's wishes. Was that a bad thing? And, as he had told Tara and me, it had been Mum's story and her business, and she had confided in him. If only they knew their actions would come back to haunt them more than thirty years later.

I boil the kettle and check my phone for messages, glad Dimitri appears to have given up sending them. I know he won't disappear quietly, that isn't his style at all. He's just biding his time; this won't be the end of it. I set a tray with a pot of tea and some cups and a mug of coffee but decide against a plate of biscuits.

'Thanks,' says Sam and Brian, in unison, as I place the tray on the table.

'Your dad has been telling us about the baby that was buried. The one your mum delivered stillborn,' says Sam.

'Yes. It was quite a shock to hear that,' I say.

89

'I'm sure,' Brian says, pausing to take a sip of tea.

Leaving the room, I go into the kitchen and try to make myself busy. The last thing I want is to hear Dad go over the story again. What will happen next? Will he be allowed to bury the baby again? Will we all be able to do that? I had a brother. An older brother who would have been thirty-six years old, if he had lived. I debate whether I should go back into the room to give Tara and Dad some moral support. But I can't help thinking about the baby who didn't even take a breath when he arrived. My poor mother having to deliver him alone. That must have been so terrifying for her. To think of her in labour and then . . . I wipe away a tear as a surge of emotion threatens to overwhelm me.

My thoughts are interrupted by an incoming call from Mark.

'Hi, Mark.'

'Hi, Josie. Tara's phone is switched off. Is everything okay? Jaz — sorry, *Jason* — said you had an emergency with your dad and you were both needed straight away. He's with the kids.'

'Yes and no. He's okay — well, kind of. His heart's fine. Tara and I are both here with him.' I pause, wondering if I should say any more. 'Look, it's a bit of a long and compli-cated story. I'll let Tara tell you when she sees you. That's probably fairer. But he's been filling us in on something that happened . . . way before we were born.'

'Oh. Okay,' he says. 'Sounds intriguing.'

'Well, yes and no. We've had a bit of a shock.'

'Right. Do you need me to come?'

'I don't think so. Erm, the police are here, Mark. I'm not sure how long we'll be. But I'll tell Tara to call you as soon as they leave.'

'Jeez. This all sounds a bit messy. Are you sure I can't come and be with you?'

'It'll make more sense once Tara can explain things. Hopefully we won't be long.'

'Okay. Thanks.'

'No worries. I'm going to give Gran a quick call,' I say, glancing at the clock on the wall. 'I had to leave her rather hurriedly. She'll be wondering where I am and what's going on.'

'Right. Well, call if you need me,' he says.

'I will do.' I end the call and phone Gran. 'Just checking in. Everything okay, Gran?'

'Yes, dear, all is fine. I've been making soup.'

'Oh, okay.' I'm surprised as I can't remember the last time she made soup. 'I'm at Dad's.'

'Is he okay?'

'He's fine. Tara and I are with him and making sure he's settled.'

'Well, you tell him I'll be round tomorrow. I can't believe I've not seen my own son since his heart went kaput.'

I try hard not to laugh. 'Gran, it didn't go kaput. Otherwise he'd be dead. It was a wee heart attack. He'll be fine.'

'Whatever. Tell him I'm coming and I made soup. Tomato and berry.'

I frown. 'Will do. I'll be home soon-ish.'

'Okay, my love. And please do take your time . . . I've got company with me anyway.'

'Oh.' I wonder if Bella, her bridge friend, has popped in.

'Yes, your lovely husband is here.'

I feel the blood rush to my head. 'Sorry?'

'Yes. Your husband.'

'Dimitri?'

'Well, unless you have another husband you're yet to tell me about?' she says, laughing.

'What is he doing at *yours*, Gran?' I can't believe what she's saying.

'We're having a cup of tea and a blether about things. Take your time. Goodbye,' she says and hangs up.

Bloody hell. This day can't get any worse. What should I do? I glance through the kitchen door, which is ajar. They're still deep in conversation, so I call Mark back.

'Josie?'

91

'Mark. I don't know what to do. It's Dimitri. He's at Gran's house now.'

'What? Why?'

'Exactly. I need to go now . . . and I'm sorry to ask, but would you mind coming, please? In case . . .'

'Of course. Wait outside until I arrive though. The cheek of him.'

In the calmest voice I can muster, I pop my head around the door of the lounge and tell them I'm nipping back to check on Gran. Looking at Tara, I hope she picks up on the severity of what I'm trying to tell her.

She narrows her eyes and mouths, 'Is all okay?'

I nod, noticing Dad is holding his head in his hands. He looks up at me briefly.

'Don't say anything to her yet, will you dear?'

'Of course I won't.' Telling Gran about this is the very least of my worries. 'I'll be back as soon as I can.' My heart is racing as I charge downstairs and open the front door, then run out onto the street and make my way to Gran's.

CHAPTER TWENTY-SEVEN

When I arrived, I was welcomed in and looked after and for that I will always be grateful. It felt wonderful to have a shower and wash away the blood and the smell of him. Nobody asked me any awkward or probing questions. Instead, there was an unspoken and gentle understanding we were there for the same reasons. To begin with it was me and three others, which grew to five and six. All of us escaping.

I don't have any clear memories of Christmas Day, which passed in a haze. I seemed to spend a lot of time sleeping, though most nights the nightmares kept me awake and shivering. Sometimes my dreams took me back to that day with clear and vivid flashbacks. Other days I wondered whether it really happened.

I didn't tell anyone anything about myself or where I'd come from. I needed to work out what to do and where to go. I couldn't stay at the refuge for ever, though. I would need to make a plan to move on before things caught up.

I tried calling her a few times, but the number just rang out until one day a message told me the phone had been disconnected.

One cold morning I sat in the kitchen and started to ball up some newspaper to start a fire. The refuge was in an old building with high ceilings and the rooms took ages to heat up. We spent most of our time in the kitchen, the cosiest room, but only after the fire had been going for a few hours. That morning my task was lighting the fire. As I prepared the grate with the paper, my eye caught a small column.

WOMAN ARRESTED FOR MAN'S MURDER

A woman has been arrested on suspicion of murder following the death of a man on Delancey Road, London, on Friday. A police source confirmed the man had been stabbed in a vicious attack.

The woman, who is 21, remains in police custody. A local said the man's death has sent shockwaves through the community.

A police spokesman confirmed that a murder investigation has been launched but said there were 'no further details at this stage'.

Seeing it in black and white made things very real and that brought a whole wave of fresh fear. I thought the best thing to do was keep moving. I had to get further away. That was when I decided to keep going north to Scotland.

CHAPTER TWENTY-EIGHT

Tara

As soon as Dad starts talking to Brian, I watch him and his colleague. Their eyes never leave Dad's face and it doesn't seem to be taking them long at all to accept what he's saying. Dad is talking slowly and deliberately, and his face is once again pained. It doesn't appear to be any easier for him to be telling this story for the second time in one afternoon. The consultant from the hospital would not be happy if she could witness the scene. Sam occasionally murmurs at intervals and Brian remains silent. Part of me wonders why they aren't shocked and why they aren't looking at each other knowingly. Then I think, in a flood of relief, that in their line of work, nothing surprises them and so this is all quite tame.

I stand up and mutter that I'll go and make more tea, which is all I seem to do these days to escape awkward situations. Standing in the kitchen, I think about how much I long for something stronger like a whisky or a vodka to help numb the shock from Dad's confession. I vaguely wonder about Josie and if everything is okay for her to hurry off like that. I'm trying to gather my skittering thoughts. Mum had a baby before us who wasn't fathered by our dad. She arrived here alone and pregnant and told nobody. She gave birth to the baby on her own and had to bury him.

I grip the worktop as sadness threatens to overwhelm me. Josie and I have a brother with a name. Jonathan. Our older brother. I think of Dad looking after Mum and keeping her secret all these years.

Something shifts in the back of my mind when I remember the day Mark and I found out I was pregnant. My periods were always on time, and after being a couple of days late I was sure I knew why. We went and bought the pregnancy test kit together and Mark waited outside the bathroom, sitting patiently on the hall floor with his knees at his chest, while I peed on the stick. I sat for a moment on my own, on the other side of the door, thinking about how much our lives would change if the test was positive and how I would feel if it came back negative. I knew I would be disappointed as I had convinced myself I was pregnant. We were both excited and full of hope and when I opened the bathroom door and waved the wand at Mark — he scooped me up in a bear hug then gently placed me back on the ground and covered my face with kisses. Was Mum excited when she discovered she was pregnant? Or did she feel scared and alone? What could make her run away at such an exciting time in her life? Did the father know? Was he interested?

I picture her giving birth to the baby alone and her panic when she realised he wasn't breathing or moving. What did she do? I can only begin to imagine how horrendous it must have been for her. How do you ever recover from something like that? I think about the size of my bump when I was six months pregnant with the twins. My belly was swollen and I was proud to show it off in my tight maternity tops and jeans. Imagine trying to conceal it from everyone. Had I been unfair on Mum and judged her too harshly for her brief messages? Rebuking myself for having such visceral feelings of anger towards her, I'm now utterly grief-stricken for my poor mother. I wonder what she will make of these latest developments. I would be completely devastated. Should I tell her?

I'm drawn out of my thoughts by the sounds of people moving in the front room and the door creaking open. Totally consumed by my thoughts, I haven't even managed to make them a cup of tea. Turning, I go out to meet them in the hallway, noticing Dad still sitting in his chair by the window. I'm glad he hasn't tried to stand up and hope now he can rest. What a day for him.

'Thanks for coming,' I hear myself saying. 'I hope you got everything you need?' How do you make chit-chat with police officers who have heard your dad confess to a historic crime?

'No problem at all . . .' says Brian, his voice trailing away.

'I hope your dad is okay. This will have obviously taken a lot out of him,' says Sam.

'You're right. It's been a shock to us all.'

'You had no idea?' says Brian.

'Nope,' I shake my head. 'None at all.'

'Right,' he says, letting out a long sigh.

Only then do I notice the conspiratorial glance between them. There's more to this than they're telling me. I wait for them to say something else, to elaborate on what they're clearly thinking.

'We were wondering . . .' starts Brian, who glances at Sam.

'Your mother went missing in 2000?' says Sam.

I nod. 'Well, not missing as such. She left us. Walked out. Why?'

Sam clicks her teeth together. 'It would be good to get her to corroborate this version of events.'

'Right,' I say. 'Well, that could be tricky as she's not in touch.'

'When did you last speak to her?' asks Sam.

I'm so shocked by her question that I can barely answer. 'It would have been when I was ten years old,' I blurt. I'm hoping they can't tell I'm lying, although technically I'm not really. I'm not sure that Messenger falls into the category of *speaking* to someone, it's more like writing to them.

'Are you sure about that?' asks Brian, his eyebrow rising as he waits for a response.

What does he mean? Why is he asking me that? Is he monitoring my social media use?

I nod. 'She sent us birthday cards but that stopped when we were twenty-one.'

'Nothing since then?' says Sam.

I shake my head. 'No.'

CHAPTER TWENTY-NINE

Josie

I run along the street to Gran's house, figuring it will be quicker than driving and trying to park. I arrive just as Mark pulls up. Waving at him, I don't wait and just open the door to Gran's house. Marching into the kitchen, I find Dimitri sitting at her table. Strangely enough, I feel some relief — relief that he is here and we can finally put an end to all of this. Every moment of self-doubt or worry that I can't live without him vanishes as he stands up and smiles without even a flicker of remorse on his face. He looks well and his face is lightly tanned, no doubt from all the time he's been relaxing in the garden. He doesn't appear to be a troubled man whose marriage is in tatters or whose world has collapsed. Every gut feeling that I tried my hardest to keep at bay during the latter years of our marriage is now coming to the surface.

'What are you doing here?' I shout.

'Josie. Darling. Not exactly the best way to greet your husband, is it?' He walks towards me and attempts to draw me into an embrace, but I duck out of his way. The smell of his aftershave makes me want to vomit.

Gran sits at her usual spot at the kitchen table watching in confusion. So much for her threat to slice off his balls. Has she already forgotten what he's done?

'Tara, darling. Isn't this a nice surprise? He said he was missing you and thought he would pay you a surprise visit. The old romantic!'

'Gran, don't you remember what happened?'

Her face is impassive. 'What do you mean?'

'We're not married anymore. Dimitri was having an affair with our neighbour.'

'Oh,' she says, her voice stern. 'Oh — I did *not* know that. Surely not . . .' She glares at him. 'How could you do that to my granddaughter? You horrible, horrible man.'

Out of my peripheral vision, I sense that Mark is standing in the hallway, clearly not wanting to intrude, but ready to step in should I need him.

'Why didn't you say anything before?' asks Gran.

'I did. You must have forgotten.' Clearly the stress of Dad's heart attack has affected her more than we realised. She also called me Tara when I arrived.

Gran turns to him. 'How could you just sit and drink tea with me and eat my shortbread biscuits? You had so many of them. You greedy man. Why did you not say anything?'

Dimitri now looks slightly shamefaced. Even if adultery doesn't make him repentant, part of me is slightly relieved to think that tricking a pensioner has embarrassed him. 'I thought you knew all about it and that you had forgiven me.'

'No!' shouts Gran. 'You're a horrible wee slime of a man. You're an utter shit!'

Mark suppresses a shocked laugh. He obviously hasn't witnessed this side to her personality. Meanwhile Gran starts her slicing motion again. If it wasn't so ridiculous it would be funny.

'Please go. You're not welcome here,' I say.

'But Josie, surely we can talk? Come on, we're good together.'

I laugh. 'No, Dimitri, we are not. Our marriage is over. This is all over. You don't belong here. Now piss off.' My voice wobbles as the emotion of the day threatens to overwhelm me. Fortunately, Mark steps out of the shadows and comes into the kitchen.

'I'll come down and collect my stuff soon,' I tell him.

'In fact, it would probably be easiest if you made yourself scarce so Josie can get her things in peace. I'll come down with her,' says Mark.

'Oh,' says Dimitri, startled to see him.

'It's time you left. Please go,' I say.

The doorbell sounds and Mark goes to answer it.

'Oh, I wonder who that could be,' says Gran.

My mouth forms an 'O' shape when I clock who is following Mark into the kitchen.

'I thought I would just come down and check if you needed a hand,' says Jason, walking over to my side.

'What are you doing here?' I wince as I realise the fragility of the situation. Things could explode at any minute, and I need Dimitri out of here before he puts two and two together.

'Jason!' exclaims Gran, walking over and hugging him. 'Would you like some tea? And shortbread?'

I narrow my eyes, shaking my head. I wasn't aware they had that kind of relationship. Clearly, by the surprised expression on Jason's face, neither does he.

'Jason . . . Jason?' says Dimitri.

Oh no. 'Okay. Now you've overstayed your welcome. Time you were on your way,' I say, pulling at his arm.

'Is this *the* Jason?' says Dimitri.

Jason frowns.

'This is Mark's work colleague,' I say. 'And it's time you were on your way.'

'Not so fast,' Dimitri says, standing his ground. His hands grip the back of the chair. 'This is the famous Jason?'

'Eh?' says Mark. 'What are you going on about?'

'There are lots of Jasons in the world,' I say. 'It's quite a common name.' Looking at him with pleading eyes, his face softens for a second. Then his lips curl in a sneer. 'This is the Jason who you had a fling with, is it?'

'Why is that any of your business?' says Jason, stepping forward and squaring up to him.

'Are you for real? Are you the one she had a fling with as a teenager?'

'We had a bit of a summer romance years ago, if that's what you're referring to,' says Jason. 'Why, what's the problem?'

'*What's the problem?*' Dimitri says, his voice mimicking Jason's. 'Are you for real?'

Oh God, how can this be happening? My arms flail as I snatch at Dimitri's arm again, trying to haul him out of the house and away, but he's like a rock, glued to the floor.

'Do you have any idea what you did to her?' he says, looking at Jason with disdain.

'Dimitri.' My voice is low and firm. 'It's time you were on your way. *Please.*'

This is what he threatened in the cards he sent. He had promised to keep it a secret. He was the only one who I told when I was heartbroken and vulnerable and now he's going to tell them all. He's going to tell Jason. 'Mark, if you don't mind. I'd like him to leave now, please. Otherwise, I'll call the police.'

In these few seconds, I stare at Dimitri in terror. I hope he will read the plea in my eyes and hear the desperation in my voice. Yet he is the one with the upper hand, and every speck of self-despair, every moment of self-doubt comes back in a tsunami of emotion. Spotting the weakness in me, he dives straight in with his final parting shot.

'You,' he says, turning to Jason. 'You're the reason that she's such a bloody mess. You're the reason that she can't conceive and that our marriage is in ruins. This is all your fault.'

'Listen, buddy,' starts Jason, rubbing his chin, 'I've no idea what you're talking about.'

Gran has started filling the kettle and Mark is watching in silence, his gaze flitting from me to Jason to Dimitri.

'You're more stupid than I thought,' says Dimitri, a look of contempt on his face.

'Hey,' says Mark, 'I think you've said enough. Out.'

'Please go now,' I say, quietly.

'Oh, I'll go, *my darling*. In my own good time.' He turns to address Jason. 'When you had your little summer fling and went back to Australia, did you realise what you left behind?'

Jason looks at me, bewildered. All I can do is shrug. Especially as I know what's coming next.

'Dimitri,' I say, pulling at him again. He shakes me off and I stumble back, hitting the wall.

'Hey,' says Jason, grabbing him while Mark clamps his arm around his other side.

Dimitri struggles, his arms floundering under their grip. 'You ran back to Australia and left her pregnant. You abandoned her and guess what happened next? She lost the baby. Now she can't conceive.'

I sink into a chair at the table.

'That's enough, you little prick. You've said enough.' Mark shoves him out the kitchen followed by Jason, and I watch them give him a firm shove out onto the doorstep.

Dimitri turns around and shouts back at them, 'You're welcome to her!' Then there's a scuffle and I hear him shout, 'Ow!'

Either Mark or Jason has punched him.

'Cup of tea, anyone?' asks Gran when they return to the kitchen.

I'm unable to speak and when I catch Jason's eye, he looks away. He rubs at his fist, and sorrow and pain twists at my gut. Then he turns and leaves.

CHAPTER THIRTY

I'm watching you, girls. I always have been. I know how much pain you're in. I'm just so sorry that you've had to go through all of this. No mother ever wants her children to suffer. No mother ever wants to abandon her babies. I don't think I'll ever be able to make it up to you. But I'll try my best.

PART TWO: BEFORE

One week earlier

CHAPTER THIRTY-ONE

Josie

I arrived home early at our terraced house in Teddington. We'd moved to Teddington because of the amazing Ofsted-rated schools and lived in a small, overpriced house in an area popular with families. The irony was not lost on me. My meeting had been cancelled and, with students finished for summer, my schedule was much more fluid than usual. I thought I would surprise Dimitri with some lunch which I'd picked up from the local deli: fat, juicy olives, pâté and freshly baked bread. My stomach rumbled during the short drive home and I had that lovely feeling of anticipation as I parked the car, pushing my sunglasses on top of my head. It was Friday and I was *so* looking forward to the weekend. Dimitri had been working long hours — he was quite a successful writer, which allowed us to live in this area, and worked mostly from home. He had a deadline to meet, but I was sure he wouldn't mind some alfresco lunch.

Walking up the path, I wondered if there was any wine in the chiller. Our supplies seemed to have dwindled of late. I slid my key into the lock and, trying to turn it, I frowned. It wouldn't budge. Strange. I knocked softly, then a bit louder, hearing music playing inside. He wouldn't hear me above that. In fact, no doubt he was in the shower, oblivious to everything else. Or perhaps in the garden? So much for his pressing deadline, I thought with annoyance. I reminded myself to breathe and smile. I headed to the end of the street and turned to walk down the back lane dodging the over-growth and nettles. I was glad I wore trousers today otherwise my legs would have been scraped and stung. Hoping that the back gate was unlocked, I gave it a bit of a shove and it fell open. Pausing to admire the blooming roses, I smiled when I spotted the open bi-folding doors. The decking looked great — a view which I didn't normally see from this angle. It would be pleasant to have lunch outside today and enjoy the sun. I walked up the steps onto the deck then into the kitchen, frowning when I heard the front door close.

'Hello?' I called. 'Hello, it's me.'

Dimitri appeared, his face red and his dark hair unkempt. He wore shorts and a crumpled T-shirt and his eyes darted around the room.

'Hi there,' I said, walking over to kiss his cheek. 'Did you fall asleep in the sun?'

'Why are you home so early?' He moved away from me, folded his arms and leaned against the fridge.

'My meeting was cancelled . . . so I thought I would sur-prise you and bring in some lunch.' I hoisted the bags onto the granite worktop, a flutter of panic starting to take hold. 'I couldn't open the front door.'

'You should have called.' He scratched his head and flicked through the messages on his phone. All the excite-ment I felt about the weekend ahead started to seep from me. 'You know I don't like surprises.'

'Oh. I thought you might make an exception. For your wife.'

'There's no need to be huffy,' he said. 'I was in the mid-dle of something. You know I don't like interruptions.'

Pushing past him, I ran upstairs. I needed to change out of my work stuff and get away from him. This was so not what I had planned for this afternoon.

'Where are you going?' he said, following me.

'I'm hot.' The collar of my blouse scratched at my throat and I pulled at it.

'Why don't you come and have some lunch first?' He pulled at my arm.

I could feel a heat rash spreading across my face and my cheeks flushing. 'I will. But I need to get out of these clothes. I'm so hot.' Bloody hormones.

'You're acting weirdly.'

Actually, he was the one who was acting weirdly. Why was he hanging around me? Why wouldn't he leave me alone to change?

'Come on,' he said. 'Let's have lunch.'

'Dimitri, will you fuck off? Stop pawing at me.' I ran up the other set of stairs to our bedroom in the converted loft. How could this have all gone so wrong? One minute I was planning a romantic lunch in the garden and now . . . now I wanted to punch him.

'You need to calm down, Josie,' he said. 'Come on now. You're starting to panic. Just calm yourself down and breathe.'

He was right behind me. I felt his breath on my neck and I wanted him to go away. I tried to pull the bedroom door closed behind me when I reached the top of the stairs. But he was too fast.

'Calm down, take it easy.'

'Stop telling me to calm down!'

'Josie. You're being irrational again,' he said. 'Come on. Take a moment and *calm down*.'

Perhaps he was right, and I *was* being irrational. The doctor did say this was possible with the cocktail of hormones I had to inject myself with. Feelings of anxiety and worry were normal, he said. I stood for a moment staring around our tidy bedroom. All the drawers in the chest were closed, the picture of us by the river on our wedding day on the dressing table, the door to the en suite closed and the shutters tilted open. Yet something wasn't right. I kept wondering whether paranoia was also a side effect of the injections. Glancing around, I started taking deep breaths, conscious of my husband's hand rubbing my shoulders. Feeling slightly more grounded, I waited for a moment. I had worked out what was wrong.

I stared at the bed. It wasn't how I had left it when I went to work this morning. I mean, yes it had been made but *not* by me. The pillows weren't plumped up the way I did it and there were just a few too many wrinkles on the duvet cover. His grip tightened on my shoulder. Had he been napping? I mean, he did look quite warm and confused when I got in. Perhaps I woke him up?

I glanced out of the window and saw the pink flowers on the trees and the blue sky. The toddlers across the road were giggling and calling out to their mum. I wriggled free from his grip and walked round and sat down on my side of the bed. Leaning over, I buried my nose in the pillow. Someone else had been here.

CHAPTER THIRTY-TWO

Tara

I lay in the bath enjoying a soak when I discovered the lump. I wasn't a regular breast checker despite the reminders everywhere. Even the local sports centres had posters stuck to the back of the toilet doors. I always looked at them thinking I would remember to check when I got home. But I didn't always quite manage to put the advice shown into actual real-life action. Other than the odd cursory feel in the shower when I remembered.

But this morning I decided to make the most of having my partner, Mark, around to keep an eye on the kids. Our twins, Millie and Oliver, had turned four and although they were fairly sensible for their age, I couldn't quite disappear and relax with them unsupervised. Because when I did have a bath and leave the door open should they need me, I tended to be hanging out the side sloshing water onto the floor, straining to hear signs of any tantrums or rows. Or failing that they would shout, 'M-u-m-m-m-m-y,' up the stairs or wander into the bathroom and ask me why my stomach was so big and what we were having for lunch.

This morning I enjoyed the solitude and poured in several generous glugs of the lavender bath oil Gran gave me for Christmas and which I saved for such rare occasions. I locked the door and climbed in, submerging myself in the warm water. I lay for a few minutes trying to flick through a magazine. But it was awkward to hold, and my eyes kept fluttering shut. Flinging it to the corner of the bathroom I closed my eyes and enjoyed the warm water.

Aside from the brightly coloured plastic letters stuck to the tiles, which spelled out MILLIE and OLI, the bathroom was a place of muted colours and calm. My haven, and one of the first rooms that we'd tackled when we got the keys to the house last summer. It badly needed an overhaul. It was the same yellow suite we had as kids — so beyond vintage. There was absolutely no sadness or nostalgia at all when the builders ripped it out and began to work their magic.

We replaced everything with a white suite and plain tiles and painted the walls a pale grey. We splashed out on underfloor heating and dark grey tiles which looked like huge pebbles. Sometimes I would lie on the warm floor at night and look up at the stars through the skylight. Complete bliss.

My towel warmed on the radiator and this morning the Velux window framed a pale blue sky. One thing that I've learned since becoming a mother is that I grow restless quickly. I'm not used to sitting down for long. I should be doing something rather than being still. I wonder sometimes if that's because I don't want to think about things. I seem to cope if I keep on moving.

After a while I grew restless and thought I should attend to some grooming, so I reached for the shower gel and slathered my legs, lathering up the bubbles. The razer glided over my skin, and I managed not to make any nicks. I turned my attention to my armpits, which were certainly needing some attention. I couldn't quite remember when I'd tended to them. As I pulled the razor over the right one, I winced when I nipped the skin. I pushed my chin into my chest, twisting my neck round to get a better look and pulling my breast out of the way — easy enough as I have very small breasts. I pit-patted my fingers over the whole area and moved down towards the nipple. I repeated it again and again. Then I did the same thing on the other side.

Everything seemed okay on the left side, and I checked it all several times to be sure. But something about the right side bothered me, a niggle which wormed its way into my head. I pit-patted up and over and around. Maybe I had imagined the lump? I was tired, that was probably the reason I was overly anxious. My fingers crawled around my breast and lingered on a small patch halfway between my nipple and armpit. I pressed and prodded and pressed again. Pulling my hand away sharply, I slapped it under the water. I was now being paranoid. It was best to leave things alone for a few minutes before I started to jump to conclusions. I could check again in five minutes or so. Focusing on my breathing, I slowly breathed in for four counts, held for four counts and breathed out again for four, holding that breath for four — a technique I heard on one of the podcasts I loved to listen to. Usually, it worked wonders in helping me settle my nerves.

My breathing certainly steadied, which was good. But as I lay in the cooling water, the bubbles disappearing, my mind raced. How would the kids and Mark manage without me? And what about Dad and Gran? I tentatively pulled my hands out from the water and started to repeat the same moves again. Sometimes my breasts got a bit sore around the time of my period. Although my cycle was a bit all over the place just now. That calmed my mind slightly, but I thought I would finish checking to be sure. Pit-patter across the skin. There it was. Definitely. A lump the size of a chickpea.

CHAPTER THIRTY-THREE

Josie

As I sat on the bed, *our* bed, and looked up at Dimitri, I knew straight away. He didn't break eye contact and didn't even try to deny it.

'Can you blame me?' he said tightly. 'I mean, you're hardly up for a romp much these days, are you?'

'I've been injecting myself with hormones. I'm knackered, Dimitri. All so I can give you a baby!' I spat the words out in disbelief.

'It didn't mean a thing,' he said, trying his best to smile at me. 'Meaningless sex, that was all. A stupid fling. But you know I have needs.'

I couldn't begin to describe how surreal it was to be having this conversation with my husband. Just a few minutes ago he had been shagging someone else, identity still to be established, in our marital bed. The one I'd woken up in that morning, a few hours ago, with my husband lying next to me with a bulge in his pants. I had realised the time and leaped out of bed to get ready for work, leaving him lying there moaning. Was this my punishment for failing to do my wifely duties this morning? I mean, you couldn't make it up.

Who took their bit on the side to their house, the one where they lived with their wife, for a sex session? What a bloody cliché. 'Are you going to tell me who she is?' I said, tightly.

He shrugged, pursing his lips. 'Does it matter?'

I glared at him. 'Yes, of course. You've been shagging someone else in our bed and I would quite like to know who that is, thanks very much.' Should I have yelled and screamed at him? Or thrown ornaments at his head? But I didn't like clutter and I didn't have anything to hand. I glanced at the pile of books on the floor next to my side of the bed. I was about to grab a hard-back Michelle Obama biography to chuck at him when I spotted something shiny sticking out from underneath the pile. Bending down, I clasped my fingers around a rose-gold hoop and pinched it between two fingers, holding it up at the light. 'Does this belong to her?'

'I don't know,' he baulked. 'Isn't it yours? I mean, how should I know whose earring it is?'

'Wrong answer, Dimitri. It is not mine.' Clenching my teeth together, I steadied my breathing. Rose gold. I *always* wore silver. However, I did know a person who loved rose gold. I even knew who had a pair of earrings like these because she bought them when I held that Stella and Dot jewellery party last year. As I topped up everyone's glasses with fizz, she tried on all of the samples, much to the annoyance of the other women who were also keen to try.

Normally I would try and rationalise things and make excuses. Surely there must be a simple explanation as to why our neighbour's earring would be lying on our bedroom floor. Maybe she came over to borrow something and dropped it? Exactly. This time I couldn't make any excuses. They were all ridiculous.

And at that moment, things finally began to slot into place. She was often here when I came back from work, claiming she was waiting for me to get back as she needed some advice about random things. There were the text messages to Dimitri, which he claimed were about a writing course she wanted to do. They had concocted the perfect

114

smokescreen. She wanted to write a novel, and he offered to mentor her. Because he was a writer and wanted to help.

'It's not a big deal,' he said, when he realised that I had pieced two and two together. 'Honestly, don't make more of this than it is.'

'Are you now saying that it's my fault that you're shagging our neighbour and one of our best friends?'

'Friend?' he said with a snort. '*Friend?*'

That just fuelled my anger.

'What kind of friend would be desperate to jump into bed with your husband at the first opportunity? No real friend would do that to you. You're better off without her . . . She feels sorry for you because you can't conceive.'

I stared at him, his arms crossed. He always got defensive when he was in the wrong.

'Look, please don't blame yourself,' he tried to say kindly. 'You've been under pressure. I understand. I've been up against it too.' He raked his hands through his hair. 'We both have a lot on our plates. You with all this fertility stuff and me with the latest deadline. I mean, it's understandable. Sometimes we have to vent our frustrations.'

'*Really?*' Was it understandable? Was this what a marriage was about? Him trying to justify his actions because of stress? I couldn't remember the last time I jumped into bed with a neighbour or a colleague because I was under pressure.

'Take some time,' he said. 'Think about how we can move on from this . . . Maybe we could go on holiday. Head off for some together time.' He tried to look at me meaningfully.

I glanced at his hairy toes. The truth was that this man repulsed me. I didn't love Dimitri. I hated him and all I could think was what an utter bellend he was. Oh God, my sister had been *so* right. Why did I not listen to her? 'Oh, fuck off and leave me alone.'

He shook his head, turned and went downstairs.

Grabbing my suitcase and a holdall from under the bed, I noticed a discarded condom wrapper on the floor. *Nice.* All I could do was start laughing hysterically. What a mess.

Wiping away the tears, I grabbed some jeans, T-shirts and sweaters, my gym gear and some papers and notebooks. Then I rummaged around in my bedside drawer for my passport and some jewellery. I went through to the shower room and swept the bottles into my washbag. I took my electric toothbrush, the only charger and the tube of toothpaste.

I paused for a minute at the door when I heard the sound of whirring. Seriously? Surely he wasn't. But the whirring continued. He had been caught in the act and admitted it, and now he was casually brewing himself a bloody coffee? While I prepared to walk out, he was happily popping pods of coffee into the machine. *Obviously* all of the shagging had tired him out and he needed a caffeine fix, poor soul. Shaking my head, I caught a glimpse of my blotchy face in the bathroom mirror. I gave it a quick wash with a facecloth. I pulled my bobbed strawberry-blonde hair into a ponytail. Biting my lip, I took a few deep breaths and reminded myself I deserved more. I took another deep breath and imagined Gran rolling out pastry at the kitchen table, and drew comfort from the image. She would wipe her floury hands on her apron and draw me into a hug. She would make everything better.

I reached into the bathroom cupboard and pulled out the nail scissors. I briefly thought about going downstairs to stab him, but went to his underwear drawer and cut a hole in the crotch of every pair of his pants instead. Then I filled a glass of water, emptying it under the duvet on his side of the bed. I repeated this several times. I knew I was being childish, but I didn't care. The thought of him pulling on holey pants and lying down on a squelchy bed made me feel *so* much better.

When I took my bags to the bottom of the stairs, he wandered through with his mug of coffee, putting it on the small hall table. 'This is silly, Josie. Come on. We've had blips before, and we've managed to move on from them.' His dark eyes bored into me and once I would have found it attractive, but not anymore.

'Blips? You've been having an affair with one of the neighbours. How do you suggest we move on?'

He took a sip of coffee. 'It was hardly an affair, rather a few romps in the sack. There are ways we can move on — a fresh start somewhere else?'

I shook my head, incredulous at his suggestion. 'What are you talking about?'

'All I'm saying is that this doesn't mean anything. There's no need for anything hasty. Let's be rational. A change of scene could be exactly what we need.'

'Dimitri, are you suggesting we move to a new house?'

His eyes lit up and he reached his hand out towards me. 'That's not a bad idea, Josie. Not a bad idea at all. What a girl you are! I mean, prices are soaring here and, well, Hampton Court might be a nice change?'

Was he for real? I batted his hand off my arm. 'Well, that would give you a fresh batch of housewives to make your way through. You could try and charm them with your wonderful chat.'

'Come on, darling. This is silly. I love you.'

Once I might have fallen for his empty words but not anymore. 'Goodbye, Dimitri. I'll be in touch to get the rest of my stuff.' I don't think he thought I was going anywhere. He stood there looking quite blasé.

'Okay, if this is what you want, that's fine. If you want to walk away and leave me and what we have together, so be it. But I think you just need some space for a while and that's fine. Call me and let me know when you're feeling better.' He turned away from me to catch a fly buzzing around his head.

That's when I slipped the laxatives in his coffee, picked up my bags and walked out.

CHAPTER THIRTY-FOUR

Tara

I didn't say anything to Mark when I came downstairs after the bath. There was no point in worrying him yet, and anyway he was tired from working such long hours.

'Did you enjoy that, love?'

I nodded. 'Yes, thanks. Where are the kids?'

'Making plans for their den in the garden.'

Smiling, I glanced outside, and a sob caught in my throat. What if I didn't live long enough to see them grow up? Would Mark manage as a single dad? I suddenly thought of my own father and got yet another insight into how he felt when Mum left. Would Mark be able to do what he did and pick up the pieces and muddle on? Although I suppose the main difference, I reminded myself, was that I would be dead and past the point of no return. Dad always waited and hoped that Mum would come back.

'You're miles away, Tara,' he said, looking at me questioningly.

'Sorry, Mark. Just thinking about how amazing it'll be to have the studio space sorted. Hopefully sooner rather than later.'

'The guys did say they should be able to start within the week, which is positive, isn't it?'

I nodded. 'When are you heading to the restaurant?'

He glanced at his watch. 'In another hour or so. Hopefully they're managing without me. Coffee?' He pulled the cafetière from the cupboard.

'Yes, please. You've read my mind.' I knew he could tell something was wrong.

'Are you sure you're okay, love?'

'Yes, I'm fine. Don't worry. I'm just thinking about stuff . . . that's what happens when I sit down.'

'Anything I can help with?' he said, walking over to put an arm around my shoulder.

'No, just the usual stuff. You know . . .' He did, as he'd listened to me plenty of times over the years talking about my mum and latterly all the stuff with my sister. He was very patient, though he did struggle to get his head around it at times. Although he knew the reason Josie and I didn't talk, I think he thought we should sort things out and clear the air. It wasn't quite as easy as that though. Mark came from a big family in Glasgow, one of four boys who adored their mother, though not so much their bullying father.

We met under emotional circumstances and were friends for a long time before anything else happened between us. I had been standing on a platform at Waverley Station in Edinburgh, waiting to take the train home after a day at work. On days like those, I wished I lived in town and had a flat nearer the hospital. The commute could sometimes be a step too far, especially after the kind of day I'd had. One of our patients, a young boy, had died, and I'd taken it badly. As a nurse, I should have been used to dealing with death, but that wee boy got under my skin. I was so fond of him, and his passing hit me hard. As I waited for the train to arrive, I tried to distract myself by wondering what to make for tea. There was a commotion on the concourse and several police appeared on the scene. They surrounded someone — it looked like a man from where I stood — and tackled him

119

to the ground. All the trains were then delayed or cancelled and the station fell into chaos as we were evacuated.

Rather than head up the stairs and exit onto Princes Street, I ran out onto Market Street and took myself up the seventy-six steps of Fleshmarket Close, holding my nose to avoid the scent of stale urine, and turned into Cockburn Street. I was in a bit of a daze and found myself in a café. I must have been quite out of it because as I stood at the counter, I had no idea what the guy was asking me. Eventually he steered me towards a chair and sat me down with a cup of tea and a flapjack. He sat with me and listened as I told him what happened that day at work and then at the station. I'd never offloaded to anyone in that way before, but he sat and listened. It was exactly what I needed that day. I left and returned to the station to catch another train home, feeling so much lighter. The following week I went back in to thank him although I couldn't remember his name. I don't even know if he told me it. He introduced himself as Mark and after that the café became my regular coffee stop on the way to the hospital. If Mark was in, which he generally was as the owner, he'd sit and chat. When I told him I lived in North Berwick he laughed in surprise. He had been looking at premises in the town as his dream had always been to live and work by the sea. The rest, as the old saying goes, is history.

He handed me a coffee and I gazed at him, reaching my hand up and rubbing it over his unshaven cheek. Who would have thought we would have ended up together and living here? I smiled at him. 'Thank you.'

'That's okay, though I wish you would tell me what's *really* on your mind,' he said.

'I've obviously overdone it with the lavender oil. It's made me feel a bit dozy . . . I should use something more uplifting to energise me next time.' I forced a laugh.

'The coffee should perk you up a bit.' He sipped from his mug. 'What's on today?'

'Well, swimming lessons with the kids later and Dad invited them for a sleepover. They're going to be delighted about that.'

He raised an eyebrow. 'I don't believe it. A night without the kids and I'm working?'

'Yes,' I said smiling. 'But it does mean that we can have a lie-in tomorrow . . .'

He moved towards me, kissing me gently on the lips and grazing my chin with his stubble. 'Very true,' he said. 'It's not that bad after all.'

'Mummy,' said Millie, flying into the kitchen. 'Oliver said Jamie's mum bought bananas from the shop and they laid spiders!'

Oliver followed close behind, his eyes wide. 'It's true! His bananas laid spiders and they're in a shoebox and they're getting the vet out and everything.'

Mark chuckled. 'I think you mean the SSPCA?'

'Do we have bananas? I don't want bananas here,' said Millie, her eyes darting about the kitchen in a panic.

'No, don't worry, we're all out of bananas.'

Mark reached into one of the drawers and pulled out his iPad and looked. He walked over and showed me the local Facebook page which Jamie's mum posted on. She had indeed bought bananas at the local supermarket which came with an extra 'gift' from Colombia. Loads of people made comments and posted pictures of various spiders, which gave me the creeps.

'Can I see, can I see?' Oliver ran over.

Mark raised it out of reach. 'Not now, Oli. Maybe later.' He grimaced at me.

He and Millie would both freak if they saw the pictures and that would mean sleepless nights for all, including Dad.

'Don't worry,' said Mark. 'It's just one of those things that sometimes happens when food is brought from far away. But Jamie's mum has done the right thing. And I'm quite sure it will all be sorted.'

'Bleurgh. I'm never eating a banana again.' Mark's words obviously placated Millie and she ran back outside.

Meanwhile I needed to remember not to buy bananas for a while. At least until there was no chance of a repeat episode happening in our house. The thought of spiders and their babies in my house made me shudder. 'I think that would tip me over the edge.'

'Can we get a tarantula as a pet?' said Oliver.

'No,' said Mark and I at the same time. 'Okey-dokey.' He shrugged and ran after Millie.

Smiling at them as they ran out into the garden, I thought of the spiders and then the lump in my breast and shivered.

CHAPTER THIRTY-FIVE

Josie

I threw my bags into the boot and sat in the driver's seat, desperate to get away yet wondering if I could do this. Did I have the strength to leave?

Turning the keys in the ignition, I briefly glanced over at Asmita's house and noticed movement at the window. Pausing for a moment, I wondered if I should go and confront her. Though I would probably end up apologising and she would try and gloss over things because that's what everyone in my life seemed to do. I decided no, I couldn't face another scene of any sort, and anyway there was a chance she didn't know that I knew. Although I assumed she must have been aware of some of the shouting and screaming. Everyone's windows and folding kitchen doors were open because of the rising summer temperatures.

Instead I flicked the finger at her window, revved the engine and screeched away from the kerb outside my home and my haven for the past five years. How quickly things could change.

I drove towards Twickenham on autopilot and after a couple of miles I found myself following the signs for the M3/A308/Sunbury/Staines and then the signs for the M25.

Fortunately, I'd filled the tank with petrol on my way back from work yesterday so I didn't need to stop. I didn't need the satnav on either. I'd made this trip dozens of times over the years and had plenty of time to think about things as I made the seven-hour journey north. Normally Dimitri and I would do this drive together and the time would fly as we chatted non-stop. We would pull off at various service stations for coffee and snacks and take turns driving, allowing the other to nod off for an hour or so when we ran out of conversation. Other times we would make a weekend of it and stop off on the way up for a romantic night at a hotel in York or Northumberland. A couple of times I found myself wiping away a tear when I thought about what happened. Why did I trust him again and again? Flicking on the radio, I managed to distract myself with some upbeat tunes interspersed with news reports about world events.

I stopped south of York to refuel and grab a coffee. Sitting in a corner of Starbucks, I sipped on a latte and watched the throngs of people passing through. I wondered where they were going with their sense of purpose. They looked like they belonged. I was envious of the young couples holding hands and the families with young children. Should I have done more to make sure his needs were being met? I mean, I did my best, but maybe that wasn't enough. Perhaps I couldn't blame him for getting together with beautiful Asmita with her dark glossy hair and full lips. I bit into a lemon and white-chocolate-chip muffin, which was sweet and cloying in my mouth. I took another sip of coffee to wash it down.

What would I say to everyone? It would be mortifying to admit the truth about my sudden arrival and Dimitri's affair. My sister, Tara, never liked him, although I couldn't quite understand why. But once I'd seen him through her eyes, I felt even more of a fool and quite sick at the way we left things at Christmas. Would she ever forgive me?

And what about work? What would I tell them? I'd have to email them to let them know I was taking some last-minute leave. Thank goodness there were no students to deal with at the moment. It was the silver lining in what had turned into a complete shit-show of a day.

Eventually I stood up and stretched, my body tense and stiff from sitting. I pulled my phone from my bag, wondering if I should text Tara and Gran to let them know I was coming. There were two texts from Dimitri but I deleted them both without reading. I threw the mobile back into my bag. I would surprise them. It would give me more time to formulate a plan.

When I joined the motorway again, the Friday traffic had started to thin out. It was just after six o'clock and I couldn't wait to drive past the Northumberland coastline. It was beautiful and so good for the soul. Part of me wondered if I should stop off there for the night. I mean, I didn't have to be anywhere. I didn't have anyone to answer to and I could suit myself. For the first time in ages, I was aware of a small sense of liberation. I kept driving, thoughts about Dimitri swirling in my head. I thought about the early days when we met at university. We were both studying English literature at St Andrews and I loved his appreciation of language and the letters he would pen me. Kind, charming and gorgeous, he helped me move on and away and start a new life. When we graduated, he swore that he only had eyes for me and like a fool I believed him.

That first summer he went to work in Cyprus with relatives, promising he would be back in the autumn to take up the job he'd been offered at a publishing company. I moved down to London to be near him and started a PhD. But he was never in touch at all that summer and when he did come to London we didn't quite pick up where we left off. He wanted some space and I respected that. He saw me when it suited him, which worked for me as I could focus on studying. Our on-and-off relationship was all right for a while until I decided I'd had enough and was about to walk away. But at that point Dimitri decided he was ready to commit and six years ago we married.

When I spotted the blue Saltire sign welcoming me to Scotland and the words Fàilte *gu Alba*, butterflies swirled in the pit of my stomach. I thought about my marriage and if I should grow up and get on with things. Should I turn around and drive back to Teddington? But I couldn't let go of that sense of ease as I made my way up the long and familiar A1. When I reached Dunbar, I pulled off to use the toilets in the garden centre. The woman at the door kindly let me in even though it was about to close. At least I wouldn't risk bumping into anyone. The chairs in the café were up on the tables and a man mopped the floors. I stepped around his bucket, mouthing an apology as I made my way to the toilets.

Glancing at my watch, I realised I would be home in less than half an hour. I joined the A1 and at the next roundabout followed the signs for North Berwick. Catching a glimpse of the sea, nervous anticipation swirled in my stomach. The roads were quiet and the sky a beautiful pale blue. I drove through Tyninghame admiring the red-slated roofs on the white and pink cottages and looked over at the fields to my right, which grew Brussel sprouts during the winter months.

I kept checking my rear-view mirror, a habit from London driving, but I was the only car on this stretch of road. The evening sun dappled through the trees and as I turned the corner, I caught sight of Tantallon Castle and the spectacular view of the sea, the Bass Rock and Fife beyond. It never failed to amaze me.

I spotted a new café which had opened up right on the cliff. Trying to keep my eyes on the road, I scanned it with interest. It looked like a shipping container. I couldn't wait to visit. Then I spotted one of Gran's neighbours coming towards me in her car. Hers was the only bright yellow car with a pink stripe around it in the town. Being spotted was the last thing I wanted, and I pulled down the sun visor to give me something of a screen. Following the road past the campsite on the right, I noticed a new development of houses on the left. The Law, a huge volcanic rock which Tara and I used to love climbing, loomed above me. I passed Tesco and followed the road round, taking a left to follow the line of trees which lined a small track. I drove slowly up it, jolting a bit over the potholes. The track widened out and the large brick entrance to the driveway loomed ahead of me. This hadn't been my planned first port of call. Yet my car moved slowly across the red gravel and I came to a stop outside the stone cottage, which now had a pale green door instead of the red one that I remembered.

The garden was still beautiful, sprawling and shielded by a hedge to give privacy from nosy walkers. The view at the end of the garden made me gasp. This was a scene I would never tire of and I knew why my mother loved it so much. I sat in silence in the empty driveway for a moment thinking. I had mixed feelings when Gran told me Tara had bought the house. Perhaps jealousy? Though I'm not sure why because I didn't want to buy it. Maybe it reminded me of everything that my sister had and I did not, including a perfect family. Standing there and thinking and being in the moment did make me feel calm. Calm. It was such a small yet powerful word and a feeling I hadn't experienced for such a long time. I turned off the ignition and slipped out of the car, walking down to Mum's favourite apple tree. I reached out and touched the trunk and part of me even wanted to hug it. I remembered the sounds which used to reassure me and ground me. Mum laughing, my sister chatting to her doll and the gentle creak of the branches on a breezy summer day. Closing my eyes, I could imagine Mum lounging in the hammock strung up between the trees. Taking a deep breath, I smiled and opened my eyes. I shivered when I spotted the garage, which was always full of spiders. Then I heard a noise, a low grumbling from the road beyond. I could hear the gentle sound of a car's engine and the crunching sound as the wheels rolled across the driveway. I turned around and stared back up at the cottage.

CHAPTER THIRTY-SIX

Tara

I groaned when I saw the car in the driveway. Who on earth was visiting? I was so looking forward to a quiet night after a long day. All I wanted to do was switch off my phone and slump in front of the TV with some crackers and cheese. When I realised there was no wine, I nipped out to Tesco to get my favourite Chablis. The shop was only a two-minute drive away and I managed to avoid seeing anyone — the peril of going supermarket shopping in a small town — and was home within ten minutes. And now, an unexpected visitor. Who on earth dropped by at this time on a Friday night anyway? I should be more easy-going, but I didn't like surprises. Then I remembered I left my phone in the house, so someone might have sent me a message. Mind you, I didn't recognise the car. Nobody was inside and I frowned. Could the builder be popping in to check the site again?

Someone was standing at the bottom of the garden. My heart started to race. I narrowed my gaze. It wasn't the builder. A woman stood staring up at me. That's when I gasped. My sister, Josie, stared back at me. I got out of the

128

car and stood waiting and watching until she slowly started to make her way up the garden towards me.

'Josie?' I said in disbelief.

'Hi,' she said, shifting awkwardly from one foot to the other.

'What are *you* doing here?' I didn't mean it to come out sounding quite like that and I cursed inwardly when she shrank back. But I was genuinely baffled by her sudden appearance. She must have got a new car since she last visited.

She gestured towards the bottom of the garden. 'I forgot how stunning the view is.'

'Yes. It is.'

'Dad's been here?' she said, pointing at the tubs of flowers at the front door.

'Yes, you know Dad. Doesn't miss an opportunity to do some gardening.' Turning to grab my bag from the passenger's seat, I pointed to the house. 'Do you want to come in and have a look? I'll give you the grand tour.'

Leading her into the hallway of what used to be our childhood home was strange. It dawned on me that this would be the first time she had been back since we moved out all those years ago. I assumed Gran or Dad told her we'd bought it. They must have, otherwise how would she have known to come here? I did think if they had told her it might have prompted her to get in touch before now . . . anyway, no point dwelling on that. She glanced at the light pouring in from the skylight in the hallway.

'It looks so different,' she said, looking up at the window above. 'Wow. That's amazing. I remember it always used to be so dark here.'

'Wait until you see the kitchen,' I said, pointing through to the back room, now also flooded with light. We knocked down a wall between the old kitchen and the dining room to make a huge living space. It was so different to the gloomy, old-fashioned room which used to be our kitchen when this was the ministerial manse. I shuddered when I thought of the orange tiles and the dark flooring, which felt so oppressive when we were kids. It was my least favourite room in the house. The rest of the house was wonderful with all of its nooks and crannies — great for playing hide and seek when we were growing up. And, of course, the garden was spectacular with its amazing uninterrupted views of the sea. Josie and I had so much fun out there as kids and it was something I wanted for my own children. I wanted them to enjoy the kind of childhood that I had, until things all went so horribly wrong.

Even though the twins were only four, they were already becoming quite excited by our plans for the garden. I planted a vegetable patch, with Dad's help of course, and Mark had plans to try and make his own cider from some of the many apple trees dotted around. We managed to clear away a lot of the junk from the garage. We had plans to knock it down and build a den-cum-office for me and the kids, with floor-to-ceiling windows making the most of the view. I'd hoped to set up a massage therapy business from home. I mean, who wouldn't be relaxed and chilled out with that view?

Josie gasped. 'How amazing, Tara. I can't believe what you've done . . .' She walked around, looking genuinely impressed by the new space we'd created. I was so pleased and relieved that she approved. 'And to think this was the most horrid kitchen ever when we were kids.' She smiled. 'Do you remember the bright orange tiles? And that horrid lino on the floor?'

'Can you believe when we moved in there were still traces of those old tiles underneath the new ones the last owners had redecorated with?' I stood lost in my own thoughts for a moment as I remembered the day the builders knocked the wall down and I caught a glimpse of my retro childhood kitchen.

Josie cleared her throat. 'I'm sorry to turn up like this out of the blue. I'd planned to go to Gran's first of all. But I kind of ended up here . . . I guess I was curious, and . . .' Her voice trailed off.

I watched as she stood for a moment not speaking, but chewing her lip — a sure sign of nerves which always gave her away.

'Tara, I need to talk to you . . . I owe you an explanation. And an apology . . .'

For a moment I was lost for words, which *never* happened. I could always chat my way through or out of most situations. But yes, she did owe me an explanation. I turned my back to her to fill the kettle. Could she really be here to apologise? My sister *never* apologised for anything. 'Are you going to tell me what this is about?'

'Um,' she said, fidgeting with her bag. 'Yes. Of course. I will . . . but do you think I could use your loo first? I'm desperate.'

'Of course. Come on, through here,' I said, showing her to the small cloakroom off the hall covered with pictures of the kids.

'They're so sweet,' she said, smiling. 'Bless them. I can't believe they're four.'

We both stood looking at the assortment of baby and toddler photos. 'To think they must start school soon . . . after the summer?'

I nodded. 'I'll leave you to it.' I closed the door behind me and walked back through to the kitchen. Picking up my mobile, my finger hovered over the screen, ready to text Mark. But why? There was nothing to tell him yet anyway.

I thought back to the last time I saw Josie, the Christmas before last, and shivered. We'd left things horribly and I'd regretted that day ever since. But she walked out and left without a backwards glance. Then she blanked all my emails and texts. She did send the twins birthday presents and Christmas presents last year. However, she refused to have anything to do with me. I only knew she was okay because she kept in touch with Gran and Dad. They said they tried to reason with her, but she wouldn't listen. She said she would only keep in touch with them if they didn't mention my name. Mark told me she would eventually wake up and come to her senses, but I worried about her. My sister was vulnerable, more so with the fertility treatment Gran told me about. I thought about going down to visit her, but I had to accept she would only talk to me at the right time and on her terms. Not being able to speak to her tore me apart. We were always close, and more so when Mum left. We wanted to stick together.

I heard the toilet flush and Josie walked back through to the kitchen. She seemed smaller. She'd definitely lost weight and appeared unsure of herself. That was new to me because Josie, as the older sister, was always more confident and the one with answers to everything.

'Where are the kids then?' she said, looking around.

Was she expecting them to jump from a cupboard? 'At Dad's for a sleepover,' I replied. 'He's become quite the doting grandfather.' Neither of us needed to say that perhaps he was making up for being a crap father.

Josie and I often wondered if Dad would find someone else to replace Mum. But he never seemed interested. He said he wanted to wait. He hoped she would return. He threw himself into work as the local church minister. I think that must have been hard for him. His role in the community meant he was even more prone to the whisperings and mutterings about where Mum had gone. Our town was smaller then and people liked to gossip. Dad left Gran in charge of raising us. Perhaps that made him into the doting grandad he was now. Maybe he felt guilty that he wasn't there for us when we needed him.

'And Mark?'

'He's working.'

She nodded. 'Of course, this will be a busy night for him. How's it going at the restaurant?'

'Really well, thanks. Seems to be as busy as ever. I guess with all the tourists and the golfers, there's never a shortage of people looking for some freshly caught seafood for dinner.' I couldn't bear to make much more small talk. I wanted her to cut to the chase and tell me what happened. 'Cup of tea?'

I asked, desperate to try and do something rather than stand there awkwardly. 'Or something stronger?' I said, pulling the wine from my bag.

'Yes, I could do with a drink.'

The wine glugged as I poured it into two glasses. Handing her one, she took a large sip and then put it down on the worktop. 'Thank you.'

'Where is Dimitri?' I tried to sound casual, but it came out accusatory.

'He's in London.'

'He's actually let you out on your own?' I tried to joke, but she didn't smile. Shit, me and my sense of humour.

She took another glug of wine and perched on the stool by the breakfast bar. 'I'm so sorry, Tara. I'm so sorry for everything.'

'For what?' I said, wanting to ensure we weren't talking at cross purposes.

'I'm sorry for believing him and not you.'

I raised an eyebrow and held my breath. This was so unlike her. What on earth happened?

'I've left him,' she said and drained her glass of wine.

CHAPTER THIRTY-SEVEN

Josie

I watched as Tara refilled my glass and waited as she took a small sip from hers. She always was one to do things quite measuredly.

'Cheers,' I said, raising my glass.

Clinking hers next to mine, she narrowed her eyes. 'Cheers, Josie . . . I hope this time you're certain.'

I tried to smile. 'About what?'

'Leaving him.'

She was of course completely right, but it struck a nerve, and I gripped the glass. I needed to remain calm. I had come here to apologise and not make things any worse than they already were.

Tara raised an eyebrow. 'Well . . . we've been here before, haven't we?'

I regarded her for a minute, sitting at her dining room table, and swept my eyes around the kitchen again. I loved what they had done with the space. It reminded me of the sort of kitchen and living area I admired when I flicked through home magazines. Bright and light with so much space. I mean, our house in Teddington was nice and our renovations had improved it hugely, with its lovely kitchen and doors opening out onto decking and the garden. But it was like a doll's house in comparison to this. I wondered if she knew how lucky she was to live here with a devoted partner and two beautiful children. This house used to be mine too. I shook myself, annoyed by that twinge of envy.

'I'm not judging you,' she said.

Damn. She always had the ability to read my mind. 'Doesn't sound like it,' I said, crossing my arms.

She reached across and grabbed my hand. 'Josie, come on. You're my sister and I love you and I want what's best for you. It's all any of us want . . .'

I thought back to the loyal sister she'd been to me over the years. Despite our differences she was always there for me, and that worked both ways. I would do anything for Tara. Dimitri had done his best to isolate me from her and create a wedge to weaken our bond. That's when the full extent of his control over me began to dawn on me. Because I'm not sure if I would have been there for her this last year. I would have come up with an excuse, manipulated and fuelled by Dimitri, to avoid helping her or seeing her. In my mind, my sister was a bitch and to blame for everything. I was utterly ashamed as I sat at the table, trying to push away the guilt now washing over me in waves.

'I'm sorry, Tara. I'm so sorry I've been a shit sister and a crap aunt to the kids. I've thought a lot about you all.' I squeezed her hand. 'Sometimes I wonder why I'm so stupid. Why did I stay with him all these years?' Tears started to blur my vision and I gratefully took the tissue she handed me from the box on the dresser.

'Because it's not quite as simple as that, Josie. It's easy for any of us to see what's going on when we're outside the relationship. Not so when you're inside and trapped. I can easily make observations and judgements. It's not quite the same when you're in the relationship with the person you love.'

Her words struck a chord and another sob rose from my chest.

'Dimitri is narcissistic and always will be.'

She was right, but her words were so final and horrible. These were words about my husband. She could never take these words back. What if I went back to him? What if we tried to make another go of things? I hadn't quite realised the extent of Tara's dislike towards him.

'It has always been all about him. From the very start, Josie.'

I nodded. 'But his charm managed to cover a multitude of sins . . .'

Tara coughed. 'He was charming enough to begin with but that soon slipped away. Remember when you almost missed Dad's birthday when he was on a deadline and couldn't come?'

I nodded even though I couldn't remember.

'And I know he made you feel bad about leaving him . . .'

I nodded again.

'And the time Gran and I came to visit?'

Another memory I had conveniently managed to forget.

'He never made us feel welcome. In fact, he went out of his way to exclude us. Think about all the times you spent with his family versus ours.'

She was right and I needed to listen to her and pull my head out of the sand. For years I had avoided hearing any of this. As we began chatting, layers of tension started to lift. We touched on some of the occasions over the years when I'd felt alienated from the family.

Family get-togethers were always about *his* family, and he encouraged me to keep things a secret from Tara. Everything she said made perfect sense. Everything she said about Dimitri was right. 'She won't understand, and she'll make it into a bigger issue,' he'd said after another pregnancy test had come back negative. Whereas if I had been able to lean on my sister and get some emotional support from her, then I wouldn't have been so wretched and blamed myself. Another thing Dimitri was good at — insinuating our inability to conceive was my fault. If I hadn't drunk that extra glass of wine . . . if I did more or less exercise. I sat for a moment reflecting on the toxic mess I'd walked away from.

'You're right, Tara,' I said. I needed time to process all of this without saying anything out loud to her until the right time. He'd conditioned me not to confide in my own family. He would twist things Tara and Gran and Dad said, to make me feel as though I was the black sheep of the family. I spent hours and hours analysing things they'd said to me to the point of paranoia. The whole thought of family and what they meant left me feeling exhausted. It was easier to make the most of the rare trips back on my own. There was less of an atmosphere than when he came with me and put everyone on edge. My face flushed with embarrassment as I thought of the awful things I said about them to Dimitri with his encouragement.

'Josie,' she said, her voice kind. 'Absolutely none of this is your fault. You've not done anything wrong.'

I knew she was trying to help. Raking a hand through my hair, I nodded. 'Thanks, Tara. But . . . well, it doesn't seem quite that way now. I'm just ashamed and . . . I feel stupid.'

'The main thing is you can see him for what he is. And Josie, it's an awful thing to say but I'm glad you don't have kids with him. I'm glad you can walk away and not look back.'

Something had been festering away at the back of my mind since I'd told her what happened. My sister, I realised, wasn't surprised to hear about Dimitri's actions. 'Tara?'

'Mmm.'

'How did you know though?'

'What?'

'That he's done this before?'

Obviously flustered, Tara stood up. 'I'd better open some more wine . . .'

CHAPTER THIRTY-EIGHT

Tara

I was laying it on thick and not even trying to be diplomatic about the extent of my dislike of Dimitri. But I couldn't stand the man and wasn't at all surprised to hear about his latest bout of bad behaviour. His philandering was the whole reason that Josie hadn't spoken to me for almost eighteen months.

He tried it on with me last Christmas when I was in the kitchen spreading whipped cream across the pavlova. He stuck his finger in the bowl, which annoyed me, and put it in his mouth suggestively. I mean, yes, he was quite a good-looking guy in a Greek waiter kind of way, if you were into that. Plus, I knew his sleazy type only too well and my sister was far too good for him. But how do you tell your sister that you think her husband is a complete bellend? How did I tell her about his latest attempt at seduction, this time with her own sister. I mean, what would I say? Tell everyone as I sliced up dessert and handed it to them? It would utterly destroy her. There was no way that I could tell Mark what happened until Dimitri had departed, as he would have certainly thumped him.

'Eh, do you mind, Dimitri?' I said, trying to distract him as if he was a little boy. 'Go and fill the kettle or do something useful. Like scrape those plates into the recycling box.'

He scowled and raised his eyebrows at me in quite a suggestive manner. All I could focus on was the fact they desperately needed a trim, which I was on the verge of suggesting. But before I said anything, he reached across the bowl of cream and put a splodge on the end of my nose. Not exactly appealing, eh?

'What are you doing, you idiot?' I said, wiping it away with the back of my hand and onto my apron.

'Oh, I do love it when you're mad. So sexy,' he said and guffawed.

Oh dear God. My brother-in-law was making a pass at me while I sorted the Christmas pudding. We weren't actually having the traditional pudding as nobody liked it, hence the meringue. I did momentarily wonder how he would have done the same trick with a steamed fruit cake. Was that where I'd gone wrong? 'Dimitri,' I said again, 'how about you go and make yourself *useful*? Go and check if anyone needs a top-up. Take another bottle of white out the fridge and a red one from the wine rack.' Over the years I'd got quite used to his suggestive behaviour and managed to deal with it, swerving times he tried to be alone with me and defusing awkward comments he tended to make in social situations. I thought I'd handled it all quite well. Until now. I couldn't work out why my sister put up with him. Sometimes I wondered if she thought he was the best she could manage.

'You want me,' he said. 'Admit it.'

'Dimitri, at this very minute in time, I would quite like you to move out my way.'

He laughed. 'It's okay, Tara. You don't have to play hard to get. I saw the way you looked at me across the dinner table.'

'What are you talking about?' I said, baffled.

He grinned. 'You kept staring at me.' He sucked air through his teeth. 'And you were doing that sexy thing with your eyes.'

'Eh?' I said, genuinely confused.

'That thing you do. When you narrow your eyes. It makes you look sultry.'

I choked back a laugh. 'Dimitri, do you know where you're sitting at the table?' I tried to contain my sniggers. What an idiot. 'Well, the clock is right behind your head and my watch is broken,' I said, pointing at my naked wrist. 'I was checking the clock for timings. I didn't want the turkey to be charred or the roast potatoes to be incinerated.'

He stuck out his chin. 'Relax, gorgeous,' he spoke slowly. 'You don't have to make excuses. That's why I thought I would try and catch you . . . alone.'

'I left my glasses upstairs and couldn't see the clock properly.' Where was Mark when I needed him? Normally Millie and Oliver hovered around me constantly any time I went into the kitchen in case they could help. They were obviously consumed with their toys in the other room. There was a peel of laughter from next door. Great. Mark in full entertaining mode regaling everyone with his restaurant tales. Meanwhile Dimitri, who was obviously either deaf or deluded, persevered.

'You're too adorable with your denials,' he said. 'But it's absolutely normal to want to give in to your desires.' He lowered his voice. 'Nobody need ever know.'

'Dimitri, you're talking a lot of crap. Are you trying out some dialogue for your latest novel? Or a possible plot point? Because I have to tell you, I don't think it's working.'

I turned away from him, ready to decorate the meringue. My cheeks burned. I had to figure out what to do. But I felt his breath on my neck, smelled his citrusy aftershave.

'Seriously? Dimitri, do you mind?'

'Not at all. You're totally turning me on.'

His hairy hands pawed at my shoulders and I shuddered. 'What. Don't. You. Understand?' I said, spinning round to push him away. 'Will you leave me alone? Go away.'

'Oh Tara! Just give into your desires.'

Honest to God, what a knob. I kept my voice low as I said, 'It's Christmas and I don't want to create a scene. But I'm so close to punching you.'

He smirked.

'You don't deserve to be married to my sister and the sooner she comes to her senses and sees you for what you are, the better. You're an utter twat.'

His cheeks burned red. 'Frigid cow!' he spat. 'You're as bad as your sister!'

Nice. 'Oops, will you look at that,' I said as I knocked my glass of Claret down his shirt. 'Clumsy me. Oh dear.' Overcoming the temptation to throw the meringue in his face, I pushed past him and bustled into the dining room. Mark glanced up at me, catching my annoyed glance, and watched Dimitri following behind, spluttering at the red stain which now bloomed across his shirt. It was like he'd been shot. If only. Josie and Gran were now in the next room playing with the twins. Dad seemed oblivious to what was going on and was completely enthralled by Mark's chat. He didn't notice the change in my mood.

'I need to go and change,' said Dimitri to nobody in particular, stomping off to put a fresh shirt on.

I managed to avoid him for the rest of the evening by disappearing upstairs to put the children to bed. Dad announced he would take Gran home along the road to her house. Feigning a headache and yawning, I went off to bed. Mark did come up to check on me but I whispered that I would fill him in later. He said things were tense between Dimitri and Josie and he heard them having a tense 'discussion' in their room.

Since they'd arrived to stay with us, I could tell Mark's patience was being tested. Not helped by the fact that Dimitri kept criticising Mark's cooking and offering helpful hints on how he should be doing it, while getting tanked into his wine supply.

The next morning, I was in the kitchen sliding a tray of croissants into the oven when Josie came into the kitchen white-faced and tense.

'Is everything okay?' I asked.

She struggled to make eye contact with me. 'Erm, well, no actually. We've decided we're going to leave a bit earlier than planned.'

'Oh. Earlier? What do you mean?' They'd said they planned to stay until at least the twenty-eighth.

'We're heading back to London today. Now.'

'But it's Boxing Day, Josie. I thought you were staying until the day after tomorrow.' I paused and gently touched her arm. 'Is everything okay?'

'Yes,' she said, looking everywhere but at me.

'Are you sure?'

She didn't reply.

'Speak to me, Josie. Tell me what's wrong. Why are you leaving now?'

Her eyes were swollen, and she'd obviously been crying. Honestly, that bloody man. What was wrong with him and why couldn't she see what a prick he was? 'Did he say something to you?'

She balled her hands together and looked at the floor. Millie sat at the breakfast bar pretending to eat Rice Krispies though she was dipping her hand into the huge red box of Heroes that Gran brought with her yesterday. She might only have been three but she was fairly intuitive. I could tell from her wee face that she knew something wasn't quite right with Auntie Josie. 'Millie, sweetie, will you go and check on Oliver, please? He hasn't come for his breakfast yet.'

She nodded, looking from me to Josie with wide eyes.

I tried to make my voice sound excited. 'He'll be *so* annoyed if he thinks he's missing out on Heroes for breakfast and you're eating them all. Especially the *Mars Bars*! Those are his favourites.'

She hopped off her stool and ran through to the next room, teasing her brother about the chocolates and the fact she was having them for breakfast. I only had a short window before things kicked off between them. I never would usually let them get away with eating chocolate for breakfast, but frankly this morning I didn't care. I only cared about Josie and what happened to make her want to leave my house so early.

'Tell me what's happened and why you're leaving,' I demanded. 'We hardly ever see you. You only come home once a year and now that's being cut short. Is it something *he* said?' It was wrong but I found it so hard to hide my contempt for him. Mark had warned me about that over the years. He encouraged me to try and reign in my facial expressions in the name of diplomacy and I tried and tried. But obviously completely failed. Josie bit her lip and her eyes danced between me and the door.

'It's just that . . .'

'What? What is it, Josie?'

I heard the stairs creaking, a sign he was on his way down.

'Tell me,' I hissed.

'I can't,' she said pleadingly. 'I can't, Tara. I don't want to believe it's true.'

'Believe what is true exactly?'

But it was too late. Dimitri appeared and stood in the doorway glaring at us both. The kitchen door flew open. Mark held a pile of logs in his arms. 'Oh, everyone's up? Great,' he said. 'Let me get rid of this lot—' he jerked his head down towards the wood — 'and I'll put the bacon on.'

'No thank you,' said Dimitri, pulling on his jacket. 'No need to do that on our account. We need to go.'

'Oh. Where are you off to? Are you going for a walk?' Mark said, confused.

'No, we're leaving. We're going back to London.'

'Oh,' said Mark again. 'So soon?'

I gave him a warning look — his tone was far too bright and cheery.

'But why the rush?' he said, trying to appear the good host.

'We want to beat the traffic,' said Dimitri.

'Traffic? On Boxing Day? I don't imagine there will be much traffic today,' he said, dropping the logs at his feet.

Meanwhile my sister continued to stare at the floor.

'Well, if you're sure we can't give you a tea or a coffee?' said Mark.

Neither of them spoke.

'What about Gran and Dad?' I asked, looking directly at Josie. 'Surely you're not going to leave without saying goodbye to them?'

143

Josie sniffed. 'Of course not. We'll pop in on the way and say bye.'

I shook my head and sighed. How I wished Dimitri would disappear on his own.

Mark gave me a conspiratorial look. 'Let me give you a hand, Dimitri. Let's put your bags into the car.'

Dimitri continued to hover. 'Are you coming, Josie?'

'Yes. I'm coming. I'll be right there . . .'

He waited and I stared at him, refusing to budge. Our eyes locked and I continued to stare until he looked away. Fortunately, at that point Mark caught on and ushered him through into the hall before I lost my temper.

'What about the kids?' I said to Josie. 'Are you not even going to say goodbye to them?'

'Of course I will. As if I would go without saying bye. What do you take me for?'

I left the question hanging there for a long moment then called them through from the TV room. They quickly appeared, hair ruffled and chocolate smeared on their pyjama tops.

'Auntie Josie is having to go home now.' I made no mention of Dimitri. Mind you, I don't think the kids noticed. There had never been much of a bond. He barely acknowledged them during his stay, other than to steal some of their Heroes, which didn't go down well.

Millie started to cry. 'Don't go, Aunt Josie,' she said. 'You promised me we would go to the beach.'

'Bye Aunt Hosie,' said Oliver, who buried himself in my sister's arms for about two seconds. He either needed the toilet or was high on sugar, as he hopped about from one foot to the other.

Josie kissed his head and he ran back to the television room. Ah, the TV. Whatever he was watching would be far more exciting than this. Josie walked over to Millie, who now sobbed dramatically. 'Shell hunting,' she said between gulps.

My heart broke watching my daughter so upset and Josie also started to cry, tears streaming down her cheeks.

'Sorry sweetie,' she said, her voice choked. 'I will make it up to you, I promise.'

I gently prised Millie out of her arms and wiped the tears from her face. 'How about you go and check on Oli, and I promise we'll do something really special later on.' She looked at me earnestly and nodded. With a last shudder, she hugged Josie again and went to join Oliver, her thumb firmly in her mouth.

I made sure she was out of earshot when I spoke. 'Josie . . . why do you need to leave? Please stay. The kids hardly see you. I rarely see you, and Gran and Dad were so looking forward to having you here a few more days. Gran especially.'

Hurt and confusion were etched across her face.

'Is it something we've done? Is it something *I've* done?' It finally dawned on me. How could I have been so stupid? 'He's said something to you, hasn't he?' She didn't need to answer. Guilt, betrayal, confusion and accusation. 'Josie. What. Did. He. Say?' I prayed that Mark kept him distracted and out of the way while I tried to get to the bottom of what had happened. But in the pit of my stomach, I knew. 'Josie,' I said, my voice growing urgent. 'What happened? What did he say?'

She started to speak and reached into her pocket for a tissue. Wiping her nose, she bit her lip and started to speak. 'He said you made a move on him . . .' Her voice trailed away.

Rage surged through me. 'And you *believed* him?'

Josie didn't answer.

'Josie. Seriously. You're going to believe that pompous prick over your own sister? You honestly think I would make a pass at him? My own sister's husband?'

Josie's tears now streamed down her cheeks, and she kept trying to desperately wipe them away. 'I don't know, Tara. I hoped you would never do that. But he insisted that you did . . . He's my husband. He said it's not the first time and he's uncomfortable being here. And . . . he's all I have.'

I took a step back from her in utter disbelief. 'For the record, Josie, I would never do such a thing to you. You're my sister, for God's sake. Even if your husband looked like Brad

Pitt — which he clearly doesn't — he's the last man on earth that I would ever think attractive.' Oops, maybe a step too far, but I was beyond caring. 'Your husband is a pretentious prick.'

Mark appeared and cleared his throat. 'Um, Dimitri's in the car. He says to come when you're ready.'

'He can't be bothered to say goodbye to his niece and nephew? Or me? He thinks he can just slope off after making wild accusations? Well . . . I'll make sure I say goodbye to him. He's not getting away with this.'

Mark hated scenes and his eyes darted between me and Josie. 'Let's calm down, shall we?' He flicked his head toward the room next door. 'Tara,' he said, warning in his voice, 'remember the kids. They're next door.'

I stormed past him, Josie close behind me, and pulled open the front door. Their car exhaust pumped curls of fumes into the air, which was so typical of Dimitri to sit there idling and not give a toss about the environment. I grabbed the driver's door and yanked it open, glaring at the smug face of my brother-in-law. 'You're a complete and utter shit, do you know that? My sister is far too good for you and one day I hope she realises what a complete fucker you are.' I felt Mark beside me, confused as to the amount of venom in my voice. Wait until I told him what happened. Then he would understand my fury.

'Well . . . I think that says it all, doesn't it, Josie?' he said as my sister got in the passenger seat.

'Josie, you don't have to go,' I said, pleadingly. 'You don't have to go with him. You can stay here. With us.'

'He's my husband, Tara.'

'He's a wanker . . . Josie, you're my sister and I love you and you will always be welcome here. Anytime. Please . . . remember that.'

But she wouldn't meet my eye, focusing her gaze straight ahead.

'Goodbye, Tara,' said Dimitri as he pulled the handle and slammed the door shut. The car roared off and I stood watching.

Mark came to stand beside me and snaked his arm around my shoulder and I burst into tears.

That was the last time I had seen my sister and the last time we had spoken.

As we finished the wine, I gave her a condensed version of events. There was no need for her to know what a sleaze he was towards me or any of the details. She was going through enough and I suspected that there was more to come.

CHAPTER THIRTY-NINE

Josie

I woke up shivering and wondering where I was. For a gentle, suspended moment, my life was okay. Pulling the covers over me, I fell asleep again for a while and woke to the trill of the birdsong outside. Lying there listening was wonderfully relaxing. I was so comfortable and warm and couldn't quite believe I was here in the tidy spare room of my sister's house. Of my old house. This room used to be my old bedroom all those years ago. Although now the floorboards were painted a pale shade of grey, the walls a bright white, and the windows had white shutters which blocked out the morning light. I hopped out of bed and tilted them open, allowing some of the morning sunlight to creep in. A moss-green rug lay on the floor and the bedspread was embroidered with green flowers. The room was still and quiet and so very peaceful. I tucked myself back under the covers and lay for a few minutes looking up at the ceiling and remembering the room when I was a child. Back then, it had pink dotty wallpaper which matched the rose-coloured carpet. The curtains were cerise pink, and I loved my jazzy duvet covered with hearts and clowns. How strange to think I lay here twenty years ago. How I wished I could rewind the clock and do things differently.

The reality and the dread started to creep through me again as I replayed yesterday and remembered what happened. Automatically, I reached for my phone to check the time. It was coming up for nine o'clock. I never normally slept in this late. I sat upright. Rubbing my temples, I recalled the late night with Tara and the wine and the apologies and the explanations. Glancing back at the phone, I scrolled through my emails and WhatsApp in case I had any messages. Yesterday, on the journey up, I turned off all my notifications. I was glad that I had. He had bombarded me with messages telling me he missed me and how I was being overly dramatic. I switched off my phone and shoved it under my pillow.

Getting up, I pulled on the dressing gown which Tara had left at the bottom of the bed and tightened the cord around my waist. I padded downstairs.

'Good morning,' I said to Tara and Mark, who both sat at the kitchen table.

'Hi, Josie,' said Mark, standing up and hugging me. 'Great to see you.'

My eyes glistened when I heard his kind voice. 'Thanks. And I'm sorry. I'm sorry I was so awful that Christmas. That he was so awful.' I sighed. 'What an almighty mess.'

He batted his hand through the air. 'Ssh. There's nothing to be sorry for. The main thing is you're here and you can stay as long as you want.'

'Tea?' offered Tara, pointing at the kettle.

'Please,' I said, helping myself.

'Ladies, I'm afraid I'll need to love you and leave you,' he said. 'I need to be in early to sort through the orders.'

'Of course.' I watch him kiss my sister on the head and give him a small wave. She's so lucky. But honestly, I'm not jealous, only happy she has a brilliant man in her life.

'I know how lucky I am,' she said, reading my mind. 'But he's lucky too,' she added, smiling. 'And he's not perfect. He hasn't yet figured out how to load the washing machine.'

'But he can cook. And he's kind. And a great dad.'

Tara nodded. 'Okay, I get your point.' She took a sip of tea. 'What do you want to do today? Are you ready to face Dad? Or to visit Gran?'

'Gran definitely. I feel bad I haven't seen her yet. I did intend to go there first of all last night . . .'

'I know, but I'm glad you came here first, Josie, and so will she be. In fact, I can guarantee it will be the first question she asks you. *Have you seen your sister?* She asks me all the time if we've been in touch.'

I cast my eyes downward, feeling guilty again.

'Don't worry, Josie. Honestly,' she said. 'None of this mess is your fault.'

My little sister, who suddenly appeared to be so much wiser and more mature than me.

She glanced at the clock on the oven. 'I said to Dad I would pick the kids up around ten. Do you want to come with me?'

'I should go to Gran first,' I said. 'And then Dad. I'll come back and see the kids, if that's okay?'

'Of course. Whatever works.'

I walked around the kitchen looking at the pictures on the windowsill. 'I love your work on the house, Tara. It felt strange sleeping in my old room. But also . . . I can't quite explain . . . comforting.'

'I'm glad. It's a lovely room. I loved that room when we were kids. I wished it was mine.'

'Oh?' I said in surprise. 'I loved your room!'

She laughed. 'And I hope you're okay with Mark and me living here now. I did want to tell you when it came on the market. But you didn't answer my calls, so . . .'

Pursing my lips, I told her Gran kept me informed and I didn't have a strong opinion either way. 'I mean, I was quite intrigued to know what you planned to do and what it looked like.'

'I must show you the photos from when we got the keys.'

Tara and I lived in the house for a few more years after Mum left. We moved in with Gran when I was fifteen and she was thirteen. That was supposed to be a temporary plan until Dad found us somewhere else to live. But it never happened, and we were quite settled at Gran's terraced house overlooking the sea. When we lived in this cottage, it belonged to the church, then Dad decided he couldn't stay on any longer without Mum. He knew the church wanted to try to raise some money by selling their properties. The manse had become too big for him to manage on his own and too costly, so selling it was the sensible option. Tara and I were heartbroken when we left because it was our last connection with Mum. We hoped she would come back while we lived there and worried we would miss her if she did return. But Dad always insisted she would find us wherever we lived.

The people who bought it faithfully forwarded on mail over the years which hadn't been redirected to Gran's house. Mind you, the local postie was great too. Everyone had a connection in this town. They knew we lived with Gran, and if anything did go astray it would always eventually make its way through Gran's letterbox. Which was just as well because every year after Mum left, she would always send us a card on our birthdays.

CHAPTER FORTY

Tara

My romantic morning with Mark didn't quite go to plan. For a start, I had a bit of a headache thanks to the wine we consumed last night. I was also desperate to give him a rundown of what happened with Josie. We were both in bed by the time he got back late from work. Other than a brief text to let him know she was here, he had no idea about what had happened.

'This wasn't quite the lie-in I was expecting,' he said, kissing me on my shoulder after listening to me talk. 'What an utter dick.'

'I still can't believe that she had to find out that way though. I mean really — in their bed?'

Mark squirmed. 'I can't even begin to imagine why he thought that was a good idea. But then he's not exactly the sharpest tool in the box, is he? Unless he wanted her to find out?'

'Maybe the idea of getting caught gave him a buzz?'

'Perhaps . . .'

Either way, it was a scene I did not wish to picture.

'How is she?'

'Better than I thought she would be. I mean, the fact she drove straight here is a promising sign. And she seems adamant that she's not going back . . . although she'll need to at some stage to get her stuff.'

'Do you think she'll stay in London for her job?'

I pulled my hands through my hair and tried to sit up, propping up the pillows. 'I really don't know what she'll do. It's early days.' I gently moved Mark's hand away from my waist where it tended to pause before moving upwards. I didn't want to push him away, but I had other things on my mind, not to mention my sister sleeping in the spare room next door.

'How was work?' I swung my legs round out of bed, stood up and stretched.

'Busy,' he said, yawning. 'And we got a brilliant review on that new website. If we can keep up the momentum it should be a fab summer, especially with the festival.'

'That's great, love. That starts the week after next?'

'Yes.'

'And what about the extra help? Is Jaz due back soon?' Yesterday's events suddenly made me aware of our own situation. What if I needed him to take over and be me? Would Jaz be there to help?

'Yeah. He's due back any day and that will make a huge difference. Especially with him knowing lots of people here too.'

Jaz was his business partner and he'd been on an extended 'research' trip to Australia, where he'd lived for several years. I think he actually just fancied a long holiday. The idea of him being back and at work suddenly seemed pressing.

'I guess I'm not getting that extra morning cuddle,' he said, smiling.

I shook my head. 'No. I've got to collect the kids from Dad at about ten. Plus I'm sure you'll want to see Josie?'

'True. I'll jump in the shower.'

He grabbed a fresh towel from the closet and, kissing me on the lips as he passed, disappeared across the hall to the bathroom.

153

I pulled on some jeans, threw on a sweatshirt and made my way to the kitchen. I just hoped that Josie slept well and her resolve hadn't broken. The very worst thing she could do would be to come downstairs and say she was going back home.

While I waited for the kettle to boil, I stared down to the bottom of the garden. It would make such a difference to have things all cleared up down there. I thought again about how perfect it would be once the summer house had been put up. The views were such a bonus and would be quite a unique selling point for my business. I returned briefly to work when the twins were babies and my maternity leave finished. However, with the cost of travel, the nursery and the fact that Mark worked such erratic and long hours, it all got too stressful and wasn't cost-effective. Gran and Dad did offer to help but I knew it wasn't fair to rely on them all of the time.

I managed to retrain as a massage therapist and worked on an ad hoc basis when I could by renting out a treatment room in the town. My ambition was to be able to open up my own business so I could share the views with people who needed some calm and relaxation in their life. But I needed to keep reminding myself to take one step at a time.

I pulled on my sandals and walked through the garden inhaling the air. How I loved this garden and the memories it held. All the parties Josie and I enjoyed at the bottom of the garden, lunches under the picnic tree on the rug, Mum dozing in the sunshine in the hammock she loved. I looked at the flourishing apple tree. It provided us with an abundance of fruit every year. Mum would whip up crumbles and chutneys and tarts. I closed my eyes and for a moment was six years old again. I could see Mum lying there, her foot dangling from her hammock, Josie talking animatedly to her dolly as she pushed her around the garden in the buggy. And Dad coming in from his parish duties and bringing out a tray with a jug of lemonade. Bending down, his knees cracked, and he gently prodded Mum and she smiled. She sat up, shielding her eyes from the sun, and then a glimpse of something, I'm not quite sure what, passed between them.

I opened my eyes and blinked. Focusing on happy memories and times should be something I did more often. Although I do sometimes wonder how different life would have been if Mum hadn't gone away. I might have pursued a different career to nursing or married someone who wasn't Mark. Those were things I would never know the answer to.

CHAPTER FORTY-ONE

Josie

Gran lived in Forth Street, a few minutes' drive from Tara's house. It was right on the beachfront with direct access to the west beach, which we spent hours on as kids. I think we assumed everyone's gran had a house like ours did. There was even a special hidden room in her attic. Her bedroom had a magic door which appeared to be a cupboard. But that opened onto a staircase which led up into the attic and a big room with a sofa and beanbags. I loved taking myself up there for some peace and quiet when I wanted to be alone.

Her stone-built terraced house had a long back garden which we played badminton in during the summer — actually, any time we could if the weather was fine. The steps at the bottom of the garden led down to the beach and had brilliant views of the harbour and Craigleith Island in the Firth of Forth.

Normally, under usual circumstances, I would walk in through the front door, which was always unlocked, and call out, 'Gran?' She always echoed back, 'Hello!' But today I hesitated. Walking in didn't seem appropriate when such a long time had passed since I last visited. Instead I rang the bell, hearing it chime, and waited. She didn't take long to answer, opening the door with her usual wide smile, which turned into a gasp when she realised it was me.

'Oh, Josie!' She put her arms out and I hugged her, smelling the familiar and comforting scent of her face cream. 'Josie, my darling girl. How lovely to see you.'

I stood back and looked at her. True to form, she looked as wonderful as always, although older, unsurprisingly, as she had celebrated two birthdays since my last visit. She had her apron over her turquoise A-line skirt and cream blouse which was covered in tiny daisies.

'What are you doing here? I mean, it's so lovely. I'm delighted you're here.'

She surreptitiously threw a look over my shoulder scanning the street behind.

'I'm on my own, Gran.'

'Oh,' she said, not looking in the least bit disappointed. 'But where is Dimitri? How did you get here?'

'It's a long story, Gran.'

She ushered me across the threshold into the hallway. 'Come on, dear. Nothing a simple cup of tea won't fix. Let's get the kettle on and you can tell me. Oh, my daring, I can't tell you how wonderful it is to see you!'

Oh, Gran. Wiping the tears away from my eyes, I followed her through the hall and into the kitchen, where I immediately let the tears flow. How I had missed this. All of this: family, security, warmth, and most of all a sense of belonging. The scent of scones baking and laundry powder stirred feelings of nostalgia at the pit of my stomach and I had to give her another cuddle to make sure I was actually here. I walked around the kitchen, looking out at her lawn and to the sea beyond. 'Gran, look at your garden and how lovely it is. And that view is stunning.'

'Well, I have to admit the beautiful lawn has nothing to do with me,' she said. 'You know what your dad is like about his gardening.'

I laughed. 'Yes. He always did prefer talking to the plants and flowers than to the rest of us.'

157

Then I glanced over at the spot where her noticeboard usually hung; it had been replaced with a blackboard.

She chuckled. 'Isn't it super? My to-do list from Ikea! Look at my chalk — I can write down what I need from the shops or things I need to remember. Then wipe the list away. Just like that. It's much more environmentally friendly than all those bits of paper that used to gather on the noticeboard.'

I couldn't help smiling when I noticed her reminder to herself, chalked on the board, to book herself into the next block of Pilates at the complementary therapy centre in the town. I gulped back another sob.

'Oh dear. What's the matter?' She reached up to give me a pat on the shoulder. 'You sit yourself down and I'll put the kettle on.'

Rooting for a tissue in my handbag, I wiped away the tears and noisily blew my nose. 'I've missed you so much, Gran.'

'My dear, you're in luck this morning because I've got a batch of scones in the oven.'

I couldn't help but laugh. 'Gran, you must have known I was coming.'

She waved her hand in the air. 'Och, you know me, dear. I've always been a bit fey.' She chuckled. 'I do like to potter and have something in the tin. You never know who might turn up.' Reaching into the cupboard she pulled out a tin of herbal teabags. 'I have this fancy stuff instead of good old Tetley's? Your sister likes it, though I've no idea why. Smells like cat pee. Mark agrees with me too. He always pulls a face when he sees it.'

'Thanks, Gran, but I'm with you and Mark on that. A cup of coffee would be fine.'

'Perfect,' she said. 'That's what I feel like too and I can use my fancy new gadget.' She pointed at the Nespresso machine on her work top. 'None of the instant stuff for me. Can you believe some of my bridge friends still have a jar?'

I laughed. 'That's like the one we've got back in London.'

'Your sister got it for me at Christmas. Makes rather nice coffee.' Rummaging in another box, she glanced up at me.

'Do you want a strong one or flavoured?' She pointed at her box of capsules. 'Vanilla, caramel or cardamom?'

'A vanilla coffee would be lovely. Let me help you.'

'You sit there, my love. I can manage quite fine, thanks.'

It was wonderful to see that she hadn't lost any of her independence. She always had been so proud about managing things herself and didn't like to ask for help. Though she would sometimes make a list up and wait for Mark to pop in. With the exception of painting, he was quite efficient with DIY, whereas Dad was not.

Gran busied herself with the coffee pods, and while it spurted into our mugs, she passed me over some plates and napkins.

'Dare I ask whether you have seen Tara yet?' she said, passing me a cup of coffee and laying down the plate of fruit scones in front of me. 'There's some butter.' She pointed at the dish.

'Yes. I drove up last night. That's where I stayed.'

Gran sat watching me, her fingers playing with the silver choker around her neck. 'Oh, I'm so glad to hear that. I was so worried about the two of you not talking.'

'And it's all my fault. I apologised to her and hope we can move on.' I fiddled with the scones, pulling out the raisins and making a pile on my plate. I always saved them to eat at the end.

'And how long will you be staying, dear? And what about your dad? Does he know that you're back?'

'No. I'll go later,' I said. 'I'm not sure how long I'll stay, Gran . . . If I'm honest, I'm not quite sure what to do anymore. I'm not sure where I belong . . .' My voice trailed away. That was when I gave her the brief, edited version, of what had happened with Dimitri. Maybe I was trying to spare Gran's blushes — or mine perhaps? I mean, telling her that he was playing away with a neighbour in our bed, well, it was all so humiliating.

Gran nodded and listened, saying very little. 'What about your job, dear?'

159

Admittedly, that threw me. I wasn't expecting her first comment to be a question about my employment status. 'I'll try and take some extended leave in the first instance. Then work something out. I don't know yet, Gran. I'm so tired. I'd like to lie down in a dark room for a week.'

'And what about Dimitri?' she asked kindly. 'Do you want to sort things out with him?'

That was a question I couldn't yet answer, although deep down the answer was there. I wasn't ready to admit it. A loud rap at the door startled us. Then an insistent thwack.

'Are you expecting someone?' I asked as the letterbox started to rattle.

'No, unless it's the postman. That new one is quite impatient.'

'I'll go,' I said, jumping off my seat and heading to the door. Pulling it open, the postman was about to shove a card through the letterbox. 'Parcel for you,' he said. 'Thought you weren't in.' He thrust the box at me.

'Well, give us a chance to get to the door. We're not all Usain Bolt,' I replied, throwing him a glare. The comment went over his head and he stalked off whistling.

I started to close the door when a hand pushed against it.

'What the . . .' My voice trailed away when I realised who it was.

CHAPTER FORTY-TWO

Tara

I was relieved when Josie left for a bit to go to Gran's. Mark collected the kids from Dad's, although he was under strict orders not to say anything to him or them about Josie being back.

'How am I supposed to do that?' said Mark.

'It's quite easy. Don't say anything. Talk about the kids and what they had for dinner last night. It's not like my dad's into chit-chat anyway.' I knew Josie would go after she had been with Gran. I was leaving her to that and not getting involved. I had enough dealings with him and Gran. It was now up to her to do her family bit.

Mark and the kids all arrived back while I was in the shower. Brushing my hair, I looked across the landing and saw Millie coming out of her bedroom.

'Hello, poppet,' I called. 'Did you empty your bag?'

'Hi, Mum. Yes, I did.' She ran towards me and threw her arms around my waist.

Bending down to hug her, I buried my nose in her dark blonde hair and sniffed.

'Mummy!' she squealed. 'Stop!'

Taking another quick sniff, I let her go and stepped back. Tears sprang to my eyes and I smiled at her. 'I can't help it though. Your head has the best smell ever! I want to bottle it.'

'Urgh. That's weird.'

I stuck my tongue out and she giggled.

'We ate loads of pancakes for breakfast.'

'Wow, sounds amazing. Grandpa made you pancakes?'

'No,' she said earnestly. 'The lady at Tesco made them. He bought them from her.'

'Ah. And what did you put on them?'

'Honey. Oli had Nutella. Like, half the jar.' She gave me a disapproving look. 'I told him you wouldn't be happy. But he ignored me.'

I laughed. 'Where is he?'

She shrugged. 'Dunno.'

'Go and check that he's emptied his bag too for me, please, will you?'

She huffed and sulkily dragged herself over to the doorway of Oliver's bedroom.

'You're not allowed!' she shouted. 'M-U-U-M, Oliver's on the iPad again.'

'Oliver, poppet. You're not meant to be on that. Anyway, didn't you want to come and say hello? Did you miss me?'

He scowled. 'You were in the shower.' He was huddled under his Hearts FC duvet cover.

Millie stood like a mini policewoman, arms crossed, looking particularly pleased to witness her brother getting told off.

'Millie,' I said. 'Please will you go downstairs and check Daddy is okay? I bet he'd love one of your special cups of tea. Then maybe later we could do some baking?'

'But Mum . . .' She was so indignant.

'Off you go. *Please, Millie.*'

She tossed her ponytail, gave me her best frown and stomped off down the stairs.

I turned back to look at my son. 'Oliver. You know the deal with this.'

He stared ahead.

'Give it to me, please. Come on . . . otherwise we might have to rethink going to the pool later.'

That did the trick. 'Sorry, Mummy,' he said, pulling it out from under the covers.

I sat down on the bed next to him and curled my arm around his shoulders. 'It's okay, sweetie, but rules are there for a reason.'

He lowered his eyes, blinking his long lashes.

'Where did you find it?'

'Daddy left it lying about.'

'Okay, I'll put it away now,' I said, making a mental note to tell Mark to be more careful about where he left things. I was completely paranoid about social media and the kids somehow getting online and being groomed by an online predator. I know they were only four but nothing surprised me anymore. Sighing, I gave him another tight hug. He didn't ever mind me burying my nose in his hair, so I took full advantage. I could smell blueberry shampoo and pancakes and maple syrup. 'Is that maple syrup I detect?'

'Uh-huh,' he said.

'Millie said you had chocolate spread.'

He shook his head. 'No, I didn't. It was all finished. Grandpa said he needs to buy more from the shops.'

Honestly, my daughter would do anything to land her brother into trouble. I sniffed his head again. 'Do you think you'll still let me do this when you're all grown up?'

He wriggled beside me. 'Mmm, yes, probably.'

'Okay that's a deal.'

'I'm hungry,' he said.

That did not surprise me. Oliver was always hungry. 'Okay, how about we go downstairs and have a rummage?'

His eyes lit up and he jumped off the bed.

'I'll be with you in a minute. I need to nip to the loo. You go and start looking.'

He ran off, calling triumphantly to his sister that it was snack time and he was allowed to have whatever he wanted.

163

I'd missed them though they'd only been away a night. The house was strange without them albeit I hadn't dwelled on it last night with Josie's unexpected arrival.

Since I'd become a mum, being apart from them was something I thought about a lot. How could my own mum leave us without saying goodbye? The thought of time away from my two made me want to vomit. I couldn't get my head around the fact my mother walked out, and it was something I thought about most days. I managed to contain the thoughts inside my head but they stirred up such a range of complicated feelings. Until recently they made me feel numb and almost apathetic towards her. I couldn't fathom how she could have left in such a hurry.

When I gave birth to the twins, I developed postnatal depression and the counsellor wondered if this had perhaps been triggered due to the circumstances of my mum's disappearance.

For days and weeks after Mum left, the town's gossips were in their element. She was having an affair; Dad was having an affair; she couldn't cope with us kids; she had a nervous breakdown; she'd gone to join a Tibetan commune; she was living elsewhere as a man. Everyone had an opinion on the matter, and although Dad and Gran did their best to shield us from it, the rumours continued to circulate and seep into my thoughts over the years. I clocked people throwing me sympathetic glances, heard the odd tut, the shakes of the head. comments were made in shops, in the doctor's waiting room and in cafés, where hands were clasped across mouths belatedly when they realised I was there. The daughter of the woman who left. Sometimes I wondered how Dad managed to stay on in the town with all the constant speculation. Didn't Mum think about the effect it would have on all of us over the years?

Each birthday the twins celebrated, I felt more and more baffled and the empathy I had towards her evaporated. Now the numbness was spiked with bouts of anger and intense dislike.

CHAPTER FORTY-THREE

Josie

Dad cleared his throat. 'Josie. Well . . . this is an unexpected . . . surprise.'

'Surprises tend to be unexpected, don't they?' I said, moving back to let him into the hallway.

'I was calling in to say hello to your gran. She normally gives me a list on a Saturday morning. I wasn't expecting to see you here . . .' He stopped and gave me a probing look. 'Have you seen Tara?'

'Yes!' I snapped, immediately feeling guilty when I saw Dad's face. I wasn't quite sure if he was embarrassed or angry. It was hard to tell with Dad, he was a man of few words. But he had a way of pressing my buttons so that I reverted to adolescence.

As he bustled past me towards Gran, I stood for a minute annoyed at what I had hurriedly perceived as his accusatory tone. His question was innocent and fair. So why did I immediately go on the defensive? Perhaps because he hadn't even bothered to say, 'Hello, how are you?' Or give me a hug? I followed him into the kitchen, where he took a seat at the table while Gran jumped up and fussed around him as she always did.

As an only child, Dad never had to compete for affection with siblings. Unlike me. God, what was *wrong* with me? I felt like a hormonal fourteen-year-old, not the grown woman I was supposed to be.

'Isn't this a wonderful surprise?' said Gran. 'Sit down, son, and I'll get you some tea.'

Dad looked over at me. 'What brings you back here then?'

I sat down at the table, tracing a pattern with my middle finger. Clearing my throat, I took a sip from my coffee cup and placed it back down with a clatter. I didn't really want to go through all of this again. 'The thing is . . .'

'She wanted to come back up and sort things out with her sister,' interrupted Gran as she plonked a mug of tea in front of him. 'It's been bothering you, love, isn't that right?'

Good old Gran to the rescue. 'Yes . . .' I started to say.

'She jumped in the car and drove up last night. You never did say what the roads were like, dear.'

Dad reached for a scone, which Gran had already sliced for him and smeared with butter. 'You've got to watch the A1, haven't you? Especially at certain times of the day. It's always on the traffic reports. And that M6. I mean, it sounds horrendous. Beats me why anyone would want to travel on it, ever.' He bit into the scone. 'This is good, Mum. Much better than the ones you get in the fancy new deli in the high street. They're doing a scone of the day, and do you know what they had yesterday? Earl Grey tea with dates. I mean, sounds disgusting.'

Gran scowled. 'Some recipes should not be tampered with. A scone should be a scone. Either plain, fruit or cheese.

'Here, take another, Josie dear. You look like you could do with some feeding.'

I sat there completely baffled as the conversation about scone recipes went on around me. Should the mixture include an egg or not? wondered Dad. He thought he would teach the twins how to make them and so wanted Gran's recipe.

'It's not so much a recipe rather than a bit of this and that. A cupful of flour, a dod of butter, some sugar and milk.'

I couldn't even begin to imagine Dad baking and how that would all go. He had never in my memory taught me or my sister to bake or cook a thing. He left things like that to Mum, and then, when she left, Gran. As a matter of fact, I was completely baffled as I sat there listening to them. Gran did catch my eye a couple of times and give me a wink, but this was so like my family. It didn't matter my world was collapsing around me, or anyone else's for that matter. Talking about mundane stuff like scone recipes and traffic reports was far easier. In a matter of minutes, they would start talking about bridge. I'd put money on it.

'How long are you staying for?' said Dad.

'This morning? With Gran?'

'No, I mean are you here for the weekend?' He reached for another scone. My dad always had a slim and wiry frame yet a huge appetite, and I often wondered where he put it all.

'I'm not sure . . . I left yesterday and came up without any plans.'

'But what about work? Surely you need to tell them what you're doing?'

I nodded. 'Yes, I've taken a couple of weeks' leave. I thought it would be nice to see you all.'

'What about Dimitri?' he said, his voice tense. 'Where is he?'

'He's not with me.' I placed my hands on the table in front of me. 'The thing is . . . well, the thing is . . .' I couldn't believe I was actually nervous about telling him. Once again, I had to remind myself none of this was my fault. 'The thing is, I've left him. I've left Dimitri. Our marriage is over.'

Dad choked on his tea. 'Left him? *Left him?* What do you mean? You can't do that!'

I pushed the chair out, stood up and walked towards the window, noticing Gran as she put a warning hand on his arm. I knew too well what Dad's views on marriage were. As a church minister, he regularly held forth on the importance of the institution of marriage and how wrong divorce was. Tara and I heard it all the time when we were growing up.

I still couldn't believe she had managed to get away with not actually getting married to Mark. I mean, in Dad's eyes, she'd had her children out of wedlock. Although that didn't seem to matter quite so much to him as the mention of the 'd' word.

It didn't matter there was a whole litany of well-documented cases of church colleagues who had indulged in sleazy extramarital affairs. Dad still thought marriage was something you worked out regardless of what went on.

'These things happen,' said Gran. 'Modern life — things are different now.'

'Is it because you couldn't have children? I mean, plenty of couples don't have children. Motherhood is not the be all and end all . . . especially when women are focusing on their careers.'

'Dad,' I said, trying my utmost to remain calm. I leaned back against the sink and crossed my arms. 'No, it's not because I can't have children, or I'm focusing on my career rather than my husband. Neither of these things.'

'What is it then? You're not . . . Oh my God, Josie.' He clasped his hand over his mouth for a moment. 'Are you gay?'

Gran let out a roar of laughter and I couldn't help start sniggering too. I honestly couldn't believe how this was all unfolding. I don't think Dad had ever spoken so much or expressed so many opinions in one sitting before. I clutched my sides, chuckling the more Gran giggled.

Dad sat back in his chair and folded his arms. 'Well,' he said tensely, 'you never know what to expect these days.'

'Oh, Dad. Would it have mattered if I'd been gay?' I didn't let him answer as I did not want to know. 'No. None of those things. I've left Dimitri because he's an adulterer . . . For all I know, he's been at it with half my street at home and he also made a pass at Tara last Christmas. So there you go. That's why I haven't been back and why we fell out.'

Gran's eyes were wide and I could tell she was shocked by this. This must all have been new information to her, which meant Tara couldn't have said a thing. Normally she was quite open-minded, but for once she was rendered speechless. Meanwhile, Dad's face paled and he tried to speak but no words would come out.

'More tea anyone?' I said calmly.

Gran exhaled a lengthy breath. 'Well, I never. I hope he doesn't show his oily wee face in these parts.'

Dad stood and walked over to me. 'I'm sorry, Josie. I had no idea.' He awkwardly patted my shoulder.

'If he does,' continued Gran, 'I'll chop his balls off.'

My eyes widened and Dad looked horrified as we watched Gran doing a slicing motion with her hands. 'Dirty wee bugger.'

CHAPTER FORTY-FOUR

Tara

When Josie came back from Gran's house, she filled me in on what had happened. 'I don't think I've heard Gran swear before,' I said, smirking. 'I wish I'd seen that.'

'It was very amusing,' said Josie. 'In fact, seeing Dad's reaction was the best thing. I mean, he was horrified. Utterly aghast, especially when she started doing the slicing action with her hands. Honestly, she's some woman, our gran. You wouldn't mess with her, would you?'

I laughed and shook my head. 'I guess she's been through a lot and doesn't care. I hope I'm like her at that age,' I said, feeling my voice catch in my throat. Should I tell her? Surely confiding in her could only help? I sat for a moment, turning my head to look outside. Neither of us spoke.

'Remind me again how you got away with not marrying Mark?' she said, breaking the silence.

I sat down on the sofa, curling up a leg underneath me. 'It wasn't a priority for either of us,' I said. 'I mean, things are different now, aren't they? Though you're right. I presented it to Dad as a fait accompli. Maybe he thought if he challenged us we would move away.' I noticed Josie flinch and chided myself as I didn't mean that to sound like an implication that's what she had done. I kept talking in a bid to distract her. 'Mark is Catholic and Gran did remind me that in her day that was taboo.'

'Crazy to think that used to be an issue, isn't it?'

'I know, and that it was such a massive issue for her and grandad. Her family fell out with her when they got married. Her parents refused to come to the wedding. Seems strange to us now.'

'Yes,' I said, nodding. 'I've tried to ask her but she said it was all in the past and better left alone.'

'It was quite common if you were brought up on the west coast,' she reminded me. 'There was a huge divide between Protestants and Catholics. So in a way we must take our hat off to her even more for standing her ground and following her heart.'

'I wish we'd met him.' Both Josie and I had tried to ask more questions over the years and it was the only time she had got cross with us so we stopped.

Josie opened up her laptop and started typing. 'I'd better send an email to work,' she said, briefly glancing up. 'Let them know what's happening. Well, at least a version . . .'

'Has he been in touch?'

'Yes. He's been trying to call and text. I mean, I'll have to talk to him eventually. But I can't face him now. I will . . . soon.'

Oliver ran into the living room and jumped onto the sofa, burrowing in beside me and sucking his thumb. I gently pulled it out, knowing he must be tired.

'Right,' said Josie, closing her laptop. 'That's that. I've requested some leave, which shouldn't be a problem as I have time owed. The campus is quieter anyway as it's summer.'

'Does that mean you're staying here with us, Aunt Josie?' asked Oliver.

'For a wee while. If that's okay with you?'

He gave her a thumbs-up.

'What about if you and Mark go out and grab some dinner tonight and I can babysit?' she suggested.

It was a lovely gesture, but I longed to put my pyjamas on and go to bed. Sleep was the only thing I wanted right now. But I didn't want to appear ungrateful. 'Thanks. That's sweet of you. I'll message Mark and find out if and when he plans to be back.'

'It must be tricky trying to find some time together. What with the restaurant and . . .' I smiled, nodding my head towards Oliver.

'Yes, I suppose so. But I guess we always knew things would be tricky to begin with. Starting any new business is, I suppose. But hopefully it will all be worthwhile. And when Jaz is back on board, things should balance themselves out a bit.' My phone buzzed.

That sounds a lovely idea if she's sure. How about that new place in Dunbar? I should be back about six.

'Mark says yes. He should be home about six.'

'Perfect. There you go. Now, how about you go and get yourself organised?'

'But the kids and their tea . . .' I said.

She flicked her fingers in the air. 'Leave that to me.'

I smiled. 'Thank you, Josie. I think it's going to be quite good having you here for a while. I might start to take advantage of you.'

'Go right ahead,' she said, smiling. 'Right, Oliver. What do you want to have for tea? You can have anything you want.'

'Anything?'

'Absolutely anything.'

I covered my ears with my hands. 'I'm keeping well out of this,' I said.

Josie's phone buzzed. I thought I could detect a glimmer of a smile on her lips as I watched her read the message.

Raising an eyebrow, I asked who it was from.

She shrugged and looked away. But there was definitely more to it. She was keeping something else from me.

CHAPTER FORTY-FIVE

Josie

My favourite place in the world has always been sitting alone on the beach. The town had two sandy beaches and the people who lived on the east side thought their beach better than the west and vice-versa. I loved them both but the one I always headed to when I needed time to think was the East Bay. It's where my sister and I came to play as kids when we got fed up with the beach outside Gran's house. The sound of the waves rolling in and out had always been a comfort. I loved the way the Bass Rock changed colour throughout the year. In the spring and summer months it was white when covered in gannets, then in winter it changed to brown when the birds flew away to warmer climates. I always thought they had the right idea. If only life was as simple. I briefly wondered where I would fly to. Tenerife or Lanzarote? Or would I go further afield to Australia?

But honestly, sitting with my warm coat on — I always forgot the contrast of the coastal temperature to London's summer heat — and my hands clasped around a takeaway latte, there was nowhere I would rather be. Especially as it was early and I had the place to myself, apart from the odd person walking a Labrador or a Cockapoo.

Finding a quiet spot was always tricky during the summer months when the town was packed with holidaymakers. Getting up early was the only way to make sure I had the beach to myself during the peak season. I would often come down here as a teenager to mull over my problems. Should I leave home and go away to university? Was my summer fling really just that? Because it felt like true love. Would Mum ever come back? And why did I feel like such a square peg in a round hole?

As kids, Tara and I would spend hours building sand-castles with moats and pebbled driveways. We would take our buckets and gather shells, using them to decorate our castles. We would fill the buckets with water from the sea to fill up the moats, which took ages. Then we would ask Gran to decide whose was better and grander. Being a diplomat, she'd always announce a tie and declare the winners would be treated to an ice cream with a chocolate flake. We played in the rock pools, using our nets to catch small crabs, which we would examine in fascination before throwing back in the water. We loved swimming in the tide-filled paddling pool. It wasn't the warmest of playgrounds, but we didn't mind. We loved being outside and digging our toes in the sand. In fact, a lot of my happy childhood memories featured the sun and warm summers — that is, until . . . well, until Mum left. Then the memories are all tinged with a grey veil, which never lifted completely.

Later, as teenagers, we learned to surf on one of the beaches further round the coast at Dunbar. That was something I kept meaning to go back and try again, and maybe I would. Surfing would probably be the perfect therapy right now. Being in the water and focusing on balancing on the board always took my mind off things.

After Mum left, Gran took Tara and I to the beach. Dad became withdrawn and focused on his work. I think we reminded him too much of what he had lost. The beach was our happy place and has remained so. Especially when I used to visit from London. I couldn't wait to smell the salty air and be back in my comforting spot, perched on the wall and watching and thinking. Dimitri used to always complain about the cold and never wanted to join me, which I was glad about. Though somehow I wished he did share and understand my love of the outdoors. But he was dismissive and always said the best beaches were warm ones you relaxed on. Now I could come to the beach as much as I wanted to without his nagging comments ringing in my ears, one of the many bonuses about being back.

I sipped from my cup and smiled at the irony of my situation. I never quite understood why people stayed in the towns they grew up in. I thought the same about people who moved away and returned to raise their family in their hometown. Shouldn't life be about moving forward? It's funny how your views can be turned upside down so suddenly.

It had been fourteen years since I left. So much had happened and yet so little had changed. This town was the place I grew up in and which I knew like the back of my hand. And although it was a beautiful spot with amazing views, as a teenager I couldn't wait to escape. I wanted to travel and see the world. I wanted excitement and the buzz of something different. I wanted to start again and reinvent myself. Even when I came back to visit Gran, Dad and Tara, I always looked forward to getting back to university in St Andrews or to work in London. Yet look where that had got me. Now at the age of thirty-two, I was childless, jobless and husbandless. Not to mention homeless. Great, eh?

Part of me didn't want to think about all that wasted time because that might spark an inner fury which I was afraid of. Those years spent with Dimitri were years I would never get back. But I didn't want this whole situation to leave me feeling bitter and angry for the rest of my life. I didn't want my failed marriage to define me in the way Mum's leaving did.

Right now, all my worldly possessions were in a hastily filled suitcase and a holdall stashed at the side of the spare room in Tara's house. I couldn't stay there long term. Especially with the next phase of the building about to commence in the next few days.

'You can always come and stay with me,' Gran said. 'And don't worry, Josie. What's for you won't go by you.'

I was aware my sister kept throwing me sympathetic glances between swiping her paintbrush over a door or wall and issuing directives to peel carrot batons for Mia and Oliver. What she didn't know was I also regularly offered them contraband snacks like chocolate buttons and ice cream. I told them it was our special auntie pact. My sister would have a fit if she knew.

I still couldn't quite get my head around the fact she now lived in the house we grew up in. Sometimes when I walked in the front door, I could have sworn it smelled like it did when we lived there. Biscuity, damp, salty. All of those things and also something extra which I couldn't quite put my finger on but which reminded me of home.

My dad preferred to avoid being at the house as much as possible, which I understood. Instead, he was focused on getting the kids to help him in Gran's garden rather than in their own. It reminded me of the times I used to help him in the garden at the manse. He would tell me about the best plants for the sandy soil and what would tolerate the salt in the earth and in the air. Rosemary and thyme were favourite herbs as they always thrived, and he always loved geraniums. They were his favourite flowers as he said they always bloomed and flourished.

Dad was heartbroken when Mum left. He truly believed they would grow old together. He aged overnight and later admitted to me he wished he'd picked up the signs she was planning to leave. He blamed himself, I know he did. Then he shut down and refused to talk about her. Mum's disappearance was one of the many elephants in the room in our family. But every family had them, didn't they?

Taking another sip of coffee from my reusable cup, I shivered. The morning air was raw, and the wind began to pick up. I stared out across the sea to Fife. I used to wonder if Mum went across there. She always said she loved St Andrews and its beaches. I'm sure that influenced my decision to go to university there. Other times I wondered if she had gone abroad. Most of all, I wished I knew if she was okay. Sometimes I wondered if she had another family elsewhere. Maybe Tara and I had stepsisters or brothers. But I couldn't allow that thought to linger for long, as if that was the case it meant we weren't enough. Over the years, I tried many times to track her down. Both Tara and I went on endless journeys to places which she talked about when we were little. But she vanished and didn't leave any kind of trail, as though she didn't want anyone to find her.

'You can't live life constantly waiting and wondering if and when your mum is going to come back,' Gran said gently to me when I wondered whether to move away from home for university. 'Your mum would have wanted you to live your life to the full, love. She wouldn't want you to put your life on hold.'

Gran's words resonated most with me and were the catalyst to move on with life. I don't think any of us could have coped without her. Even though she had lived through a war, being widowed very young and breast cancer, she was always positive and resilient. She regularly told me, 'Tomorrow's another day, love. You will get there.'

I thought about all the things Gran had done and memories flashed through my head. Teaching me how to make soup with a handful of lentils and chopped vegetables; showing me how to rub the butter and flour together then adding sugar and milk, sometimes a handful of grated cheese or plump raisins, to make light and fluffy scones. Although mine never did turn out quite like hers. I smiled as I thought of Tara and me standing on stools in her kitchen watching as she bustled around the kitchen and waiting for our next instructions on what we were going to make. Shortbread, jam, fruit cake, chocolate truffles and pancakes. She taught us to make them all and so much more. Most of all, she reminded us every day that we were loved, even though the woman we loved most in the world had abandoned us.

For a while, I admit, I would do something nice to remember her on the date that she left: 30 June. Some years I went to the cinema on my own, other times I would treat myself to a massage or a coffee and cake. I would always wonder if that would be the year she would return. It had been a while since I'd marked the anniversary of her disappearance. Tara and I hadn't talked about Mum for some time now, but I know she was always on my sister's mind.

I sat scrolling through the pictures of Dimitri on my phone. My finger hovered over them, wondering if I should delete them all. My heart actually ached at the thought my marriage had come to an end. All these years when I thought we were happy. I wiped away another tear, even though I surely shouldn't have any left. My phone pinged as another text dropped.

This is ridiculous. When are you going to come to your senses and come home?

His texts were becoming briefer and angrier. He'd stopped apologising. Although I'm not quite sure if he'd ever started.

Twenty years had passed since I last saw Mum. I don't think I missed her any less. I had to accept she wasn't there. Once again, I would have loved to have had the chance to talk to her right now. To go for a walk along the beach and ask her advice. I sighed. This wasn't the first time in my life I felt her absence so acutely. What would she say about Dimitri? Would she advise me to leave him? Would she be angry at him? Or would she tell me all marriages deserved another chance?

How I longed to be able to hug her and have her tell me everything would be okay. It was now highly unlikely she would ever return, especially after all these years. Which did make me sometimes wonder why she bothered to keep in touch. What was the point in the birthday cards? Was it to make us feel like she cared and to remind us she hadn't forgotten us?

CHAPTER FORTY-SIX

Tara

I saw the GP this morning and she said she would refer me straight away to the Western General Hospital in Edinburgh. 'They should see you within two weeks. I'm sure it's nothing to worry about,' she said. 'However, I do always think we should be thorough with these things.'

I tried watching her expression as I lay topless on the couch, as the bunched-up paper towel I lay on scratched at my back. But she looked thoughtful as she carefully prodded and poked at the area I had shown her.

'I can definitely feel something. But it could be a wee milk duct or a hormonal thing, which is quite common after pregnancy. But I always like to get a second opinion.' She leaned back and turned away, peeling her gloves off and throwing them in the bin. Then she pulled the curtain behind her. 'I'll leave you to get yourself sorted out, dear. Take your time.'

I sat, legs swinging, while I pulled my bra back on and slipped my sweater on top. Then I swished the curtain out of the way and sat down beside her at her desk.

'I'll refer you today,' she said, eyes fixed on her computer screen. She paused for a minute as she tapped at the computer. 'Do you have private insurance? I always think it's worth asking if you do.' She blushed slightly, shrugging apologetically. 'It can speed things up a bit.'

Did that mean she thought I was an urgent case? Did she know something she wasn't telling me? Oh God, I couldn't stand it.

She must have seen the distress cloud my face. 'Please try not to worry, Josie. I know how stressful and anxiety inducing the waiting time can be.'

I looked at her and she swivelled her chair to face me. 'Honestly, I do. I've been through it myself and I'm quite sure things are all fine. I asked about private insurance because I know they would see you in the next couple of days up in Edinburgh, which would lessen the wait for you.'

I took a sharp intake of breath. 'Thanks for your reassurance . . . but no, we don't.' Everything we had was tied up with the bloody restaurant right now or the renovations on the house. Maybe going ahead with the plans for the summer house shouldn't have been such a priority. Maybe this was all a sign that we had to make sure our lives were in order and think about our health instead. I mean, the garden studio wasn't a burning issue. This was a wake-up call for us all. If I had cancer and only a few months to live, then we would all need to start planning for that. Mark would need to learn how to be more efficient around the house. I would need to tell Josie about all the things the twins did and didn't like and all their little particular habits that only I knew about. As for Gran and Dad . . . well, I wanted to cry. I couldn't die. Nobody would manage without me.

'You should receive the letter soon,' said the doctor. 'Try not to overthink or worry too much. More often than not, these lumps are not sinister.'

Yes, but there was always that one time that it was sinister, the voice in my head screamed. *Sinister*. A word I would have used to describe a horror film. Not something inside my breast.

'Does breast cancer run in the family, Josie?' she said.

She was a new GP to the practice, and I didn't expect her to know the complicated ins and outs of everyone in the whole town, which was currently expanding at a rapid rate thanks to the new-build developments on both sides.

'Well, my paternal grandmother had breast cancer around fifteen years ago.'

'Okay,' she said, making a note. 'And do you know what type?'

I frowned. 'It wasn't hereditary. Definitely not.'

'And what about your mother?' she asked.

'What about her?'

'Has she been healthy?'

I gripped the seat of the chair, trying my best to blink away the pooling tears in my eyes. 'Erm, I'm not sure.'

'Oh,' she said, surprised.

Should I say something? How I hated this. Wiping my eyes with a tissue, I sighed. You would think I was used to explaining. 'Erm, we're not in touch. I haven't seen her for years . . . she left us when we were children.'

The GP's face flushed crimson. 'Oh, Josie. I'm sorry if I've put my foot in it.'

'No, don't worry. You weren't to know.' I paused. 'I guess at times like this though it would be quite handy to know if she was healthy and well. Or whether my sister and I were likely to inherit a genetic condition.'

'Okay, so you have a sister too?' She peered at me over the top of her glasses.

'Yes. She's two years older than me.'

'And has she ever had any issues with her breasts?'

I laughed, trying to lighten the mood. 'Not that I know of, although she did used to say she wished they were bigger.'

'Okay, well, once we know what's what with you, Tara, it may be worth getting your sister checked out too. Just in case.'

Great. This was all working out swimmingly. And my bloody mother wasn't here to ask, once again. The story of my life. Thanking the doctor, I walked out of the medical centre, clutching my bag, feeling all too aware of the intense feelings of anger threatening to overwhelm me. My bloody mother. Why had she done this? Where had she gone? And why did it still bother me so much? Maybe things would have been easier if she had died. At least we all could have moved on with our lives.

I got into the car and made the short trip home. When I arrived back at the house there was no time to wallow in self-pity for the builders had arrived and were raring to start.

'Hi, love,' said Mark when I walked into the hall and dumped my bag.

'Remember you're picking the kids up from nursery?' He kissed me on the cheek, grabbing his car keys from the bowl on the radiator cover. 'And the guys are going to start demolishing the garage today.'

Great. My head was starting to throb and the thought of a demolition crew banging and clattering a few metres away was not helping. 'I thought it was tomorrow?'

'Yes, that was the plan, but they finished the other job early and thought they may as well crack on here.'

'Great,' I said, trying my best to muster up some enthusiasm. 'Where is Josie?'

'She's popped down to see your gran.'

'I think I'll go and join them,' I said, reaching to pick up my bag.

'Okay, love. I'll call you later. How was the gym?'

'The gym?' What was he talking about?

'Yes,' said Mark, 'the gym. Where you've been . . . that's why you asked me to take the kids to nursery this morning.'

'Oh,' I said, shrugging. 'Fine, I suppose. I wasn't feeling in the mood. Had to wait ages to get on the machines, which was a bit annoying.'

He looked at me quizzically. 'Is everything okay?'

I sighed. 'Yes, I'm fine. A bit tired and fed up. I'm sorry for moaning.'

He hugged me towards him, and I wanted to bawl into his chest. He smelled lovely as always and I reminded myself

182

how lucky I was to have him. We all were. If I was going to leave my children motherless then I couldn't have chosen a better man to be their father.

'Hey,' he said, tilting my chin upwards. 'What's up?'

Shit, my bloody eyes were watering. Again. 'Nothing. I'm fine, honestly. It's been an emotional couple of days with Josie coming back and all that she's going through. And I probably didn't run long enough at the gym. Not long enough to release the endorphins.' I hated lying to him.

He kissed the tip of my nose. 'Take it easy, love. You do a lot with the kids and your gran and your dad. And now your sister . . .'

'I'll be fine,' I said. 'It's better to crack on with things. I'm sure once all the renovation work is done, that will be better.'

'Okay, well, call me if you need me. Jaz is supposed to be back today, so that should make a huge difference — which means I'll be around more to help with things at home. Like painting, which you know I'm so good at.' He winked and I couldn't help but laugh. Mark was a man of many talents, but painting wasn't one of them. I hoped Jaz being back would actually keep him occupied at the restaurant for a bit longer. It was safer when he wasn't at home trying to help with anything to do with paint, as he ended up getting in the way. 'Maybe when the garage is down you could focus your attention on the garden. It will be great to have the summer house up and running and even better if the garden's looking good too. I think the kids will love it.'

'Do you think your dad will let me do that though?' he said, raising an eyebrow. 'You know your dad and his green fingers.'

'I think he will. He seems to be more focused on Gran's garden at the moment.' Normally Dad would immerse him-self in his gardening projects and I was surprised he hadn't wanted to do more here other than the pots at the door.

I thought about him in his top-floor flat which over-looked the harbour. Gran always described it as his 'ridiculous' flat. I think that was because the stairs could sometimes be too much for her to climb. She never liked to be caught out of breath. Gran and I have tried our best over the years to introduce splashes of colour here and there with cushions and potted plants and throws from one of our many excursions to Ikea. He seems to humour us for a bit and then puts them away, removing the colour and therefore the joy. I did sometimes wonder if he would wear black if he lived on a Greek Island. He certainly embraced the persona of a dour Presbyterian Scotsman. Mark had often asked me what it was like growing up the daughter of a minister.

'Dull,' I always said. 'Hard work. We got called Bible bashers at school, though Josie and I couldn't have been more different.' We rebelled against our dad's strict regime. 'Thank God for Gran.' She wasn't your typical granny who wore rollers to bed and always baked. Well, yes, she did always bake, but she also did things like slip some cider into her shopping trolley when she knew we had a party coming up. There was no way Dad would have approved. And if we did try to buy it ourselves, we had to overcome two hurdles: first of all, being underage, and then even when we were of age, we didn't want anyone telling tales on us to Dad, who disapproved of alcohol.

She always stayed up late for us when we were at a party. That way we didn't have to creep back and try and shimmy up a drainpipe after sneaking out when he thought we were in bed. Josie and I had a lot to be thankful for and it was all down to Gran.

'How long do you think Josie will stay for?' asked Mark, pulling on his jacket.

'Mmm, I'm not sure. It's nice having her here but . . .'

'What do you think she's going to do about Dimitri?'

'I don't think she'll go back to him, if that's what you mean. But who knows what she's going to do moving forward? All her life is down there.'

He nodded. 'Sure is a tough one. If only she hadn't married such a twat.'

184

'It's whether she goes back and starts a new life for herself there or whether she has a fresh start completely and moves away.'

'How would you feel if she came back here?'

I stared at Mark. 'I would actually be fine . . .' It's not something I would have admitted to a few months or even weeks ago. But things had changed, and having her here was good for the twins. Especially if the family dynamic was all going to change. Much as I hated to admit it, perhaps this was as good a time as ever to try and contact Mum again.

CHAPTER FORTY-SEVEN

Josie

'I wish I had some more friends.' There, I had said the words out loud. Wouldn't it be nice to call someone up and go for a chat and a coffee? I loved being reconciled with Tara and I adored her as much as anyone can love their sibling, but that was the thing. She was my family and therefore she had to be connected to me.

Seeing a friend at one of the local coffee shops here would be such a nice thing to do. So many trendy cafés had sprung up and I actually yearned to check them out. But I'd lost touch with school friends long ago and most of them had moved on and away. Anyway, how could I ring them up out of the blue? I couldn't help but have twinges of envy when I curled up on the sofa and watched reruns of *Friends*. I had always loved that show and the close and easy-going relationships they all had with one another. The laughter, the camaraderie and the support they gave each other was something I'd never had. After laughing my way through an episode I was left feeling bereft. It didn't matter, I now realised, I was married to my supposed soulmate — his words, not mine — and I always had someone to go home to. But now I was lonely and alone. Maybe if I had more confidence, I would go out alone. But the thought terrified me.

The truth was I had let my friendships drift. After school, I couldn't wait to move away and start a new life, so I let friendships lapse and avoided coming home during the holidays as much as possible. When I did come home, I was always too busy seeing family. Of course, when I moved to London I did little else but work.

I liked to rush home after work to see Dimitri, telling myself I was being a good wife. He told me how much he enjoyed having me to talk to of an evening as he got so lonely and isolated during the day. Well, obviously that *wasn't* the case as he'd had quite the daytime social life. However, once again, hindsight was proving to be quite illuminating. In the cold light of day, it seemed Dimitri's writing career always took priority over everything else and that included my life, family and friendships too. He had published two successful novels which made a modest income, but he behaved as if he was some kind of superstar. And he was a pro at nurturing and manipulating the tortured writer thing. Nobody could possibly understand his art and creativity and his self-expression. In order to fulfil his talent, he could only write full-time and there was no chance he would be able to hold down a second job as that would be so limiting for him. He did the odd bit of tutoring over at Kingston University, but he moaned about that constantly — except when some of the young female students pandered to his ego. My regular full-time salary buoyed us up, although he insisted his writing income allowed us to have the lifestyle we did. I was left wondering, what lifestyle exactly?

Aside from the odd coffee or lunch with colleagues at work, it was very much me and him and occasionally Asmita. I'd fallen out with Tara and the only contact I had was the odd conversation with Gran. My world was me and Dimitri. His life was Dimitri, himself, certain neighbours and anyone else who commanded his attention and then me. On reflection, he always thought it was fine for him to have female friends but bristled if I mentioned a male colleague. Something else that was starting to strike me as odd was his thing about locks in the house. He always insisted we didn't have a lock on the bathroom door in case one of us fell. I have to admit I found that a bit unnerving when I wanted to lie and soak in the bath undisturbed. He would wander in whenever it suited him, despite my protests. I now realised that was just wrong. 'I love you so much I miss you,' he said when he wandered in and sat on the toilet seat. 'What if you drown? Or hurt yourself?'

He also insisted on a joint bank account, and although my salary was paid into that, he knew nothing about the current account I'd kept in my maiden name and had been surreptitiously saving money in for months. I read an article about savings and finances which featured a case study from one woman who insisted on keeping things separate. It must have struck a chord with me. Perhaps I wasn't so stupid after all.

My phone beeped and I glanced at the message, shaking my head in disbelief when I saw who the sender was.

When are you coming back? Dimitri's in bits. Me too. I don't know what to say other than sorry. A x

I pressed delete. I was in the house alone this morning and had promised Tara I would help by painting the back door. She'd already given it a coat but asked if I would do the last one. The builders had demolished the garage, which now lay in bits in a skip, and so at least I didn't have to worry about flying dust and debris sticking to wet paint. I decided to make myself a coffee to take outside. As I came down the stairs, I saw the pile of letters on the mat. Picking them up, I carried them through to the kitchen and propped them on the dresser. A pale-yellow envelope stuck out and I pulled it from the stack, panicking I had forgotten their anniversary or Mark's birthday. A typed label was stuck on the front and addressed to me. Who on earth would send me a letter here? Nobody knew where I was. Opening it, a card with a picture of sunflowers on the front fell out. His handwriting was scrawled inside.

I know where you are and what you've done. It's time to come back. This is ridiculous. We belong to each other. If you don't come home soon then I'll come and get you. I love you, Josie.
       Yours as always, Dimitri

It didn't matter I was safe in Tara's kitchen and hundreds of miles away from him, he knew exactly how to get inside my head. More worryingly, he knew exactly where I was. I shivered. It felt as though he was watching.

CHAPTER FORTY-EIGHT

Tara

When I came home this afternoon, Josie was unusually quiet and wouldn't say what was wrong apart from being a bit tired. She'd done a brilliant job of the back door, which was perfectly finished. I'd chosen a chalky pink colour, which matched the roses in the garden and set off the blonde brick-work rather nicely. She said she wanted to go and have a lie-down for a bit, if I didn't mind.

She was probably feeling out of sorts without her stuff around her and very much in limbo. However, I was also on edge and having her here was triggering memories of myself which I didn't particularly like. When Josie announced she was coming home for good, part of me was pleased. But if I'm honest, I was a bit annoyed she was returning after swanning off and living in London for so long. Sometimes I wished I had done the same, but I couldn't leave Dad and Gran. Not after everything they had done for us over the years. Then when Mark and I met, and I soon fell pregnant — well, that was that. Where would we have gone? He was at the early stages of launching the restaurant here; we could hop on the train and be in Edinburgh in twenty-five minutes and come home to our town by the sea. I'm actually not convinced I would have gone to live anywhere else, but it's just nice to think that perhaps I could have.

I absolutely never planned to have any children, never mind twins. I always liked kids, but I didn't see myself as the motherly type. But Mark changed all of that. He's from a large Glasgow family and I saw how happy he was when they all visited. He had three brothers. His mother always said how great it was having a full and busy house when they were all growing up. I was so glad things had turned out this way. The kids grounded me and gave me a focus. Now I couldn't imagine my life without kids. I absolutely wasn't ready to leave them. I *wouldn't*.

I decided to make the most of the builder-free garden and took my coffee outside and sat on the small patio, which was cracked and sprouting weeds. It was a warm afternoon and I sat admiring the view.

Picking up my phone, I scrolled through Messenger for the twentieth time since yesterday. There hadn't been a reply to my message although I could see she had read it. I kept watching for the series of grey dots which showed she was composing a response.

If someone wanted to find you then Facebook was the ideal platform. Years ago, I had created my profile and kept all my settings open to the public. I wasn't fussed that all and sundry had access to my posts and pictures because I hoped Mum might be watching. I regularly uploaded news about my life and when I fell pregnant with the twins, I did a regular update on how I felt with photos of my growing bump. When they were born, I made euphoric announcements with loads of pictures, showing me holding them in my arms wearing their pink and blue Babygros. I hoped surely if she was watching she would get in touch, especially when she realised she had become a gran. But there was nothing at all from her. I had scoured all the possible profiles which might be her and which shared the same surnames. But all my searches came up blank. I think that was when I slumped into a spiralling depression. After that it was a long time before I posted on Facebook again.

Until one day, when the twins were about six months old, I happened to check my Facebook messages. A red notification flashed up against the white speech bubble and when I opened it, I saw the name: M. J. Smithson. June was Mum's middle name. I was so excited I was barely able to bring myself to click on it. Wanting to savour the moment for ever, I stared and stared until I could contain myself no longer and clicked.

Congratulations, Tara. Delighted to hear you're now a mum. Love you always. X

No explanation or lengthy letter detailing the past six-teen years and what she'd been doing since she'd walked out. It was short and to the point. But at least it was *something*. She had been in touch and that meant she still cared. She was still my mum. I thought about telling everyone else and sharing the news with them. It may sound awful, but I didn't want to. I wanted to keep it as my secret. I didn't tell anyone. Not even Mark. But that message from her and the random ones that followed were the things that helped me work my way through the awful period of postnatal depression.

Her communication was erratic over the years, and she would only respond when I contacted her. Never the other way around. Her replies were always brief, which frustrated me hugely and latterly angered me. Why wouldn't she tell me where she was? Why wouldn't she tell me where she had been? And most of all why wouldn't she answer all the questions I asked her about leaving? Sometimes I would write lengthy let-ters to her, chatting about the twins and my life. Other times I would rant, pouring all my anger at her into the messages, and press send quickly before I changed my mind. I couldn't really blame her for not replying. What did I expect?

But surely she had to reply to this question about the lump and breast cancer? I checked again and slipped my phone into my pocket. I would have to wait. That was all I could do. Picking up my cup, I went back inside. Hauling the load of coloured washing from the machine, I shoved it into the basket.

'Never ending, isn't it?' said Josie, who appeared in the doorway of the kitchen.

I puffed in response. 'Yip.'

'Come on, let me help you.' She took the basket from me, perching it on her hip.

'Thanks,' I said. 'Feel better after your nap?'

'I do, thanks. You should have one.'

Laughing, I said, 'I'd love to nap but there's never time, what with the kids and the renovations and trying to help Gran . . .'

Josie stared at me, cutting through my thoughts. 'That's an easy one,' she said. 'I'll go over and stay with her and keep her company. I know she's perfectly capable, but I could run the hoover about and catch up with some of the things she's finding trickier?'

I desperately wanted to ask how long she was planning to stay here in North Berwick and whether or not she was going to return to Teddington for work. But I knew my sister, and Josie had obviously said all she wanted to say about Dimitri for the moment. She was doing her deflection tactic, focusing on someone else rather than her solving own problems. She was exactly the same when we were kids. 'That's not a bad idea,' I said. 'It would be good to be with her.' It also took the pressure off me worrying about her while also worrying about everyone else.

She put the basket down at my feet and put an arm on my shoulder. 'I'll go and get my stuff organised, shall I?'

Part of me wanted to scream at her. Wasn't she even going to hang up the washing first? But I said nothing. Because that's what I do.

As she walked away, she pulled her phone from her pocket, a beep notifying her of a text.

Watching her scan the message, I tried to work out who it was from, but her face remained neutral.

'Everything okay?' I asked.

'Yes,' she said over her shoulder.

'You're sure?'

'Yes.' She turned around. 'I'll go and get my stuff.'

After a few moments, I heard the crunch of a car pulling into the driveway and looked out. It was Mark and Jaz. 'Josie!' I shouted. 'Look who's here!'

CHAPTER FORTY-NINE

Josie

I walked up the stairs slowly, twirling a strand of hair around my finger. I was a nomad. Off to pack my bags and go to the next place until I worked out where to go and where I belonged. I could hardly go back to Teddington and that street. Not now *everyone* knew what had happened. Someone had helpfully posted all the details on a Teddington community Facebook group, which was the equivalent of having a town crier walking around for days shouting out all the salacious details to the community. I was fully expecting the *Daily Mail* to have it up on their sidebar of shame. The story had all the perfect ingredients for a juicy scandal: he was a low-grade celebrity because of his books and his connection to the nearby university, she was a beautiful housewife with young children, and all the stark details were there for the taking, including allegations that the academic wife — yes, that's me — walked in on them and offered to join in. A journalist could also describe the value of our house and the leafy suburb we lived in, which was ideal for families. It fitted the bill perfectly. That was why my bloody phone kept pinging with text messages, no doubt from concerned neighbours and friends, and Tara kept looking at me with concern.

I would need to go back to get all my stuff. But for the moment I couldn't face it. I was now starting to wonder whether I had ever loved him. Did I only love the idea of having a husband? Anyway, what kind of man sent weird, threatening cards to his wife?

Heading off to stay with Gran was pathetic, but what if he was watching the house here? It would be safer for Tara, Mark and the kids if I moved, and at least Gran's house was nearer to the police station should we need help. Tara had enough on her plate without my drama adding to her stress. I think she had taken too much on with this renovation project but there was no point in telling her. She wasn't very good with being offered advice although she was quick to dish it out. Earlier she had told me I should make the most of being back. 'It's not a bad place to be, Josie,' she said.

I laughed. 'But it's so clichéd, isn't it? Coming back to my hometown by the coast with a broken heart and my tail between my legs. Next, you'll be telling me I should open up a bookshop or a cake chop and fall head over heels with the local widower who's also a member of the RNLI, and when he's not busy being a superdad, he's busy saving lives at sea.'

That had made her laugh and me too. I should focus on writing the book I had always planned to. Tara was right, I had lots of options and this was a chance to start again.

As I packed my bags for Gran's house, I heard her shout to me we had a visitor. That was when my heart started to thud. Was it him? He must have posted the card to me yesterday or the day before. Would he be here already? Wouldn't he wait a few days and leave me in suspense? There was no way I was going back with him. I didn't want to and he couldn't force me. I mean, he was actually quite strong. Would Tara be able to stop him? My breath was ragged as I tried not to panic. Shit. Maybe we should call Mark for help. Looking out of the window, my shoulders sagged with relief when I realised it was Mark. Phew.

196

Then when I spotted who was getting out of the car with him, I gasped. Was I seeing things? I blinked hard and looked again. Was this a bad joke? A surge of nausea threatened to choke me, and the blood rushed to my head. My legs started to tremble, and I sat down. I would need to feign illness or something. What on earth was he doing here? Jason? After Dimitri, he was probably the next person in the world I hated most. He must have gained a new nickname in Australia. Jaz. That was why the penny hadn't dropped. Tara didn't know what had happened with us either all those years ago, so she wouldn't have thought to tell me who Jaz was. She was oblivious to the connection.

'Josie!' she yelled. 'Come on, someone's here to see us. And he wants to say hello to you.'

Shit. Rooted to the spot, I tried to move but couldn't. Tara ran upstairs and bounded into the room. 'Mark has popped in with Jaz. Are you coming down?'

'Uh, I'm getting organised to head to Gran's.'

She threw me a quizzical look. 'Okay. This won't take a minute. He said he remembers you from before.'

'Who?' trying my best to stall for time.

'Jaz?'

'Oh. I don't know anyone called Jaz.' I was getting desperate.

'You'd better come down and say hello,' she said, lowering her voice to a whisper. 'Otherwise he'll think you're being rude. Come on,' she said, grabbing my arm.

I had no choice but to follow her downstairs and into the kitchen where he stood with Mark. He turned around and our eyes locked. 'Josie . . .' His voice trailed away.

'Jason,' I said sharply. That was all I could manage. I couldn't believe he was standing in Tara's house and was now in business with my brother-in-law and this was the first I knew about it all. What on earth was the name change all about?

'Good to see you,' he said, coming over and kissing me on the cheek.

His lips burned into my cheek and I stepped back.

'Do you remember Jaz?' said Mark, glancing between us in confusion. 'He said he remembers you from way back.'

'Yes. Though you were Jason then,' I said drily. 'How are you?'

'Not bad, thanks. You're looking well.'

I didn't reply and I could tell Tara was wondering what was going on. 'What's with the new name?' I managed to say.

'It wasn't my choice, it has to be said. I'll blame it on moving to Sydney.'

'What, did you become a jazz musician or something?' My tone was acerbic, but I couldn't help it.

'I'm so sorry I didn't realise you two knew each other,' said Tara.

'We don't,' I said quickly, noticing Mark raise an eyebrow at my sister.

Jason, or *Jaz*, cocked his head to the side in bemusement. 'It was a while ago now, wasn't it, Josie?'

'Yip. Look, sorry, I don't mean to be rude but I'm gathering my stuff up. I'm heading over to Gran's.'

'I don't think there's any rush,' said Tara.

Looking at my watch, I nodded. 'She's expecting me. I'd better go. Bye, Jason.'

'Yes. I'm sure I'll see you around.'

'Fancy a coffee, mate?' said Mark.

I turned to go back upstairs and fetch my bags. Tara followed me behind. 'Here, I'll give you a hand.'

'Thanks. Though I don't have much stuff.'

'I didn't realise you know him,' she said, grabbing a bag.

'I don't. Sometimes I spoke to him at the pub and stuff. You would have been too young.'

'He's quite easy on the eye though, isn't he?' she said, smirking.

'Erm, I didn't notice.'

'Are you sure?' she said. 'Because I noticed a bit of a spark between you.'

Switching the subject, and trying not to reel in horror, I said, 'Thanks so much for having me. Tell Mark too. I'll never, ever forget it.'

'Don't be daft. You're only a few minutes away. And you're welcome back any time.'

There was a guffaw of laughter from the kitchen. I rolled my eyes and reached to take the bag from her. 'Thanks, Tara.'

PART THREE: NOW

CHAPTER FIFTY

Our mum left us when we were kids. She left us sleeping home alone. She just walked out and never came back. I mean, what kind of mother does that? I never really understood what happened. It was all brushed under the carpet.

Dad got on with the job of raising us. Suffice to say, we didn't have a happy childhood. He was a very angry man.

But I've learned not to judge. What's the point? Nobody ever knows the whole truth. Anyway, aren't there always two sides to a story?

CHAPTER FIFTY-ONE

Tara

A ripple of unease spreads through me as I think about everything that has happened today. The police eventually left, telling Dad they would be back in touch in due course. He seems greatly relieved he has unburdened himself after carrying such a massive secret over the years. He has started talking about a proper burial for baby Jonathan and he actually looks as though a huge weight has been lifted from his shoulders. I was glad to see his colour had returned and was happier at leaving him. Yet there is something I can't quite put my finger on. Something about the way Sam stared at him for a moment too long over the designer rim of her glasses. The way in which Brian hesitated when he told Dad he would be back in touch. Clearly, in their eyes, this isn't finished business.

I'm desperate to know what happened to Josie and why she had to run off so suddenly, leaving me to deal with the police alone. She must have had a very good reason, and the dread flits around my stomach as I wonder what it might be. She isn't answering her phone and so I sit in the car, trying to call Mark, but the phone won't connect. Then a text drops from him to say I should go straight home.

Just go home. I'll explain all when I see you. All okay. Josie with your Gran. Both exhausted, I think. Leave them until tomorrow. I'll be home soon.

I'm actually quite relieved I can go straight home. I honestly want to stick my fingers in my ears and shout. I'm not sure I can face any more family dramas today. Then I wonder where the kids are if Mark isn't back yet. I turn the keys in the ignition as another message beeps. Mark must have read my thoughts.

PS, kids fine and Jessica's mum at house with them

I press my foot on the accelerator and head straight back, arriving as she's getting in the car. Mark must have beaten me home. She pauses and walks over to me. Rolling down my window, I say, 'Thanks so much for helping us out. Again.'

She gives me a wee wave. 'Don't be daft. I only popped in to drop Millie's jacket off from the other day. Your friend, Jaz, was here. He looked a bit agitated so I said I'd wait until Mark got back. Honestly, don't worry. My mother-in-law's staying with us at the moment anyway, so at least it gave me a break from her relentless questions.' She laughs.

I force a smile, but I'm desperate to get inside without appearing rude. 'Well, thank you. I owe you one.'

'No worries at all. Take care. Bye!'

Running into the house, I almost trip over the kids' shoes scattered across the hallway and automatically pick them up and put them in the crate by the door. I hang up their coats, which never quite make it onto their pegs but are flung underneath them on the floor.

'Hi, Mummy!' shouts Oliver. 'Jason was here and Jessica's mum came, and we got to eat lots of chocolate.'

'Ssh,' shouts Millie. 'Don't tell her.'

'Oops.' His face flushes and he sticks out his tongue at his sister.

I laugh, watching them both scamper upstairs.

'Hi, sweetheart.' Mark walks towards me and pulls off his sweatshirt.

'Hello. What on earth has been going on?' I ask.

'I could ask you the same thing,' he says, kissing me lightly on the head. 'Do you want to start or shall I?'

I follow him into the living room and we sit close together on the sofa, where I give him a condensed version of events at Dad's house. He remains silent as I explain what has happened, his eyes widening from time to time.

'Jeez,' he says, rubbing a hand through his hair. 'That is *unbelievable*. I mean, who would have thought it . . . and your dad keeping it quiet all these years. That must have been awful.'

Neither of us speaks for a moment and I can feel his puzzled stare focusing on me.

'A baby. Your poor mum. And dad . . . I'm sorry, Tara. What a shock.' He holds my hand, massaging my fingers as he speaks. 'What a day, eh?'

I watch as he rubs my hand. 'Well,' I start, 'what about you? What happened at Gran's?'

He draws his hand away from mine and starts clenching and unclenching his fingers. 'I probably should let Josie tell you herself,' he starts. 'But . . . well . . . Dimitri turned up at your gran's house.'

'*What?* When?' I can't believe what I'm hearing and a spark of worry courses through me. 'Are they okay?'

'It was this afternoon. That's why she made such a sharp exit from your dad's. We think he must have been there for an hour or so before Josie arrived.'

I narrow my eyes, thinking back to her abrupt departure. 'She did look agitated when she left, but I was in the midst of another situation.'

'That's why she called me to ask for help.'

'She did?' I'm so glad Josie thought to phone Mark rather than turn up to try and deal with Dimitri on her own.

'Yes — she called me, and Jaz said he would come and sit with the kids so I could go.'

'Ah.'

'When I got there, he was holding court with your gran, like the prodigal son.'

'What?' Now I *really* can't believe what I'm hearing.

Mark is drumming his fingers against his leg. 'It's as though your gran had forgotten everything that had happened between him and Josie, which is a bit of a worry. Maybe the stress of everything? But, yes, they were sitting drinking tea, eating shortbread and having a blether.'

I press my head back against the sofa. I can't begin to imagine how poor Josie must have felt when she arrived and saw them chatting together. 'And what happened next?'

'Well, Josie was trying to get rid of him. But Jason turned up. I think he was worried about Josie when I told him Dimitri had turned up out of the blue — but that's another story. Dimitri put two and two together and worked out who Jason was.'

'What?'

He nods. 'You can't make this up, right?'

'And?' I say, wondering what on earth he is going to say next.

'He said he knew all about Jason. That he was the guy who had broken her heart and left her pregnant.'

My heart stops. 'Pregnant?' I shook my head in disbelief. 'Pregnant? Josie? What do you mean?'

Mark grips my hand. 'I know. It was a shock when I found out. It was a shock to all of us. I don't think anyone knew. Well, apart from Dimitri.'

'What happened?' I say, my voice a whisper.

'She lost the baby . . .'

'Oh, Josie.' I can't bear to think of what my sister has gone through and that she's had to deal with it all alone. I wipe away a tear. My poor sister. 'Why did I not know?'

'Tara, you were only, what, sixteen or seventeen? She was living away from home. It was when she started at St Andrews. There's no way you could have known. So please don't start blaming yourself for something out of your control.'

I smile gratefully at him. 'But Jason . . . how could he have left her knowing she was *pregnant*?'

'That's the thing though. Dimitri's announcement was brand-new information to him . . .'

206

'Oh shit. How did he take it?'

'I don't know. He took off not long after we ejected Dimitri. He looked pretty shell-shocked.'

'No wonder,' I say. 'Poor Josie and poor Jason.'

'That wasn't all. Dimitri said the miscarriage was the reason Josie couldn't conceive. He effectively blamed his current state of affairs on Josie and Jason.'

A swell of rage threatens to overcome me. 'If I could get my hands on that pathetic little turd . . .'

'I was about to hit him myself but Jason beat me to it. And he did punch him quite hard.'

That made me feel slightly better, admittedly. But it did nothing to appease the sadness I felt for Josie and for Jason.

'Mummy, we're ready for our bath now!' shouts Millie from upstairs.

'I'll do it,' says Mark.

'No, let me. I'd like to do something nice today. Reminds me I'm a mum in the midst of all this madness.'

He pulls me into a hug and holds me tightly. 'I love you, Tara.'

'And I love you. I'm sorry you've been pulled into this crazy family stuff.'

He laughs. 'Just family stuff,' he says. 'Nobody's perfect.'

Hours later, I lie awake and restless once again. When did life become so complicated?

I pad downstairs and sit on the sofa, open my laptop and click on my Messenger items and start to type.

I'm so sorry about baby Jonathan. I didn't know. Dad told us today. I can't even begin to imagine how that must have felt. Sending you lots of love and hugs. Tara x

Then I press send. I'm not sure whether it's the right thing to do. But I want her to know I'm thinking of her and I'm sorry. Placing the computer on the coffee table, I sit back and curl up, drawing the blanket around me. Closing my eyes, I try to sleep but I can't quieten the competing noises in my head. I tuck my hands under my armpits, feeling the small stone in my breast. It is definitely still there. Surely the way everything in my life is panning out right now, it will only be bad news. Sighing, I lie back wondering how to break the news to Mark. At least I don't have to wait this out much longer. The appointment is the day after tomorrow.

CHAPTER FIFTY-TWO

People liked to talk and gossip. Especially after what had happened. Being a single mother was hard enough without the added stigma that surrounded our circumstances. I could hear the whispers and feel the stares. That's why I moved away. Though the sorrow never left me. How could it? I was living with a constant reminder. I had to be mother and father to my child and it wasn't easy. I had to teach him how to be resilient. Maybe I was overly critical and harsh. But he needed to learn how to survive in this world. Perhaps I could have been more affectionate. I do wish I had been more warm and loving.

CHAPTER FIFTY-THREE

Josie

'It wasn't your fault,' the nurse said to me as I sobbed. I remember the day as though it was yesterday.

'It's just one of those things, sweetheart. It wasn't meant to be.' She bustled around and handed me some tissues. 'Sometimes nature has a way of looking after us.' The university nurse was from Ireland and her lilt was reassuring as she did her best to comfort me. But although I appreciated her kindness, it didn't help. This was my fault. All of it. I should have taken more care with everything. I should have taken the morning-after pill when the condom split, instead of assuming everything would be okay. I shouldn't have drunk so much vodka during freshers' week. I shouldn't have considered an abortion when I found out I was pregnant. I should have taken folic acid and done more to look after myself. There were so many things I should have done but didn't and this was my punishment. It was my fault I had miscarried and lost the baby.

I had woken that morning in my room in the university halls of residence with awful cramping in the pit of my stomach. I had only known I was pregnant for a couple of weeks and hadn't yet told anyone, mainly because I was petrified and confused.

When I went to the loo, I was bleeding heavily, and it was clear I was losing the baby. I must have been about fourteen weeks gone. Somehow, I managed to get myself to hospital, where I was taken for an ultrasound. The doctor squirted some jelly onto my stomach and glided the wand over it. I hoped and prayed there would be a heartbeat and this was a false alarm. I made a promise I would do everything properly from now on if we were given another chance. But I knew. And as the doctor focused her gaze on the screen, all I could see was a dark hole and all the hope I'd been desperately trying to cling onto started to evaporate. There was no sign of any heartbeat, she said, pointing at the sac. I think she must have wondered if I understood what she was saying because she said the foetus had died. She apologised for my loss and handed me a wad of paper towels to wipe away the gel. With a swish of the curtain, she was gone, and the nurse was left to pick up the pieces.

Other than Gran, I didn't tell anyone what had happened. I tried to get on with being a student. I went out with so-called friends who didn't notice I was glum or restless. I joined the running club and kept on moving. Then I met Dimitri and everything changed. Looking back now, I realise I was vulnerable, and he must have seen that in me. I was, I suppose, looking for someone to look after me and love me. He was looking for someone he could use and manipulate. I fitted the bill, perfectly.

Years later, when we were having difficulty conceiving, we were out for dinner at an Italian restaurant in Kingston. We were sitting by the window overlooking the river and I had drunk more wine than I normally would. This led to me letting slip I had been pregnant before, so my body knew how to conceive. Dimitri's eyes locked onto mine as he accused me of blaming him.

'Are you saying this is all my fault?'

That wasn't what I was saying at all, but he continued to twist my words and talk about the miscarriage, which triggered all the dormant memories from before.

'Have you ever considered this is your fault, Josie?' he said. 'Maybe it's karma. I mean, you had your chance, and you didn't look after yourself properly and so it's your fault you lost your baby. Maybe the universe is trying to tell you something.'

I was so shocked I couldn't speak. Who was this man sitting across from me who was supposed to be my husband?

'Maybe you're not supposed to be a mother.'

He signalled for the bill and picked up his jacket and walked out without saying another word. I was left to pay for our meal and made my way home, alone, in a state of confusion and sadness. Was this really all my fault?

Now as I lie here in the bedroom at Gran's house, I realise of course it wasn't my fault. But what a day. First Dad's confession and then Dimitri showing up unexpectedly and blurting out my secret to the one person who should have been told the truth. I can't begin to think how I will explain all of this to Jason. But the Irish nurse, all those years ago, had been right. It wasn't my fault.

CHAPTER FIFTY-FOUR

I pressed the photograph of my daughters to my lips before gently placing it back on the dressing table. It was a beautiful summer's day and the girls were out at the Sunday School picnic on the beach. I had offered to go and help but Gordon insisted that I have some time to myself. He suggested I take the train into Edinburgh for the afternoon and perhaps visit an art gallery.

'You know you'll end up doing housework if you stay at home,' he said.

He was right. But when they left, and the house became still, I decided that I would rather make the most of the peace and quiet and stay at home. I wandered down to the hammock which was strung between the trees at the bottom of the garden. The sky was a dazzling blue, the sun warm and the breeze rustled through the leaves. I hopped onto the makeshift bed and lay there enjoying the view ahead, the Bass Rock glittering in the North Sea.

Dozing in the sun, I smiled as I heard the birds chattering above. Bees buzzed past and hovered around the pink tea rose bushes. I breathed in huge gulps of the warm, salty air and enjoyed the feeling of the sun kissing my cheeks. Soon, my eyes fluttered shut and I dozed peacefully.

Then I woke abruptly. A knot twisted in my stomach as though I already knew what was about to happen. The sound of footsteps crunched slowly over the gravel driveway. My heart rate accelerated as shock and fear kicked in. Shifting myself in the hammock, I shielded my eyes from the sun and looked up at the house. The figure on the drive turned and stared straight at me. The moment I had been dreading for years had finally arrived.

CHAPTER FIFTY-FIVE

Tara

This morning, after dropping the twins at nursery, I go straight to Gran's house. I sent Josie a quick message last night, letting her know I was thinking of her and we would catch up properly today.

I ring the doorbell and wait for her to answer. When she opens the door, I can't help but notice how exhausted she looks. Dark circles loop under her eyes, and her cheeks are hollowed. Hugging her, I whisper, 'I'm sorry.'

'Thanks, Tara. But honestly, I'm okay. Him turning up was just a bit much.'

'I'm not surprised,' I say. 'I'm glad he's finally got the message and gone.'

'Mark was great . . . but I'll need to talk to Jason properly. I wasn't expecting to ever see him again or have my secret brought up like that.'

'He'll be fine, I'm sure he will be,' I say, trying to reassure her.

'Hope so. God knows what he must think of me.'

I don't respond. Mark has given me snippets about Jason's life, but that's his story to tell, not mine. He seems a

215

resilient guy and I'm sure he'll be okay once he gets over the initial shock.

'You do realise the fact you couldn't conceive has nothing at all to do with you having a miscarriage?' I say, finally breaking the silence.

'It's only been since I came up here that I've been able to accept that. How convenient for Dimitri to be able to blame me for it.'

'I think your body is extremely clever. It's protected you and done you a massive favour.'

She shudders. 'You're right.'

'Where is Gran?'

'She's gone back to bed.'

'That's not like her. She's usually up and about so early.'

'She was up early,' says Josie. 'But she was tired so went for a lie-down. She's worrying me a bit. She seems to be forgetting things — she forgot about Dimitri and me.'

'Do you think she's stressed by what happened to Dad?'

'Mmm, maybe,' says Josie, but she doesn't sound convinced. 'I haven't been able to tell her about, well, what Dad told us yesterday.'

I sigh. 'That's one we should do together, when the time feels right. Do you fancy heading out for a coffee? I'm desperate for one.'

She stifles a yawn. 'If you don't mind, I'll pass. I'm a bit of a state. I need to email work and I'm going to try and catch the doctor about Gran.'

'Okay. I tell you what — how about I go and buy us some takeaway coffees?'

'Thanks, sounds perfect.'

I walk along the high street, pulling the corners of my jacket up against the wind blowing down the road, which is flanked by three-storey buildings. It certainly doesn't feel like June, more like October, which is a shame as it doesn't bode well for a good summer. Mind you, I think, so far not much has pointed to this being a great summer. Everything that could go wrong has gone wrong.

I spot Sharon, Jessica's mum, across the street and wave. She crosses over.

'How are you, Tara? You've had *quite* the couple of days . . .'

'Yip. You can say that again.' I wonder what exactly she's referring to and what she knows. I assume Brian will tell her most things, albeit off the record. I wait for her to continue.

'I heard about your brother-in-law.'

'Who from exactly?' I ask, my voice clipped. I wasn't aware that was public knowledge. Unless . . . though surely not? Dimitri hasn't complained to the police, has he?

'Um . . . well, he went to the station last night and claimed he'd been assaulted.'

'Seriously?' My temples start to pulse. 'He made a complaint?'

'Yes. Um, I probably shouldn't say anything,' she says, lowering her voice. 'Brian wouldn't be happy. Promise you won't tell anyone this came from me . . . but he accused your husband's business partner of punching him.'

'Yes, he did thump him, but he deserved it,' I say, my hackles rising.

'Oh, I didn't mean anything . . . I'm just saying what I heard.'

She probably doesn't mean anything malicious, but I hate the thought of people gossiping about my family. There's already so much they can talk about — they don't need any fresh fodder.

'And don't worry. Brian gave him his marching orders.'

Breathing a sigh of relief, I say, 'Well, thank God for that.' I want to keep moving. I can see a couple of other nursery mums making their way along the pavement towards us. 'Thanks again for last night and for watching the kids. I do appreciate it.'

'No problem at all. Look, I just wanted to let you know, Tara.'

'Thank you. I appreciate it.' Turning to go, she puts a hand on my arm.

'And I'm sorry about the body in your garden too.'

'Thanks. I am too.'

She starts to say something else but stops.

I wait, growing anxious at the impending arrival of the two nearing women. 'Were you going to say something else, Sharon?'

'I . . . no, nothing,' she says.

'Okay.' But my heart sinks as there is something else, it's written all over her face. 'Catch you later.'

She smiles. 'Will do.'

CHAPTER FIFTY-SIX

Josie

I owe Jason an explanation but where do I even begin? Should I apologise? I have no idea what the etiquette around such a situation is. Am I supposed to say sorry for losing his baby he didn't know he had? Or sorry I didn't tell him I was pregnant and by the time I had plucked up the courage to make contact it was too late?

More than forty-eight hours has passed since the showdown with Dimitri. I've tried chatting to Gran but she doesn't seem to want to be drawn on it and I still haven't summoned up the courage to tell her about the bones. She isn't herself, which is worrying me. I managed to talk to her GP over the phone, and he said I should bring her in and have her checked out. However, Gran dismisses any suggestions I make. What can I do?

Dad isn't ready to see her yet, understandably, but eventually Dad, or more likely Tara and me, will have to tell her about the baby and what happened with Mum. I'm quite sure Gran would have been horrified she wasn't told any of this when it had happened all those years ago. I can understand why Dad wouldn't have said anything to her though. That would have been the last thing Mum would have wanted. Gran did always say she was very private, and I couldn't help sense she disapproved of that particular personality trait in Mum. Mind you, I'm sure Gran has plenty of her own secrets which she chooses not to divulge to all and sundry. She *never* speaks about her late husband, and even when we asked about him when we were growing up, she said it was too difficult to talk about.

On more than one occasion I've found Gran upstairs sitting on the window seat in her bedroom, staring out to sea. Even when I'd gently called her name a few times, she was completely lost in her thoughts. I knew a woman of my age couldn't expect her grandmother to give her all the answers or tell her what to do. I knew I had to decide for myself and the answers were inside me. Tara had tentatively asked me whether I was going to talk to Jason. The only bit of information she could tell me was he was apparently mortified he'd lost his temper and whacked Dimitri.

I sit on my bed, wondering where I will end up next. Staying here, with Gran, is only a short-term solution and I need to go back to Teddington eventually. I can't hide here for ever. Sitting with my knees bent, I lean my head back against the wall and close my eyes. Taking a moment, I breathe in for four counts, hold for four counts, then breathe out and repeat this several times. Opening my eyes, everything is suddenly clearer. I pick up my phone and quickly type a text.

A couple of hours later, I'm outside the Seabird Centre watching and waiting. Mums and grandparents with kids stroll past, holidaymakers stop to take photographs of the view and I glance over at the few brave paddlers on the beach. I hope he hasn't changed his mind, and look down at my phone. No new messages. Turning around, I lean over the railings and watch the birds diving into the sea and skimming its surface. It has turned into a warm afternoon and the sky is a bright blue, but the cool breeze makes me shiver and I'm glad I've worn a cardigan.

Feeling a hand on my shoulder, I turn to find Jason behind me.

'Hi,' he says tentatively.

'Hi. Erm, thanks for coming,' I say, sounding like an awkward teenager.

He points to the beach. 'Shall we walk and talk?'

'Good idea.' Relief sweeps through me as I realise how much easier it will be to talk to him without having to maintain eye contact.

'How are you?' he asks.

'Okay.' I shrug. 'It's been a bit of a strange few days. Or strange few weeks, I should say.' I attempt a laugh.

He coughs to clear his throat. 'Mark told me what happened with Dimitri. I'm sorry.'

'Oh . . . don't be.' The sun is pleasant on my face, and it actually feels okay to be walking along with him. Though we're dawdling rather than marching, this is comforting. It means he isn't in a rush to get this over and done with.

'He sounds like a nasty piece of work and I'm sorry.'

I wave my hand dismissively. 'You have nothing to be sorry about. None of this is your fault . . .' I take a gulp of air. 'I'm mortified you found out in that way. That was never my intention, and he had no right to say anything to you.' We continue in silence for a few minutes. The only sounds are the water lapping the sand and our feet crunching on shells. 'I didn't tell you because you'd gone back to Sydney. I was in shock, and I wasn't quite sure what to do.'

'Josie, I don't quite know what I would have done either if you had told me. I would have been shocked, for sure. Would I have come back?' He shakes his head. 'I was so much younger and I had a life over there.'

'You don't have to explain what you would have done hypothetically speaking,' I say. 'There's no point.'

'But maybe I would have. I missed you . . .'

'Oh.' I was *not* expecting that.

'You didn't reply to any of my letters.'

'Letters? What letters?' I say, confused.

'I wrote quite a few times but never had any response.'

I shake my head. 'I never got any of your letters. Where did you send them?'

'To your gran's house.'

'But she never gave me any letters,' I say, confused.

He places a reassuring hand on my arm. 'I'm sorry. I don't know what happened. But I promise you, Josie, I did write to you.'

Wiping away the tears with my sleeve, I oscillate between sadness, confusion and regret. Why hadn't Gran passed on his letters? He must have felt so hurt and humiliated when I didn't reply and to hear about the miscarriage from Dimitri. 'I'm so sorry for all of this, Jason.'

'None of what happened was your fault,' he says, his voice quiet and soothing. 'These things happen, Josie.'

'What made you so wise?'

'People change. My granny always used to say things happened to you at the right time. *What's for you won't go by you, son.*'

'True,' I say. 'Gran says that too.' We continue walking in silence. 'Hopefully we're older and wiser now.'

'I'm sorry you had to go through that, and you didn't think I cared.'

'It was awful,' I admit. 'It was all such a shock — the pregnancy and coming to terms with it and wondering what to do. Then the miscarriage and not telling anyone what had happened . . . well, that is until I met Dimitri.' I think about how vulnerable I must have been and how I perceived his attention as kindness when actually he had taken advantage of me.

'And is that why you couldn't have children with him?' he asks, his voice cautious.

'No. It's easier for him to blame someone rather than himself. We'd been having IVF treatment for quite a while. Every round was unsuccessful, and I was actually starting to question what we were doing. It was horrible and made me feel like crap. Meanwhile, Dimitri was *entertaining* our neighbour.'

222

'I'm sorry. You didn't deserve that.'

'Well, your granny was right. It must have happened for the right reason. I'm actually glad the IVF didn't work and I'm glad I woke up and realised what a shit he was.' We had reached the end of the beach and took the path up towards the golf course. 'I can't tell you how relieved I am to think I'm free of him.'

'And what will you do next?'

Shrugging, I laugh. 'I'm not quite sure. I guess take one day at a time.' We amble along, side by side, any awkwardness now gone. 'How about you?'

'What do you mean?'

'Do you think you're back for good or will you go back to Sydney?'

He frowns. 'No, I won't go back there.'

'Don't you miss it?'

Taking a sharp breath, he says, 'Yes and no. I had a life there and I enjoyed it . . . but it was time to come back.'

'I'm assuming that you settled down,' I say, pointing at his ring.

He stops in his tracks. Turning, I'm shocked when I see the pained expression on his face.

'What is it?' I say, trying to quell the panic in my voice. 'Did I say something wrong?'

'No, Josie. It's me. I'm not used to people asking me personal questions. I tend to keep myself to myself these days.'

Tilting my head to the side, I wonder what on earth is wrong. I'm about to speak when he takes a step towards me.

'It's . . . well, yes, I was married. But my wife . . . well, she . . .'

God, he's going to tell me she had an affair too, like Dimitri. What is it with people? As I stand there looking at him, his dark eyes locked on mine, I wonder how anyone could be unfaithful to him. He's pretty much perfect.

'My wife died.'

'Oh.'

Neither of us speak, and although I'm desperate to say something wise and comforting, I have no words.

'It's okay,' he says. 'I mean, I haven't told many people this. Well, obviously they know my wife died. But they don't know what happened. Usually when I say I'm widowed, that's enough for people. They change the subject and make their own assumptions.'

'I'm so sorry,' I say, wondering why Mark and Tara have never said anything to me.

'Mark and Tara respect my privacy and they're not even aware of the whole story . . .'

'It's okay,' I say, tightening my cardigan around my shoulders. 'You don't have to tell me either.'

Confusion flits across his face. 'I don't *have* to, but I want to tell you, Josie. There are not many people I can talk to anymore or want to talk to.'

'Okay,' I say, reaching to squeeze his shoulder. 'If it would help, tell me.'

'My wife died a couple of years ago. She was . . . she was murdered.'

CHAPTER FIFTY-SEVEN

A chill ran down the nape of my neck as I walked towards her. She had aged. Her hair was lank and tinged with grey and her skin sallow.

'Hello,' I said, awkwardly.

'Hello, Mary.'

There was something in her tone that I didn't like. It was barbed, edged with menace. Though I couldn't blame her.

'How did you find me?' I asked.

She laughed. 'Is that it? No "How are you?" No "How nice to see you, Nancy"?'

She was right. I was so shocked I didn't know what to say. Despite having had plenty of time to prepare.

Her eyes stared past me towards the house. 'You've done all right for yourself, haven't you?'

'I . . . guess . . .'

'Yes, you have,' she said.

'What happened?' I said quietly. 'What happened that day when I left? You said it was self-defence.'

'Pah. Well, turns out they didn't believe me. The police turned up not long after you left. They cuffed me straight away. Even when I said he had been beating me for years.' She reached into her bag to pull out a pack of cigarettes. She lit one and greedily sucked in the nicotine. Exhaling the smoke in small circles which floated above her head, she

225

walked down towards the bottom of the garden and leaned against the small wall by the hammock.

I followed her vaguely, thinking how easy it was to fall back into my role, always doing as I was told.

'The police weren't interested. They just wanted me locked up for killing him.'

'But why?'

She looked at me as if I was pathetic. 'Because they didn't care. Apparently, it's okay for a man to beat his wife black and blue, but if she tries to defend herself, that's a different matter.'

CHAPTER FIFTY-EIGHT

Tara

I take the train into Edinburgh, watching as we speed past golden fields, and the sky changes from pale to deep blue as we near the city. Closing my eyes, I wonder how different I might feel on the return journey. Isn't there a saying that a brush with death makes you appreciate and notice your surroundings a bit more? I will certainly try my best to do that from now on, regardless of the outcome. I check my phone *again* in case Mum has replied to my message, but there's nothing. I can tell she's read it, and I long to see the three grey dots moving about like a Mexican wave. But the box remains blank. Perhaps I shouldn't have said anything about the baby to her. Was telling her I knew a step too far?

I've told Mark I'm in Edinburgh to meet an old friend for a coffee and have organised for Josie to collect the twins from nursery. She doesn't think to question my plans at all. Why would she? As far as she's concerned, I don't tell lies. The train terminates at Waverley Station and I step off onto the platform, following the passengers up the steps to Princes Street. Watching the Cockapoo ahead of me with its owner, I can't help but smile. Its tongue is hanging out, which makes it look as though it's grinning. I have about an hour until my appointment. I had planned to take the bus along to the Western General, where the breast clinic is located. However, it's a nice day and I don't want to be cooped up on a bus with loads of other people, so I decide to walk. A quick check on Google Maps shows it will take me about forty-five minutes. Moving will keep me distracted; better that than sitting for ages in a waiting room with an out-of-date celebrity magazine filled with pages of people I've never heard of. I start heading along Princes Street, admiring the gardens to my left and the castle perched above. It's fairly quiet, which is pleasant because as of next month the city will soon be rammed with tourists and turn into a no-go area for people like me.

I cross over and keep walking down and across the bridge at Water of Leith. My heart rate has now sped up and a line of sweat gathers at the base of my spine. I'm going to end up at the hospital out of breath and with sweat patches on my clothes. I slow my pace slightly when I realise I still have twenty minutes until the appointment. Following the signs for the Breast Unit, I walk slowly, hoping I won't see anyone I recognise. It's very busy, which I find disconcerting. Until today's appointment, my daily life has been going on as normal, and I have no idea of the stress so many other people face. Spotting the signs for the Ladies, I duck in and sit for a minute catching a sob in the back of my throat. I pick up my bag and stand by the sink. That's when I really examine myself in the mirror. Why on earth do I find it so hard to ask for help? I mean, I'm quite happy to accept practical offers of help from Dad and Gran and Jessica's mum, Sharon. But I never want to burden anyone with my problems or worries. Even my own partner. Mark would be so sad if he knew I was doing this alone, and that makes me feel awful. I stare at my pale reflection in the mirror and vow to tell him everything when I get home.

I make my way through the maze of cream-coloured corridors until I see the blue lettering of the Breast Clinic and the automatic doors open. Standing on the threshold, I hesitate, knowing as soon as I go in I will find out one way or the other. The woman at the reception looks up and smiles at me, but I can only manage a grimace. I walk over to the desk.

'Hello. What's your name?' she asks. According to her name badge, pinned above her right breast, hers is Annetta.

'Um, Tara,' I manage, as I pull the letter from my bag.

'Thank you,' she says, in a clipped Polish accent. 'Take a seat in the waiting room and the radiographer will call you when ready.'

Thanking her, I stuff the letter back into my bag and walk towards the waiting room. There are several people sitting there, heads bowed as they flick through magazines. One woman clutches her husband's hand. Another young girl sits with her mother. I sit down alone in a corner and wish I had brought Mark with me for the moral support. I pick up a magazine and flick through articles on how I should make the perfect cake or decorate the ideal snug in my house. Rapidly turning through the pages, the words blur and I can only just about focus on the photos. My mouth is dry, and I jump every time the door opens and a name is called.

A young girl of fifteen or sixteen leaves the room with whom I assume is her mother, and I think of Millie being here at such a young age and how awful that would be. Her mother's face is white as she holds the door open for her daughter. I watch as the woman gripping her husband's hand unfurls her fingers from his and gingerly stands up. She walks slowly towards the door, looking back at him for reassurance. Time passes slowly as I wait for my name to be called and when it is, I almost don't realise. Then it's my turn to make the lonely walk across the vinyl floor, my eyes focused straight ahead, and I think actually I *should* have brought Mark with me. At least after this bit, he would be waiting for me with a reassuring smile or a hug. I'm not sure I'm strong enough to do this bit alone, but I've left myself with no choice.

'Hi, Tara, how are you?' The radiographer gives me a reassuring smile. 'I'm Nel and I'll be looking after you today. Try not to worry, my love. I know it's easier said than done.

But it's all straightforward and hopefully we'll find out what's happening.'

Hopefully? What does she mean hopefully? Not definitely? I need to focus my mind and so focus on Nel's reassuring dimples and her nose stud. 'Did that hurt?' I ask, trying to make light of a situation which can't be made light of.

'Not a bit,' she says, laughing. 'But the one I had done on my belly did.'

I smile at her.

'Now, have you had this done before?'

I shake my head, clasping my hands together tightly.

'Okay, well, what I'm going to do is take two x-rays of each breast. Now, this bit may be a wee bit uncomfortable. But if we can do it properly it will only last for a few seconds or so.'

'O-Okay,' I stutter.

She points to the chair where I can leave my things and pulls a curtain over to give me some privacy, which is pointless given I'm about to expose myself. I take my top and bra off, gently folding them and placing them on the chair. Then I wait, awkwardly, not knowing whether to cross my arms in front of me or stand with them swinging by my side as though this is all normal. Nel helps me to position my breasts between what are like two metal bricks. She's right, it is uncomfortable.

'Are you okay?' asks Nel, noticing me wince.

I nod, trying to blink away the tears on the rim of my eyes.

'Some people find the pressure a tad sore. I'm sorry.'

'That's okay,' I say, biting my lip. 'The doctor thinks it's maybe a blocked milk duct. I've got twins though they're four now and I stopped breastfeeding years ago.' I reckon if I can keep talking that will keep my mind off things and stop the tears.

'Twins. Crikey. Well done you. What are their names?'

'Millie and Oliver.'

'Lovely names,' says Nel.

230

'Thank you. Even though they're twins, they're so different from each other.'

Her brow is furrowed. She doesn't speak but focuses ahead.

'Sorry, Tara, I need to concentrate for a minute. Don't worry, I'm just not great at talking at this point — multi-tasking is all too much for my brain.'

I wish she would hurry up.

'That's it, all done,' she says. 'Told you we would have you sorted in a jiffy.'

Smiling gratefully at her as she moves the clamps away, I thank her and turn to change.

'Okay, Tara,' she says kindly when I reappear through the curtain. 'The images will be looked at by my colleague.'

'Oh,' I say. 'How long will that take?'

'Hopefully not too long. You head back to the waiting room and wait for the consultant to call you back in.'

'Okay.' I'm desperately trying to scan her face in case she gives anything away. But her expression remains neutral. 'Try not to worry.'

As I take a seat, the same one as before, in the waiting room, I try not to stare at the woman in the corner who's sobbing. Shit. This is so surreal. And soon I'll be told what's wrong with me. I dip my head and stare at the ground.

CHAPTER FIFTY-NINE

Josie

'What happened?' I whisper, staring at him.

'She was stabbed to death. She had gone to the shops near to our house . . . we needed milk and I was going to go but she insisted she needed some air.' He gestures to the path ahead which takes us through the woods and alongside the park.

I hesitate. 'Are you sure?'

'Yes, it's probably easier to keep moving as I tell you this.'

'What happened?'

'She got to the shop and was about to go in when she saw a young guy in distress. She stopped to check he was okay and he stabbed her. Just like that.' He falters. 'If only I had gone . . .'

'What happened though? Why did he target her?'

'It was a young guy with mental health issues. Anna was in the wrong place at the wrong time.'

'I'm so sorry, Jason. I had no idea.'

'Why would you though? I haven't seen you for years and, well, it's not something I talk about. I did to begin with, especially when I told people I was widowed. They asked me how she died and I told them. Probably too bluntly. But I was left dealing with their shock and tears.'

'I can understand why you stopped telling people. God, I can't imagine.'

'Yes. It never gets any easier, to be honest. That's why I try and avoid it altogether. It's like a festering wound though, always there.'

'How long ago did it happen?'

'Three years. I tried to get on with life. I did. But it was too hard. I can't help thinking if I had gone to get the bloody milk Anna would still be here.'

'Is that why you came back?'

He nods as we cross the bridge, stopping for a minute to look at the babbling brook. 'Yes. I didn't feel I belonged there anymore. Everywhere reminded me of her and all our memories together. I felt rootless and so lost.'

'And does it feel any better being back here? Has it helped?'

'Being busy has helped and having a different focus has been good for me. But it's still there, the pain is always lurking . . .' He starts to walk again and I follow, smiling at a young family walking past.

'Did they catch the guy?'

'Yes, straight away,' he says. 'I don't quite know if it helped or not. I mean, he was obviously not right in the head. That was the irony. Anna was so kind and empathetic. She was always trying to help people.'

I don't know how to respond. As we walk together and follow the path back down towards the beach, I thank him for being so open.

'I appreciate you telling me, Jason, and I won't tell a soul,' I say.

'Thanks, Josie. Telling you felt like the right thing to do.'

As we reach the Seabird Centre, I reach up and hug him. 'I'm so sorry this happened and I'm sorry you lost Anna. If you ever want to talk, I'm here.'

'Thanks. You never know what people have gone through, do you? That could be said for all of us.'

'True.'

He looks at his watch. 'I'd better get back to the restaurant. Mark will think I've gone AWOL. Thanks for listening.'

I smile. 'Any time.'

As his eyes linger on me for a moment, I sense my heart skip a beat. He's looking at me in a way that makes me think that he's feeling *something* too. And it's not just gratitude for being a good listener.

'It's been good talking to you, Josie and, well, maybe we could catch up again and talk about other things? Feels like it's been a bit doom and gloom,' he says with a self-deprecating laugh.

'I would like that,' I say, knowing that I'm blushing.

'Great,' he says and smiles. 'See you soon.'

As I watch him walk away, I have to sit down on the bench to collect my thoughts and take a breath as I think about the effect he's having on me. Then I think about what he's been through. Bloody hell. I thought I was having a tricky time, but what I've gone through is nothing compared to poor Jason.

The alarm on my phone goes off, a reminder that it will soon be time to collect the twins from nursery. Tara said she had an errand to run in Edinburgh and was meeting a friend for coffee. I know she's lying and there's more to it. But what can I do? There's no way I can challenge her on it. Anyway, Jason is right, none of us truly knows what anyone else has been through or what is on their mind. Although I do have a fair idea in Tara's case. I'll have to wait for her to tell me in her own time.

CHAPTER SIXTY

'Why didn't you call me? Why didn't you help?' Her eyes were cold and accusing. 'Ten years I was in prison. Ten bloody years of my life I won't get back.'

I stumbled backwards. 'I . . . I'm sorry. I didn't know. I didn't know what to do. I tried ringing you . . . but nobody was ever there.'

'You didn't try hard enough though, did you? You just left me there to clean up the mess. Your mess,' she said coldly.

'But you told me to go. You told me to leave while I could. You practically pushed me out the door and told me to get away as far as possible.'

'I didn't think I'd end up in prison though. For something you did.'

My heart was beating fast and my throat was tight. It was as if we were back there that day. I heard her words ringing in my ears. Just go as far away from here as you can and don't look back. You need to think of the future. *I didn't know what to say because she was right. I was a coward for running away that day and leaving her to pick up the pieces as usual. But she told me to go, said it was the best thing for me and the baby.*

235

CHAPTER SIXTY-ONE

Tara

The consultant says it's a benign hormonal condition. The lump in my chest is not cancer.

'Are you sure?' I say, stunned.

'Yes. It's noncancerous,' she says, smiling reassuringly.

Relief whooshes through me. 'Why is it there?'

'Well, as I'm sure you know, breasts come in all shapes and sizes. There's fatty tissue and glandular tissue, the tissue which produces milk when you're breastfeeding.' She glances back at her notes. 'You had twins and breastfed them?'

'Yes,' I say. 'For six months.'

'Sometimes milk ducts can become blocked when you breastfeed. Sometimes hormones can make your breasts feel lumpy. There are a variety of reasons which can cause benign lumps. But you did the absolute right thing by getting in touch with your doctor, especially as you said you hadn't noticed it before.' Clasping her hands together, she leans towards me. 'If you lean forward over a sink and look at your reflection in the mirror, you can sometimes find dimpling or puckering of the skin. That is something to be aware of. Or if a lump is very painful. But as I say to all my patients, it's

236

always better to be safe than sorry. That's what we are here for.'

I'm not sure whether to laugh or cry with relief. 'I was so sure I had cancer.'

She nods. 'I think that's quite natural. We all tend to assume the worst. But actually, most lumps we see prove to be benign.'

'What should I do now?'

'Nothing at all.'

'But will it go away?'

'Hopefully . . . although can I check what contraception you're taking?' She looks back at my file and scans the notes.

'I have the implant in my arm.'

'Ah, okay. That makes sense. That might be what caused it.'

'Really?'

She nods her head. 'It's not a common side effect but you wouldn't be the first case I've seen.'

'Should I have the implant removed?'

'That's up to you, Tara.'

I immediately want to claw it out of my arm and resolve to contact the surgery as soon as I get home. If hormones are creating lumps in my system and causing me this amount of stress, then I want it out. Mark can go for the snip. Thanking the doctor, I walk out of the room and float along the corridor like a lead weight has been removed from my whole body. Relief and adrenaline are still coursing through me and I want to scream and shout to everyone I'm fine. But I check myself. Not everyone will have good news and I need to be mindful of that. I'm one of the lucky ones.

When I arrive back at Waverley Station, I have some time to wait until my next train and so I sit in a coffee shop nursing a coffee and eating a muffin. Every mouthful tastes delicious. I couldn't eat breakfast this morning as I felt so sick with nerves, and since I found the lump I had lost my appetite. This is a sign things are on the up. I don't have cancer, Dad is okay after his heart attack and we know why the bones were buried in the garden. Josie is away from that prick of a husband and hopefully Gran is just going through a wee blip. We need to celebrate the positive things in life and appreciate every minute we can with each other. I vow to make more of an effort to spend time with Dad. I'll be more honest with Mark and ask for his support in the future. I'm so lucky, and this scare has given me a real jolt. I send him a quick text telling him I love him and can't wait to see him. When I realise I have ten minutes to go until my train leaves, I go to M&S to buy a bottle of champagne. I may as well start celebrating tonight.

As I stand waiting in the queue for the self-service till, I spot Sharon paying. She looks as though she's been on a bit of a shopping mission, given the pile of bags at her feet. Calling out to her, she glances up and when she sees me her face flushes. Strange, I think. I wonder if everything is okay. She bends to pick up her bags. Assuming she will wait for me, I quickly pay for the champagne and stuff it inside my handbag. Then I go outside to find her. Looking around, there's no sign of her anywhere. Wondering if she's anxious about catching the train, I head over to the platform, where I see her showing her ticket to an inspector. She's walking briskly even though there are still a few minutes before the train departs, and heads to the top of the train and steps onto the first carriage. She doesn't look back. I'm confused as to why she's been so rude. Unless she wants to sit and read her book alone without feeling she has to chat to anyone on the journey home. But all she had to do was say hello. I certainly am not going to chase her and insist she talk to me, so I walk further to a different carriage and sit down.

My phone buzzes.

Love you too. M x

I smile and focus on the fuzzy feel-good factor from earlier. Thinking about the champagne, I wonder if we could even have it outside in the garden later. It's been a lovely afternoon apart from the slight breeze, and our garden is nicely sheltered. Hopefully now things have been resolved with the builders' discovery, we can ask them back in to carry on with their work.

Smiling, I reply to a couple of texts and check on emails as the train pulls out of Waverley, then I shut my eyes. I must have dozed off as when I open them, we're a minute or two away from arriving at North Berwick. Deciding to check my messages one last time, I click on Messenger to see the three grey dots at Mum's icon moving. She's in the middle of composing her reply.

CHAPTER SIXTY-TWO

Josie

Tara will be home any minute and I hope she's okay. Millie and Oliver and I have baked her a cake and they've covered it with chocolate buttons. They're now slightly hyper since more of the buttons went in their mouths than on the cake. But Tara doesn't need to know that.

'When will the builders come back?' says Oli, when I suggest he play football in the garden as long as it's away from the foundations.

'Soon hopefully, then you can crack on with plans for your den.'

Millie has started sucking her thumb and watches us intently for a minute. Pulling her thumb from her mouth, she says, 'Why did the builders stop?'

Shit. I was hoping Tara and Mark had covered this with them. 'Um, well, sometimes builders need to stop to have a rest.'

Millie eyes me suspiciously. 'But why do they need a rest?'

'They need a holiday like the rest of us.'

'Are you here on holiday, Auntie Josie?' says Oli.

'Kind of,' I say, feeling as though I'm being interrogated by someone from Scotland Yard.

'Will you go back to London?' asks Millie.

'Maybe. I don't quite know yet.' Crikey, where is Tara? I hope she won't be too long.

'What about your house and your things? You'll need to go and fetch them.'

I nod.

'And what about that man?'

'Dimitri?'

'Yes. We don't like him.'

'Millie . . . stop being rude,' says Oli sternly.

'Don't worry. I won't be seeing him again. He's not very nice.'

'Why did you marry him? Daddy says you should only marry someone nice.'

'Is that why he and Mummy aren't married? Doesn't he think she's very nice?' asks Oli. His bottom lip starts to tremble, and he looks at me for reassurance.

This needs an intervention. 'Your Daddy is absolutely right. You should only ever marry *or* live with someone you love. And you don't have to get married. You can also still love someone and have a family with them without being married.'

'That's right. He said that to us too.'

Oliver smiles, everything seemingly all right in his world again. How I long for life to be simple.

'Mummy!' squeals Millie. 'She's back!'

Oh, thank God. Tara is smiling and runs towards Millie and Oliver, scooping them up for a cuddle. 'Hello, gorgeous little people. Have you been good for Auntie Josie?'

'Yes and we baked you a chocolate cake!' blurts Oliver.

'Ssh! That was supposed to be a surprise,' Millie says crossly.

'Oops.'

Tara laughs. 'How have they been?'

'Angels,' I say. 'And Oli is right, they have been busy making you a cake.'

'Wow, how lovely,' she says. 'Shall we go and fetch some?'

'Yes!' they both shout and run inside.

'Wash your hands, please!' Tara shouts after them.

'How was town?'

'Good, thanks,' she says, her eyes shining. 'In fact, bloody great. And hopefully things can only get better now.'

'I hope so, Tara, I really do. It would be nice to have a bit of a quiet life for a while after the last few weeks. Although we still need to talk to Gran.'

'Let's do it tomorrow. And tonight, let's focus on the positive things. Look, I picked up a bottle of fizz on the way home. Let me just go and get some glasses. Mark said he'll be home soon as Jason is covering things tonight.'

Pulling my phone from my pocket, I start to type a message and change my mind. Tara comes out clutching two champagne flutes and I delete it and put the phone away.

It's time for us all to move forward.

CHAPTER SIXTY-THREE

'What was prison like?' I asked.

'What do you think?' she said, her eyes flashing with menace. 'Not exactly a picnic. It certainly wasn't the way I was expecting to spend my twenties . . .' She paused and took another drag of her cigarette. 'But there were plenty of women like me. Women who had killed in self-defence but ended up in jail.'

'How did you get out?'

She shrugged. 'A good lawyer took pity on some of us and has been working through the cases. Got my conviction overturned.'

'Oh. That's . . . that's good.' Even as I uttered the words I wanted to claw them back.

'Good,' she sneered. 'Yes. Good, or something like that.'

'But I don't understand. How did you find me?'

She tapped her nose and shrugged. 'Contacts.' She flicked her gaze around the garden again, noting the swing and the toys on the lawn. 'So, the baby? How is he or she? Must be about ten now?'

I stared back at her, trying to choke back a sob.

'What did you have? I'm desperate to meet my niece or nephew.'

I felt sick. 'Um . . . the baby . . . there is no baby.'

CHAPTER SIXTY-FOUR

Tara

I'm topping up Josie's glass and about to tell her about the good news at the hospital, when I hear a car pull into the driveway.

'That must be Mark. I'll go and fetch him a glass and check the kids haven't devoured the cake completely,' says Josie.

'Sure.' I smile and take another sip from my glass. I sit back for a moment and enjoy the feeling of being relaxed. I want to share it with Mark. I walk round to the front to greet him but am stopped in my tracks. What on earth is happening now?

'Josie!' I shout when I see who has arrived. 'It's Sam and Brian.'

Josie is by my side in seconds. 'Is everything okay?'

We both look at them with concern. Brian scratches at his chin. 'There's been a bit of a development we need to talk to you about.'

'A development? What do you mean?'

'The bones in the garden,' says Sam.

'Uh-huh, you know who they belong to.'

'Yes, well, we have an issue,' says Brian. 'Can we sit down?'

Just then Mark does arrive, and his face is etched with worry when he walks over to us. 'What's the matter now?'

'There seems to be a problem.'

'What with?' asks Mark.

'We need to speak to Tara and Josie. Maybe you could keep the kids occupied?' says Brian, tilting his head to the window.

Millie and Oliver stare out at us. Waving at them, I say, 'Okay then. Mark?'

'Sure, I'll sort the kids. Shout though if you need me.'

'Are you happy sitting out here?' I say, leading them round to the table and chairs by the patio.

'That's fine . . . sorry,' he says when he spots the wine cooler. 'Are we interrupting a celebration?'

'Kind of, but it's obviously short-lived. I can tell you have something serious to discuss. This doesn't seem like a friendly social call.'

Raising my eyebrow at Josie, I gesture for everyone to sit down.

'This is not really protocol, Tara. But given our personal connection and the fact that your circumstances have been a bit tricky of late . . . well, I thought this was the best way to break this to you.'

'Break what?' I say, my heart now starting to thud faster. Is this why Sharon had avoided me at the station earlier? Does she know what this is about?

'What is it?' says Josie, her voice bolder and more confident than mine.

Sam leans forward, stepping in for Brian, who is clearly struggling for words. I wonder if he's ever been responsible for such a big case. North Berwick isn't exactly known for its high crime rates.

'There's been a development with the discovery in your garden,' she says. 'While we don't disagree with anything that your dad said the other day, we believe there's more to this.'

'What do you mean?' asks Josie.

245

'I mean that we're not just talking about the discovery of a premature baby's remains.'

'I don't understand,' I say, the blood now rushing to my head. 'What are you talking about? Please can you get to the point?'

'Okay,' she says, steepling her hands together and speaking slowly. 'The builders discovered bones in your garden and our forensic teams took them away for analysis.'

I wait for her to continue.

'They believe that some of the bones do belong to a premature baby, which has been verified by your father. However there were more bones, bigger bones.'

'What?' whispers Josie.

'You mean someone else was buried there too?'

'Yes,' says Sam.

Brian tries to kind of smile at me, but grimaces instead. 'I'm sorry to have to tell you this, girls . . .' He looks gravely between us both.

What is he going to say now?

'We have good reason to believe that the bones belong to your mother.'

CHAPTER SIXTY-FIVE

Josie

'How could it be Mum? That's absurd!' shouts Tara.

I'm surprised at the venomous tone in her voice. 'There's no way it can be her. You've made a mistake,' I say, rising to my feet and knocking the flutes to the ground. They immediately smash, and I crouch down to pick up the pieces.

'Oh dear. Leave it for the moment,' says Sam.

'No!' I shout. 'The kids might cut themselves.'

'How can it be Mum? It can't be Mum,' says Tara in disbelief.

'I'm so sorry to have to be the bearer of bad news. But we have every reason to believe the body is your mother.'

'But it can't be,' I say. 'She sent us birthday cards every year.' I stare at Sam, willing her to say something, and when she doesn't, I want to hit her.

'She sent us birthday cards every year,' repeats Tara. 'How could she have done that if she was dead and buried in the garden?'

'You said the cards stopped?'

'Yes,' I say. 'When we were twenty-one.'

Brian shrugs. 'Maybe someone else sent them? A well-meaning friend or relative?'

'No. No! Who would do that? And why?' Tara jumps up from her seat and stands on a piece of the glass. 'Ouch!' She starts to cry.

Mark runs out. 'What's the matter. Is everything okay?'

'I've cut my foot,' says Tara, pointing at the blood dripping from her toe.

'Okay, love,' he says, walking over to her. 'Don't worry, I'll go and get a plaster and something to clear this glass up with.' He looks at me questioningly but what can I say? How can I tell him when I can't even begin to get my head around it myself? My mother is dead? *Dead?*

'I don't believe you,' Tara says, sitting back in the chair and holding her foot. 'I think you've got it all wrong. You should make sure you do all the proper tests before you start making wild accusations.'

The blood drips onto the patio and I hope Mark hurries up. He appears with some tissues and a bandage and gently tends to Tara's foot before sweeping up the rest of the glass.

'The kids?' asks Tara.

'They're fine. They have cake and the TV is on.' He puts a hand on her shoulder. 'Is everything okay? You're so pale, Tara. You look as though you've seen a ghost. Do you want to tell me what's going on?'

Tara nods, but the tears are now sliding down her face, so I step in. 'The police have found other bones.'

'Other bones?'

'Yes, in addition to the ones belonging to Jonathan.'

He stands up straight, looking confused. 'And who do they belong to?'

'That's the thing,' I say. 'They're saying they belong to our mother.'

'Bloody hell. But how?'

'We don't know,' says Tara quietly. 'We have no idea. Until a minute ago we thought she was alive.'

'What happens now?' says Mark, looking at Sam and Brian.

'We came to give you a heads-up . . .'

'A heads-up?' says Mark.

Brian nods. 'Yes . . .'

'There's more?' I ask, quietly.

'Yes,' says Sam. 'Given your dad's recent health scare, we thought it would make sense for you to accompany us to his house.'

'But why? Wouldn't it be easier if Tara and I went and told him ourselves?' I feel a twist of sorrow at the further pain I know Dad will have to endure when he hears the news about Mum. This could potentially be the last straw for him. He will be utterly devastated if we tell him, after all these years, she's actually dead.

Sam clears her throat. 'That's the thing. We need to be with you.'

'I don't understand,' I say, looking at Tara. 'Do you?'

'No. Please let us tell him ourselves, privately. This will not be good for his heart.'

'Unfortunately, that's not an option,' says Brian. 'We have to be there . . .'

'Why?' I ask, confused.

Sam has clearly lost patience with her colleague because she abruptly answers. 'Because we need to take him in for questioning. We think your mother might have been murdered.'

CHAPTER SIXTY-SIX

'What?' she said in disbelief. 'There's no baby? What do you mean?' Her voice was edged with threat again and as she moved closer to me, I edged back.

'Did you lie to me?'

'What do you mean?'

'Did you lie to me about the baby?'

'No!' I shouted. 'Why would I lie about being pregnant?'

She shook her head and narrowed her eyes. 'Because it let you get away.'

I felt my pulse racing and I wanted to vomit. 'How can you say such an awful thing?'

'Quite easily,' she said, her hands now on her hips. 'I've had more than enough time to think about things, you know. Do you have any idea what it's like to be locked up? Not knowing when you'll be free to live again. I've had plenty of time to ponder on why you never got in touch. Hours and hours spent sobbing in my cell. I couldn't understand why you left me to rot.'

'The baby died. I lost him . . .' The guilt started to wash over me. I pictured her alone in a small cell with a narrow bed. Suddenly it was like we were back in the flat that day all over again. I could hear her promising that everything would be okay. Urging me to run. She said I had to leave for the sake of the baby. That she would sort it all. Just *like she always had. Over the years I had somehow managed to block things out and convince myself that I hadn't done anything wrong. If I hadn't killed him then he would have killed me.*

But what sort of person was I to leave my own sister to pick up the pieces?

CHAPTER SIXTY-SEVEN

Tara

The next few days seem to pass in a blur. Dad is taken in for questioning and released pending further enquiries. He looks completely broken and haunted by this latest development and keeps insisting he has no idea what the police are talking about. He's been waiting all these years for Mum to return. Why would he have killed her and buried her in the garden?

The thought Mum has been so near to us all shocks me so much, I feel paralysed. I can't believe it's her though. Who sent us all of those birthday cards? And *who* has been messaging me? Who else could have done that? Someone well-meaning or someone very sick? I refuse to believe she's been dead and buried under our garage all these years. But the police insist it is her and Dad stresses he knows nothing. Someone must.

I can't help thinking about the day I found the jewellery in his drawer. Why does he have that and why has he never told us? Is it feasible he could have killed her and kept the jewellery as some kind of trophy? I think of Dad and his gentle demeanour, and I shudder when I remember all the times I left the kids with him. They keep asking if they can go and visit and I keep making excuses. I don't want them anywhere near him.

What if my father *is* a killer? It's always the people you least suspect, and being a church minister is the perfect cover for him. I don't understand why he would kill her though and pretend she's still alive. Unless he's completely deluded? And why does he keep insisting he knew nothing about it?

Josie is as shocked as I am and has her hands full dealing with Gran. She's managed to tell her about Jonathan's bones in the garden, which she seems to have accepted. However, we can't yet bring ourselves to tell her about Mum's body or Dad's arrest.

'She's sleeping a lot,' says Josie, when she calls to give me an update. 'A lot more than usual. I don't see the point in adding to her anxiety just now. At least not until we have the facts.'

'Do you think we'll ever have the facts though?' I say quietly. 'We'll only know what happened when there's a confession.'

'I don't believe Dad would do such a thing.'

'Did you ever for a minute think Mum was dead?'

She pauses. 'No, Tara, I didn't. I mean, over the last couple of years I've wondered if she could still be alive. But I assumed she was living a full life elsewhere and life here was too much for her.'

'We were too much?' I whisper.

'No,' she says firmly. 'We weren't too much. But we don't know what else was going on in the background, or what had happened to her before. Remember she ran away from something once before — when she came here.'

'That's true.' I pause. 'Does anyone ever know the truth about anything?'

'What about Dad? Are you going to see him? He keeps asking after you and is getting quite agitated.'

Sighing, I say, 'I will, but I can't get my head around it all.'

'You don't really think he had anything to do with it?'

I don't reply immediately.

'Tara . . . think about the man who disappeared down south and his body was found in the back garden . . .'

'What had happened to him?'

'His son had killed him.'

'What, and nobody knew?'

'No. He told people his dad had moved abroad, and because they were a quiet family nobody thought to question it. Then apparently the son walked into the police station one day and he was arrested.'

'That's bonkers, Josie.'

'Not really. His conscience obviously got the better of him. What I'm saying is, Dad is a man of the church. Do you think he would have been able to live with this lie all these years?'

'But he managed to live with the other one about the baby?'

'Okay,' she says. 'But it was slightly different though. That wasn't his fault and he was trying to protect Mum. He didn't do anything wrong.'

'Who would have killed Mum?' I ask, clenching my hands in frustration.

'I don't know,' she says. 'And Tara, we might never find out what happened that day. But we need to try and focus on supporting the family we have left. I think you should go and talk to Dad.'

'Okay, I will. I promise. I'll pop down to Gran's later. I've made her some soup. Hopefully you can persuade her to eat some. She's lost a lot of weight.'

'Yes, I'll certainly try. The doctor thinks she's maybe got a virus doing the rounds. He said to make sure she gets plenty of fluids and rest. In fact, I can hear her calling me. I'd better go.'

I end the call and stay at the kitchen table for a moment, thinking again how surreal this whole situation is. Should we be putting up some kind of gravestone in the garden? It's been used as a cemetery all these years, after all.

What I can't work out is who has been pretending to be Mum on Messenger? I switched off my mobile a couple of days ago to avoid the constant buzzing and pinging from nosy locals. Pressing it back on, I wait for the Wi-Fi to connect and watch as lots of texts arrive and notifications on WhatsApp and Messenger ping. As expected, people want to check everything is okay and whether they can do anything. I'm not in a rush to reply to any of them. I flick onto Messenger and check for something from Mum. She still hasn't replied to my message about Jonathan, despite the dots appearing that day when I came back from the hospital. She must have changed her mind and deleted it. Who am I kidding? *She* wasn't Mum. I keep scrolling through the contacts to find her icon and frown. The profile for 'Mum' has gone. It's obviously been deleted.

CHAPTER SIXTY-EIGHT

Josie

I walk over to the bookcase and tip my head to the side as I look at the rows of Dad's books on divinity and theology, peppered with the odd sporting memoir and detective novel. Until Mum left us, Tara and I had attended Sunday School routinely, and there was absolutely no question of us not believing. Yet somehow around then, or just after, we stopped going. Dad no longer made church a priority. It was almost as though he had lost his enthusiasm for the faith which had driven him and grounded him for most of his life. I pulled out an old and well-thumbed Bible. Why are so many people so resolute in their beliefs? Was I envious? What made you a believer or not? I'm quite apathetic about religion as there's so much hypocrisy attached to the various denominations. So much goes on behind closed doors, yet people in power within churches abuse their positions and act like Gods in their own right.

Dad has always been gentle, appeasing and thoughtful, more so after Mum left. I wonder how often he has read his Bible since he retired. This one has a cream cover and his initials embossed in gold. I open it and see a handwritten message from Gran:

> *On your new role with the kirk. I'm so proud of you.*
> *Love, Mum* x

I smile at her brief dedication. She always has been sparing and straightforward with her praise. I flick through the delicate pages, wondering if he has a favourite verse or one that's particularly poignant for him. Then a card which was tucked inside flutters out and lands on the carpet. I stoop down to pick it up, looking at the artist's impression of Tantallon Castle on the front. Dad received a lot of cards from his congregation, thanking him for funeral services and christenings he had conducted. I prise it open.

> *To Gordon,*
> *May your dreams all come true and your happiness be fulfilled. May you for ever be honest and authentic and be blessed with the life you deserve.*
> *Love always, M.*

It's dated the week after Mum went missing. Frowning, I put it back feeling grubby. None of this is any of my business. I can hear the floorboards creaking, Dad is obviously coming through. I quickly slide the Bible back onto the bookshelf, hoping he won't notice it's been disturbed. I manage to compose myself before Dad opens the door.

'I'll never tire of that view,' he says, coming to stand beside me in the window.

'It's always changing. No two days are the same.'

'Do you think Tara will visit soon?'

'Yes, Dad. She said she would come later.'

'And the kids?'

'I'm sure she will bring them soon,' I say, putting my hand on his shoulder. 'Now, how about a nice cup of coffee? I could definitely do with one.'

'Thank you, dear. I couldn't have done all of this without you.'

'It's okay, Dad. Just a day at a time.'

'But what if everyone keeps thinking it was me? What if we don't ever find out what happened to your mum?'

I can't reply as I don't know what to say and my mind is now tempered with worry over the card inside the Bible. Why would she have sent it the week after she left? Especially if she's supposed to be dead? Instead, I walk across the room, calling over my shoulder, 'I'll go and make that coffee.' Nobody's perfect, and I shouldn't interfere. I've already learned my lesson from what I've done to my sister. I tried to do something to help her but instead it's completely backfired.

I pretended to be Mum on Messenger, so that Tara had some kind of hope in her darkest days. I always did wonder what I would say to her if she told me about the messages from Mum. But she never has. She clearly wants to keep it to herself. Surely we're all entitled to our secrets?

CHAPTER SIXTY-NINE

So she became me and I became her. Of course I knew what happened to her. I read the papers and the coverage of her trial. Granted, there wasn't much as she was just a woman who had killed her poor unsuspecting husband. The coverage was sympathetic towards him, as you would expect. Back then beating and raping your wife was acceptable. Women defending themselves was not.

I was glad that I changed my name to hers when I started life again.

I suppose it was all too good to be true. My fresh start at life turned out to be quite short-lived.

Who would have thought that I would end up becoming me again?

CHAPTER SEVENTY

Gran

I'm upstairs in the window seat looking out at the sea. Then when the light starts to dim, I move over to the bed and lie my head back on the pillow. A sharp pain pounds between my eyes, and my head feels as though it needs to be emptied of all the rubbish jostling about inside. My pulse throbs in my temples. Why is my family falling apart again? How can this be happening? I'm tired, so tired.

I hear Tara and Josie's concerned whispers and I know they're trying to protect me from more bad news. It seems to be one thing after another these past couple of weeks. I'm glad they told me about Mary's baby and so sorry about what had happened. I'm also disappointed Gordon has kept that secret from me. We used to tell each other everything. Now my maternal instinct is waning, and I can't face seeing him yet. This is something he will have to figure out on his own. It's all getting too much for me to cope with.

I always suspected Mary was hiding when she arrived out of the blue all those years ago. She came with nothing from her past and said little about her upbringing. She was so shy and retiring and I always wondered about her real story. I was sure she had left trouble behind her and always wondered if it would one day catch up with her again.

CHAPTER SEVENTY-ONE

*It wasn't meant to happen. She just caught me completely by surprise
with her harsh words and her threats.*

'You always have been so gullible and easily led, Nancy,' she said.

*It felt strange to be called by my proper name again. My sister
Mary was older than me by about half an hour and always reminded
me. You would think she was my mother the way she told me what to do
and what to think. Except our mother had left us when we were kids,
so what did I know?*

'What do you mean?' I asked her.

'When I told you that you'd killed him, you believed me.'

I didn't understand. 'What do you mean?'

'It was me who killed him. I stabbed him.'

That's when I shoved her in fury, and she fell.

CHAPTER SEVENTY-TWO

Gran

I went to the manse that evening to collect some things for
Gordon, who was still at the picnic with the children. Mary
was curled up at the bottom of the garden, fast asleep on the
grass. I gave her a wee nudge. But she wouldn't move. Her
face was white and her lips pale.

I sat there for a moment, holding her hand and staring
at her. What should I do? I thought of the girls, they were so
young. What had happened? I stood up to go inside and call
for an ambulance but then I saw *her* come out of the house. I
couldn't believe it. What on earth was going on? I looked at
Mary lying on the ground and then Mary walking towards
me and I thought I was going to faint.

CHAPTER SEVENTY-THREE

She was also there that night. She arrived just as I was about to call the police. I don't think she could believe there were two of me. I had never told anyone anything about my past.

She never liked me. I was never good enough for her son and I think she knew this was her chance to get rid of me.

CHAPTER SEVENTY-FOUR

Gran

Mary walked towards me, her face ashen, and her eyes wide with fear.

'What's going on?' I asked.

'I can explain,' she said. 'She's my sister.'

I bent down towards the woman on the ground. 'We need to help her,' I called. 'Come on, help me lift her up.'

Mary came towards me and together we tried to help the woman who looked like Mary sit up. That's when I saw the spade and I remembered Gordon had left it there earlier when he was planting those roses. There was blood. So much blood.

'Oh God,' she said, her voice trembling. 'I can't feel her pulse.'

I leaned over desperately trying to find some sense of life about her. But she was right, I couldn't find a pulse and she'd stopped breathing.

We sat with her between us, in silence.

And that's when Mary told me about her sister and what she had done.

'We need to go into the house. We need to call an ambulance,' she said.

'No,' I said.

'What do you mean no?'

'I mean no. We need to think. Can you imagine how this will look — woman found dead in local minister's back garden? Not only that but she looks as though she's been whacked across the head with a spade.' I looked at her and thought of my son and two granddaughters and I knew what I had to do. 'Down there,' I said, pointing over at the foundations which had been laid for the new garage being installed in the next week or so.

'What?'

'We need to put her down there.'

'Bury her?' she whispered.

Something flitted across her face, I couldn't quite put my finger on it. But she didn't argue. She took the spade and went down to the bottom of the garden, digging a deeper grave for her sister. We gently placed her body in the hole, working silently to cover her with earth and sand.

'What about Gordon?' she said.

'He must never know about this,' I said. He could never *ever* know what really happened. It would destroy him. It was so very wrong, but I didn't have another or a better solution.

'It's time you left,' I said, looking at her fixedly.

CHAPTER SEVENTY-FIVE

'If the police find out what you've done, they may send you to jail,' she said.

After hearing about my sister's experience, that was the last thing I wanted. My choices — for I do believe we all have choices — were to own up and face a life in prison, where I would be lucky if I saw my daughters again.

Or to run. At least I could watch from afar.

I had to decide.

A life behind bars that would affect my kids' lives?

Or let them think I had walked away?

Not easy, is it?

Don't judge me for what I did. Because if you were in my position, what would you have done?

CHAPTER SEVENTY-SIX

Gran

I focused on becoming the best mother and granny I could. I made them fresh scones, I always had a pot of soup simmering on the stove, and I knitted scarves, repaired socks and made prize-winning Halloween costumes. I let them stay with me when they were teenagers so they could stay out late at parties and their father didn't know what they were really up to. I even kept Josie's miscarriage a secret from everyone else when she asked me to.

Everyone wished they had a granny like me, the girls used to tell me. I was the greatest gran on earth. They used to give me cards with soppy messages like 'To the Best Gran Ever' and 'To a Wonderful Gran on Mother's Day'. I was not the greatest gran at all. I was bad and I had done a very bad thing. I loved those girls with all of my heart and more, but they should have been told the truth from the start. That their mother was never coming back. The sound of them crying at night for their mum would never leave me.

They certainly didn't need to know the whole story of what happened. My version of the truth would suffice.

CHAPTER SEVENTY-SEVEN

Darling girls,
    *I'm sorry that I have to go. I love you more than you
will ever know.*
    Love always, Mum x

    *I carefully folded the paper and tucked it inside an envelope, sealing
it shut, then left the letter propped up on the kitchen table next to the
fruit bowl.*
    I removed my jewellery and gave it to her.
    *'Hurry,' she said, 'before they come back. Take her car and don't
stop. Keep going and don't ever come back.'*

CHAPTER SEVENTY-EIGHT

Josie

Gran's breathing is becoming laboured and her voice strained. I can't believe this is happening, that she has hidden her illness for so long — that she is dying. She tries to grip my hand and I stare at her wispy, white hair which frames her wrinkled face. Her skin is pale, and I reach out to touch her cheek. It's cold and soft under my fingertips. Glancing out the window, I notice the sky has changed colour from dark blue to deep pink. I look at the picture of me with my sister wearing our red pinafores. A hazy memory appears from somewhere. Of Mum smiling. I picture my sister and me eating cake at the café in Jenners in Princes Street. That was the day Mum took us shopping and bought those dresses.

Her voice is croaky as she speaks. 'I found her.'
'Who?'
'Your mother . . .' Her voice trails away.
'You found her?'
'Yes.'
'What do you mean you found her, Gran?'
'Curled up at the bottom of the garden. Fast asleep.'

Another scene I can imagine, Mum lying in the hammock strung between the two trees. She used to love lying and looking at the view.

'She was on the ground and wouldn't move. She must have fainted.'

My heartbeat quickens. What was she going to say?

'Her face was white and her lips were blue,' says Gran, her eyes fluttering as she speaks. 'I tried to help her up. I thought if I could just get her to have some water and get her in the house that she would be okay. But . . .'

'What?'

Gran moistens her lips. 'I managed to rouse her. But the spade was on the grass and your mum stumbled and she fell back . . .'

'What do you mean?'

'There was so much blood. I sat for a moment, holding her hand. I was shocked. I didn't know what to do. Then it was too late . . . and I thought of you girls — you were so young. And your dad.'

'But Gran . . . you gave us hope. We thought she would come back. We thought people would assume she had run off with another man. You made us think she had left us because she didn't love us anymore. Can you imagine what that felt like?'

Gran nods and reaches for my hand again. 'I know what I did was wrong. But I truly thought I was doing the right thing. I wanted to give you hope, because if you didn't have hope you would have nothing.'

'So you buried her?'

'I wasn't thinking straight . . . It was wrong of me. I should have called an ambulance or the police. But I panicked.'

Shifting slightly in the bucket seat, I pull my hand from hers and start drumming my feet on the ground. I want to scream and punch the wall. For a moment I vaguely wonder what her white room would look like with smears of colour

271

and some texture. Maybe I should rifle through her make-up and press it onto the walls which are now closing in on me. To think this was always my safe place and refuge.

I no longer know the woman lying in front of me. She's a liar. Standing up, I hover over her, wanting to reach for the pillow. Instead I sink back into my chair and wait.

Her eyes open and they're watering. 'I'm sorry, dear,' she rasps. 'I don't expect you to forgive me.'

I stare at my beloved gran in front of me who always tried her best. She puts everyone first before her own needs. Yet did she?

'Did you send the birthday cards?'

She eventually nods.

I now understood why there were no pictures of my parents in her house. It would be a daily reminder of what happened. The lives ruined and the tainted memories. It seems Gran was in the habit of acting on what she thought best and keeping secrets. Then I think about Jason's letters I never received. But how different could my life have been if I'd known Jason hadn't abandoned me? If I'd known mum hadn't chosen to leave? Will I ever know what kind of psychological toll that has left on both Tara and I growing up. Grief is something that you can, if not heal from, at least understand. At least not blame yourself for. Abandonment leaves a different kind of mark.

'Josie,' she whispers. She points to the drawer by the bed. I reach over and open it. Inside is a letter.

'For the police.' It's the last thing she says.

272

CHAPTER SEVENTY-NINE

Tara

It seems Gran has been hiding quite a few things from us. She's not been well for a while but decided to just keep going regardless. Treatment would have been an option for the cancer if she had seen the doctor, but it turns out she was self-medicating with painkillers for some time. She told me she always wanted to die in her own bed, in this house. We've been taking it in turns to sit with her. She's upstairs now with Josie.

Dad and I are sitting here together in the kitchen waiting. We've drunk endless cups of tea and made small talk about the weather and anything else aside from what's happening now. His mother is dying yet he seems oddly detached. Maybe I need to accept there is no normal way to behave in the face of extreme stress. He's had quite the time of it and I know the finger of suspicion is still hovering over him while the police continue their investigation into Mum's death.

'Why did you have Mum's jewellery?' I suddenly ask.

He looks up. 'What?'

'Mum's jewellery. Why do you have her jewellery in your drawer?'

His face flushes and he clenches his hands together.

'You never told us she'd left it.'

Dad sighs and doesn't answer to begin with.

'Why didn't you tell us?'

'She didn't leave it for me, Tara. I found it.'

'Where?' I whisper.

He rubs his hand over his jaw. 'I found it in your gran's loft one day when I was looking for some papers.'

I don't understand. 'Why was it there?'

'She said your mother left it behind and she thought it would upset me if I saw it. So she stashed it in the loft.'

I shake my head. 'But she had no right to do that.' Then the stairs creak, the sound of Josie coming. When she walks into the kitchen her face is white and she's clutching an envelope.

'What's that?' says Dad.

I look at my sister expectantly.

'It's from Gran. It's her confession to the police.'

CHAPTER EIGHTY

Gran

Now they have an answer and know she will never return, they can try and move on with their lives. And now I'm at the end of mine, it's time for me to go. I've said all I need to and I'm truly sorry for all the hurt. But I've made sure she will *never* come back.

DAILY POST

A woman who told police she killed another woman and buried her in a garden has died.

The woman was due to be questioned on suspicion of murder following the discovery of human remains at a house on the outskirts of North Berwick.

Police Scotland said the ninety-year-old had confessed following the discovery of the woman's remains. In her death-bed confession, she admitted to killing the woman by accident around twenty years ago. It is understood the woman died following a blow to the head.

The dead woman has been identified as Mary Smithson, wife of the Very Rev. Gordon Smithson. It was thought Mrs Smithson had left home twenty years ago. Police have not released the identity of the woman who made the claim several weeks ago.

Neighbours described their shock at the body's discovery, with one telling the Daily Post: 'Who would have thought such a thing would happen in a quiet place like this? We always wondered what happened to Mary and now we know. We would never have suspected that was what happened.'

Following a search of the garden, triggered by building work, officers discovered remains which were later confirmed to be human by a forensic pathologist.

'Thanks to this woman's confession, we have been able to piece together the exact circumstances surrounding Mary Smithson's disappearance twenty years ago. This has brought closure to her family at what has been an extremely difficult time. I would like to thank the community for their support during this investigation. There will be no further comment on this case, which we are satisfied has now been resolved.'

CHAPTER EIGHTY-ONE

Josie

I stand in Gran's bedroom and look out the window. I always loved the view from this room. As a little girl, I would hop on the narrow window seat and watch the changing sky, the foaming waves, the gannets and the gulls diving into the water. This room was always a safe place. Gran would let me try on her beads, press her Coty powder puff onto my cheeks and smudge some rouge on my lips. I always looked up to her and admired her strength.

She was my hero. A tear slides down my cheek. I'm not sure how to grieve a person who I didn't actually know. Instead I've been grieving the loss of a mother who was taken away from me. I always thought I'd done something wrong to push her away. Perhaps if I'd been a nicer child she would have stayed. The same thoughts have tortured Tara and me over the years. Neither of us could understand or rationalise why our mum would just leave without saying goodbye.

I'm not sure how I feel about Gran anymore. We held a small private funeral for her yesterday. Despite everything that has happened, it felt like the right thing to do. At least it gave us all a sense of closure. The other day we found a sepia picture of our late grandfather hidden away in a drawer. He looked like a movie star with his brooding looks and his crisp RAF uniform. We also found some old papers and letters which helped us piece together what happened to him. Our grandfather took his own life which explains why Gran didn't want to talk about it. There was so much stigma around suicide back then. Knowing the truth about what happened to him gives us a bit of context to our family history and explains why Dad is the way he is. It sounds like Gran was tough with him when he was a child. He told us that she didn't show him much affection. He realises now she was trying her best to be a mother and father to him when she was also grieving such a painful loss. That explains why he's always been a bit unemotional and hands-off. Losing our mum just heightened that detachment.

I sigh. What a sorry mess. Despite it all, she was still a loving gran to me and Tara. I'm not sure that's something that we'll ever be able to reconcile.

The sky has changed from dark red to a pale powdery pink. I can see the outline of Bass Rock perched in the sea beyond, glittering as though covered with diamonds.

Gran has left the house to me and Tara. We've decided that I'll live here for a while until I figure out what to do next. I want to have time with Tara and Dad. I need to be with my family.

Glancing at my watch, I realise it's time to go. I'm meeting Jason for a coffee this morning. I smile wryly. I don't think we'll ever run out of things to talk about. Drama seems to be a common theme in our lives.

I look back at the view once more. I know there will be lots of processing and grieving to do in the coming weeks and months. I hope Tara and I can move on and start to heal. I'm so relieved to finally know what happened and to know that Mum is dead. Even if it's sad, at least it's the truth.

EPILOGUE

I've had to move on more than once in my life and not dwell on the past. Doing that gets you nowhere. I kept my part of the deal. I never returned and just kept a watch on you girls from afar. Of course, I did think about coming back. But I knew how unsettling it would be, and something always held me back. Which I'm glad about. I always wondered if she worried I would return. How would she explain?

I've tried not to judge myself or others. I've tried not to criticise. I've tried to learn from the lessons of the past and be kind to myself and others.

But it's hard when you've made a mistake.

I didn't want my sister to die. That was never my intention. Maybe it was a good mistake though. Because I've never felt guilty. For years she let me believe I had murdered my husband and I had to run and become her, Mary.

Now I'm Nancy again and Mary's dead.

Since it happened, I've spent so much time in anguish, blaming myself. It was a failure on a massive scale and I thought I'd managed to separate the failure from who I was.

But no.

Her lies caused this all to happen. And mine. Perhaps if I'd been more honest from the start then none of this would have happened. I've had plenty of time to forgive and be compassionate. But I can't forgive

279

her because what she did means I've lost my girls. They think I'm dead and there's no going back. How could I even begin to explain what happened? It pains me to know I will never see my daughters again or meet my grandchildren.

The only other person who knows the truth about what happened is now dead. And her confession and version of events has made sure I'm definitely gone. There's no way for me to become Mary again. Mary is dead.

I'm just glad I sent my girls the birthday cards. That was the very least I could do.

THE END

ACKNOWLEDGEMENTS

I would like to thank the Choc Lit and Joffe Books team for their incredible support and encouragement. A special thanks to Jasper Joffe, Emma Grundy Haigh, Kate Lyall Grant, Nina Taylor, Sam Matthews and Kate Ballad for all of your hard work which I so appreciate.

Thank you to my editor, Laurel Sills, whose amazing eye for details helped to strengthen and shape this book. Thanks also to Matthew Grundy Haigh for wonderful copy-editing and Julia Williams for incredible proofreading.

Thank you to the very talented Nick Castle for the brilliant cover.

When I wrote this novel, I wanted to set it somewhere a bit different to a city location, hence my choice of the seaside town of North Berwick. This book is work of fiction and so certain creative liberties have been taken in terms of the place, setting and police procedure.

As always lots of people have supported and encouraged me during the writing and publishing process of this book including Douglas Wight, Alasdair Hill, Frankie Greenwood, Frances Wells, Lynne Hill, Garry Hill, Lindsey Thomson, Sandra Duguid, Sue Kennedy and Karen Brougham.

Finally, I am so lucky to be surrounded by women who inspire me every day with their stories of courage, strength and determination in the face of adversity. I must express my gratitude to those who have shared their insights into so many themes in the book including fertility treatment, caring for ageing parents, domestic abuse and breast cancer. Hopefully Tara's story is a reminder to us all about the importance of breast awareness. Thanks to Julie Watson and all the women I have worked with at Women's Aid East and Midlothian. You are all an inspiration.

THE CHOC LIT STORY

Established in 2009, Choc Lit is an independent, award-winning publisher dedicated to creating a delicious selection of quality women's fiction.

We have won 18 awards, including Publisher of the Year and the Romantic Novel of the Year, and have been shortlisted for countless others. In 2023, we were shortlisted for Publisher of the Year by the Romantic Novelists' Association.

All our novels are selected by genuine readers. We are proud to publish talented first-time authors, as well as established writers whose books we love introducing to a new generation of readers.

In 2023, we became a Joffe Books company. Best known for publishing a wide range of commercial fiction, Joffe Books has its roots in women's fiction. Today it is one of the largest independent publishers in the UK.

We love to hear from you, so please email us about absolutely anything bookish at choc-lit@joffebooks.com

If you want to hear about all our bargain new releases, join our mailing list: www.choc-lit.com/contact

Milton Keynes UK
Ingram Content Group UK Ltd.
UKHW041045200824
447137UK00010B/87

9 781781 897683